Click, D

Click, Double-Click

James Calum Campbell

First published 2015
by Impress Books Ltd

Innovation Centre, Rennes Drive, University of Exeter Campus,
Exeter EX4 4RN

British Library Cataloguing in Publication Data
A catalogue record for this book is available from the British Library

ISBN 13: 978-1-907605-72-7 (pbk)
ISBN 13: 978-1-907605-73-4 (ebk)

Typeset in Sabon
by Swales & Willis Ltd, Exeter, Devon

Printed and bound in England
by imprintdigital.net

Contents

*The quincunx of heaven runs low, and 'tis time to close
the five ports of knowledge.*

Sir Thomas Browne

Prologue

Ministry of Defence
Whitehall
Westminster
London SW1A 2HB
9th Jan

Angela MacVicar, MSP
The Scottish Parliament
Horse Wynd
Holyrood
Edinburgh EH99 1SP

Dear Angela,

   With respect to recent developments in our overlapping constituencies, it has been drawn to my attention that you have expressed some dissatisfaction with the Ministry of Defence, and the Home Office, in their respective dealings with the Scottish Government, Legislature, and Police Scotland. While in no way wishing to interfere with the activities of the Scottish Parliament, the Prime Minister wishes to make it clear that any official inquiry must now be held under the aegis of the British Government. If there has been a threat to national security then there is nothing to be gained by making wild – and in my view unfounded – allegations concerning conspiracy theories and a so-called 'Third Man'. If you insist on portraying an unfortunate local difficulty as some international terrorist plot you will do untold damage to trade relations with some of our overseas partners. The body politic, and the Fourth Estate, will respect, specifically, Defence Advisory Notices 03 and 05. This matter is no longer devolved. It is reserved. The Select Committee has opted for an independent inquiry, to be held *in camera*. The matter is therefore now *sub judice*. Any attempt to undermine these procedures will be in contempt of court.

The inquiry will be led by the distinguished Law Lord, Fochabers Dalhousie.

Sincerely,

George Grierson.

The Scottish Parliament
Pàrlamaid na h-Alba
Horse Wynd
Holyrood
Edinburgh EH99 1SP
10th Jan

The Rt Hon George Grierson MP
Ministry of Defence
Whitehall
Westminster
London SW1A 2HB

Dear George,

Enc.

Before you get on your high horse, take a look at this. I draw your attention to the appendix.

Don't leave it on the sleeper, now. There's a good chap.

Angela

37dn: Run in – Emergency Room mistake (3)

I

If I were a loner, disgruntled, disaffected, malcontent, camouflaged in my army surplus fatigues, interested in guns and
the Internet, and with a massive chip on my shoulder, I would
choose to carry out my mass shooting on a university campus.
These places are so vulnerable – not like an airport, where
policemen stand on corners with index fingers curled round
the triggers of semi-automatic weapons, where the bored customs officers x-ray you with their icy stares; or a bank, or
a mall, or a hospital emergency department. Even a garage
forecourt has CCTV.

But look at this. I strolled past a Checkpoint-Charlie-style
security barrier for vehicles where the attendant didn't give
me a second glance. Now I have the run of the place. I could
start at the top of the dell in the student halls of residence,
grim flat-roofed pueblos stacked like a shanty town in a natural amphitheatre of craggy woodland. Then I would cross a
bridge over an artificial lake and ascend the windswept landscaped lawns to the first of the classrooms and lecture theatres and labs, walking quickly now, a figure stepping briefly

out of the December mist and then disappearing into it again. Miss out the sports centre where too many people might be inclined to have a go. The arts centre and the contiguous students' union next – where I would be likely to cause the most damage. And, if I got that far, if I were still on my feet, the administrative offices – the communications hub – but, if I were quick enough, I bet they would still not know. Shock and awe. How far would I get before anyone had a glimmering that something calamitous was happening? Look at these young women wandering about as if hypnotised, biting their nails, texting. They have no idea what's round the corner.

But I am not a loner. Nor am I disgruntled. Hence my interest is purely theoretical. Yet I choose to start this account here, with this observation, because I am sure it occurred to me on the first occasion I set foot on the grounds of James Clerk Maxwell University College, the time I missed my station and detrained one stop further up the line and had to walk back through the campus to find Princess Margaret's. And that is odd, because that occasion certainly predates my meeting Alan Bletchley, and why should my thoughts turn in that direction then? Maybe my memory is just playing tricks on me.

I reached my destination dead on time. I stepped into an overheated, overcrowded waiting room.

'Dr Cameron-Strange?'

'Yes.'

The charge nurse literally threw the blue scrubs at me.

'Changing room's down the hall. You're wanted in Resus.'

I walked straight in, to a diplomatic incident.

'. . . tell your hapless Cas officers to quit faffing about *and* wasting my registrar's time *and* –'

'But he only did what he was asked to do. You can't –'

'No no no. *You* said –'

'It doesn't really matter what I said. The point is –'

'But you *said* –'

They stopped and swung round as I entered. I hadn't a

6

clue who they were. I guessed one was a manager and one a clinician. I couldn't divert my eyes from the purple throbbing pulsation on the clinician's left temple, nor quell my sickly fascination at the way he inserted italicised words into his sentences at unusual points. '*Would* somebody' – the angry eyes focused on me – 'would *somebody,* would somebody *please* sort out this apology for a Casualty, this circus, this *menagerie.* . . .' He wanted us to know he was at the end of his tether because he had spent a lifetime in the company of dolts.

I said, 'What do you need?'

He paused, momentarily mollified.

'Somebody to stitch this guy up . . .' pointing a thumb behind without looking.

'I'll do it.'

'Praise the Lord!'

I said nothing.

'Right. Fine! Fine!' He turned on his heel and left Resus.

The manager said, 'You ought not to kowtow to him. He'll be back, looking for some flunky to carry out his skivvy work again.'

And I said nothing again. I wasn't going to pick a fight with him either. Instead I put half a dozen stitches into an eyebrow. It took me about three minutes. Then I found the male changing room and put on the blue scrubs, hung a stethoscope around my neck, and went back out to track down the charge nurse.

'Hello again!' I gave her a broad grin. 'I'm Alastair.' Cordial working relations are important. But she was having none of it.

'Sister Mackintosh.' She didn't smile and she stared impatiently over my right shoulder as if appealing to someone to call her away. 'Yes?'

'Nothing, just saying hi. What's that noise?'

It was a thump thump thump, felt viscerally, as if in the bowels of a ship's engine room.

'It's just the gig.'

'Gig?'

'Didn't you know? Kosh is playing Clerk Maxwell tonight.'

It meant nothing to me. I thought first of a tennis match. Then an electric guitar riff marauded through the department, strident and raucous, even from a mile away. Rock concert.

'Ah. Are management giving us some extra help?'

She snorted. 'You *are* the help. Excuse me.'

There then followed a night of carnage, murder and mayhem. I didn't much mind. I had come across the bridge from Edinburgh just to work a single shift in a struggling emergency department. Just to help out. Rumour had it the Director, Mr Trubshaw, was 'impaired'. I hadn't troubled to research the nature of his impairment. The emergency medicine community in this country is very small, and there was plenty of gossip, but I chose to avoid it. I would cross to the dark kingdom for a night and do my bit.

I could see they were in trouble. Overworked and understaffed, just struggling to react to the tide of human misery pouring through the antiquated Victorian portals. The fabric of the department itself was not fit for purpose. Frankly, it was a dump. But I didn't say anything. It wasn't my place. Pompous StR swans in from regional Centre of Excellence, the ivory towers of Little France, to make sniffy comments as to how they were doing everything wrong. I would keep my head down and just see as many patients as possible, as safely as possible. First, do no harm.

It was all pretty predictable bread and butter stuff. There were distressing numbers of drunken women. I was reminded of pictures you occasionally see on the news on TV of buxom girls in tight dresses and heels crawling across inner city pedestrian precincts vomiting copiously across the cobblestones. Pimply youths with vulpine features stared hungrily at them with glazed predatory eyes. Next day in the campus sports complex locker rooms they would boast to one another, 'Man, I was *ratarsed*!'

Every so often the noise from the concert would waft

through the department. There was the support act, a chanteuse, a local celeb. It was a voice full of plangent protest I recalled with nostalgia once the main act came on. Kosh indeed.

There were all the usual slings and arrows – a heart attack, a stroke, an ectopic, a ruptured aortic aneurysm . . . I had two junior doctors on with me, Harry and Jenny. They had the bedazzled look of rabbits transfixed by approaching headlights. Jenny asked me about a teenage girl who was staring up at the ceiling in a strange way. I recognised a dystonic reaction to some drug, heaven knows what; it's called an oculogyric crisis. I got Jenny to give her an intravenous injection of benztropine and watch her get better on the end of the needle. Then we discharged her home. Later on, Jenny brought me a toddler who she thought might have fractured his forearm, but it was just a pulled elbow. I showed Jenny the simple manoeuvre that resulted in instant cure. Jenny asked if the boy needed an x-ray? No, he could go home. I was amused that Jenny was beginning to think I was a magician who could conjure instant cures. Then Harry attempted to adopt my cavalier attitude and he reversed a hypoglycaemic coma in an elderly diabetic with a bolus of intravenous glucose. He discharged the gentleman but I cut him off at the pass and sent him to the physicians. He was on glibenclamide. Very long half-life, glibenclamide. A trap for young players.

Then we all went into Resus and sorted out the carnage of a drunken road crash on the M90 and we liaised with ambulance and police and surgeons and intensivists and a couple of golden hours went by as the walking wounded and the worried well once more stacked up in the waiting room. At about 4 am I grabbed a quick sandwich and a coffee and I started again on the backlog. I wanted to clear out some of the low echelon stuff, and when I went out to the waiting room to bring in the next patient, I rumbled somebody – a recidivist, somebody with what the cops call 'previous'. It wasn't difficult; the combination of intensely dark skin and carrot red hair was disconcerting. Let alone the starey eyes. I mentioned it to Sister Mackintosh. 'See that guy? He's a frequent flier. I've seen him over the bridge. There's a Health Board warning out about him. Drug seeker . . . Munchausen's . . . maybe both, I can't remember. Various aliases.' It came back to me. 'Noxolo Pacharo.'

'*You've* got a good memory.'

I'm fascinated by the euphony of names. I collect them. I think of all these fabulous names of the Maori and Polynesian kids I used to come across in Auckland – Airport and Society and the lovely September. 'I bet you he's not Mr Pacharo tonight.'

She consulted a list. 'Purchase Gentleman.'

'Fantastic. Ask him if he's Noxolo and I bet he buggers off.'

I was vaguely aware that the nurses had quarantined some addict or other in some remote location, not because he was infectious, but because he was a waste of space. There was some running joke about his predilections I didn't quite pick up on. 'Give him the Scrabble. He can play with himself.' Then there was a flap and a panic call to Resus and in the space of just a few minutes occurred the event which certainly at the time I considered the most significant episode of the night. A six year old child who, as I subsequently learned, had been sent home in the afternoon with a diagnosis of croup had returned, by ambulance, *in extremis*. I walked into Resus and, behind the green uniforms of the paramedics huddled over the trolley, I could see the shadow of life preparing to depart from the clammy envelope of blue-black skin, and the bizarre upper limb athetoid movements of an incipient respiratory arrest. At the head end of the trolley a paramedic was vainly attempting bag-mask ventilation. I grabbed a laryngoscope off the equipment rack behind him. 'Quick look?' He moved to my left. I snapped open the blade of the laryngoscope and turned the child into the supine position. He didn't resist. I opened his mouth and laid the blade along a tongue the colour of a ripe aubergine.

'Suction.'

There it was. The sullen dark purple plum of the swollen epiglottis.

'Tube. Size five. Cuffless.'

I aimed for the bubbles. The tube passed without difficulty.

'Bag him.'

Already the staff nurse had attached the Laerdal with its accessory reservoir.

'100% oxygen. 15 litres a minute. Get a line in. Chop chop.'

The pulse oximeter on the tiny finger that had failed to pick up a signal sprang to life. Pulse 140, saturations 60–70–80–90%.

'Tape.' I used Elastoplast to secure the endotracheal tube and make certain it could not fall out. Harry had inserted an intravenous catheter in the kid's right arm.

'Midazolam. Just a trickle. I don't want him to wake up and pull the tube out.'

The charge nurse called out the vital signs. 'Temp 39.8, BP 90/60, sats 100%.'

'Good. Put him on the oxylog.'

Suddenly the double doors of Resus swung open and a consultant anaesthetist, a big grey-haired middle-aged man in theatre greens with a flapping green coat stomped in in his white theatre boots like a gunslinger entering a saloon in the Wild West. He wore his surgical mask loose below his chin like a bandana.

'What the hell's going on?'

For the first time that night I felt a surge of impatience at the oppressive bullying culture and the ethos of bad manners endemic in this dysfunctional department. Lighten up for God's sake! Why am I going to explain myself to a stranger lacking the courtesy to introduce himself?

Keep it together, don't lose it. It's not worth it. You'll walk out of here in the morning and you won't ever need to come back.

I kept it as brief as possible. 'Six year old. Came in in respiratory arrest. Epiglottitis. Intubated, ventilated, stable.

11

ICU have been informed.' I cocked an eyebrow at Harry and he nodded and went to the phone. The gunslinger walked slowly round the patient's trolley and stopped at the oxylog and took one long comprehensive look at the nursing record and the vitals on the oxylog. Then he took one long comprehensive look at me. He nodded once, curtly, and disappeared back through the double doors. Suddenly we were knee deep in intensivists and paediatricians and I was able to leave. As I passed Sister Mackintosh at the door she whispered, without looking at me, 'Great save.'

I hate compliments in medicine. And now, fresh from my near-death experience, I was impatient with the needy, the sore backs in the waiting room who ought to have seen their GP during the week. Now I might be tempted to say something I would regret. 'You come in here, with your petty, paltry preoccupations . . .' I might make a mistake. And thus it was that I came to meet Mr Bletchley, the man the nurses had corralled away. 'Take your sudoku with you!' Meanwhile a manager with a clip board was frowning and muttering something about breaching the four hour rule.

'Computers have crashed!' announced the clerk at the front desk, cheerily. We had the usual fatalistic IT exchange. 'They're great when they work.'

I wish I could tell you that I had some presentiment, but quite honestly the consult was prosaic to the point of dullness, and lasted barely ten minutes. He had been triaged into the Gloom Room, a broom cupboard reserved for relatives, specifically for the task of imparting bad news. ('I'll just go and gloom the rels.') I knocked and went in.

The room was almost featureless, a parsimonious closet in olive green containing little more than an ancient Formica-top table and two plastic chairs. A single garish strip light on the ceiling, a small wooden cross on the wall and, on the shelf beneath, a Gideon's bible. That was about all. I looked across at the sole occupant of the room, and for a second I was startled. D. H. Lawrence – the spectre, I suppose, of D. H. Lawrence – was seated motionless, hands clasped on the table.

Close-cropped red hair and beard, a gaunt, almost phthisic face, and these piercing eyes. I glanced at the ED chart. Alan Bletchley, thirty nine years old. Presenting complaint: *addict*. Triage category 6. The demographics had been handwritten – of course . . . the outage. The triage category was sarcastic. The lowest level of acuity is triage category 5.

'Mr Bletchley?'

The eyes stared briefly in my direction.

'Yes.'

I sat down opposite him and extended a hand across the table. 'Pleased to meet you Mr Bletchley. I'm Dr Cameron-Strange.'

'Yes.'

He was hoarse, and barely audible. He did not shake my hand. It was like speaking to somebody through a thick plate glass window.

'What troubles you tonight?'

He glanced at the chart and back at me. There was a long pause.

'Addiction.'

I was impatient with the pauses. I didn't have time for the pauses.

'And to what are you addicted? Sex? Drugs? Rock'n Roll?' I rolled my eyes in the direction of the university campus. It was a stupid thing to say, a hangover from the epiglottitis case. Euphoria. Adrenaline.

He didn't smile.

'No.'

He was so monosyllabic that my imagination began to fill in the gaps. Studied at Durham. Social Sciences. Plays the Northumberland pipes. 'Cigarettes? Alcohol? Gambling?'

'No.'

'What then?'

He stared at me fully for one minute without speaking.

'Crosswords.'

I stared back at him.

'Crosswords?'

13

'Yes.'

I gave out a single yelp of laughter. I couldn't help it. Actually, I wasn't entirely unsympathetic. I'm a bit of a crossword addict myself. Still, I didn't make much of an effort to conceal a sense of hilarity.

'Crosswords. *Ahem*!' I was already rehearsing the anecdote for my colleagues in Edinburgh next week. You wouldn't believe this guy I came across on Friday night . . .

'What's your job, Mr Bletchley?'

'Cruciverbalist.'

'You're a compiler?'

'Yes.'

He always gave a one word answer, like the solution to a cryptic clue. I had a notion that there was a great avalanche of words all pent up inside him, yet he only dared discharge one at a time, otherwise he would start screaming.

'Are you professional?'

'Semi.'

'Well, if you can get paid for it, maybe it's not such a bad addiction.'

It was not a question, so he chose not to answer it. I began to nurse an ambition to put him into a more expansive mood. Perhaps if my questions were more open-ended.

'What is it you are looking for tonight?'

Another long pause. It was surely a manifestation of major depression, this retardation of thought – the inertia, the agony of the effort to move through the slough of despond.

'Help.'

'Why do you need help?'

He was struggling. His features were twitching. In a moment he was going to start weeping. I began to regret that I had been off-hand with him. I repeated my question.

'Why do you need help?'

He shrugged.

'It's the bottom line.'

After all the monosyllables, it was like a torrent. The trick of good psychiatry is to distinguish the real from the sham. I don't claim to be any good at it but, looking into these frightened eyes, I thought, this man is at the end of his tether.

I picked up the ED chart and rose and excused myself.

'I'll see if I can get you some help.'

I found a phone and with some difficulty tracked down a liaison psychiatrist and tried to make a referral. In Middlemore Hospital in South Auckland I had good rapport with a liaison psychiatrist. I knew her and she knew me. I could pick up the phone and say, 'Sue, I know this is a strange one, but I've got this guy here who says he's addicted to crosswords. Yes, I know. I haven't got the time, but there is an atmosphere of psychosis in the Gloom Room and I have a sense if he is lost to follow up there will be a crisis.'

But I wasn't in Middlemore. I was a stranger in a strange hospital. As soon as the phone started ringing out I regretted initiating the call.

'. . . llo?'

I had woken somebody up.

I gave the story as succinctly as I could. God knows the details were patchy enough.

'*What?*'

I could picture the psychiatrist, struggling between sleep and wakefulness, perhaps making faces of helpless incredulity at his wife, now also awake, wondering if somebody was playing a bad practical joke. I ran the details past him again. The silence down the line spoke volumes. I could imagine him taking the phone receiver from his ear and holding it out at arm's length and squinting at it as if he were pricing an antique.

'Who are you?'

I identified myself again, told him I was doing a locum. He then ran off a check list in a tone of suppressed anger.

'Your patient, has he self-harmed?'

'No.'

'Is he a danger to others?'

'Not that I'm aware of.'

'Is he suicidal?'

15

'Well . . .'

'Has he indicated he has a plan?'

'No.'

'Does he show first rank features of schizophrenia?'

I said, lamely, 'The room has an atmosphere of psychosis.'

'Well, doctor. You've diagnosed the room as schizophrenic. What about your patient?'

I could hardly blame him. I relented. 'You're quite right. I'll put in a cold referral.'

'I see. Now I'm going to tell you what I think of you phoning me up at –'

I saw him glancing at the luminous digits on the bedside clock – 'five in the morning.' He went on to give me a piece of his mind and a short sharp dressing down. I took it on the chin.

'I'm terribly sorry.' The line was abruptly disconnected. There you go. Bouquets and brickbats. I would just have to make a paper referral to the community mental health people. I hung up and retraced my steps to the Gloom Room.

But the man named Bletchley had departed.

II

Since the death of my wife, just over a year ago now as I write, in a car crash, I admit I have retreated into the life of the mind.

I don't want to make too much of this. I admit it's relevant. It pertains. But it is not crucial. Of course, at the time, I completely decompensated. I almost gave up. Two things kept me going. One was my work. After the obligatory compassionate leave I found I could function in a detached robotic kind of way. It lent structure to an otherwise pointless day. The other motivator was Caitlin Roy, my sister-in-law, Mary's younger sibling. At home in her parents' place (Gloucestershire – people cross the Irish Sea for work) she annexed herself in her room and lay on the bed in the foetal position, facing the wall. I did not chide her. I did not tell her to pull her socks up. I looked at her and I saw an image of myself. We both had to decide whether to survive, or to go under. Destitute as I was, I was yet oblivious to the extent of the damage and the diminishment wreaked on me. Hadn't I also turned my face to the wall? I only needed to look at my weekend after the night shift at PMH. I'd got back to my Marchmont flat midmorning. We were having a preternaturally mild winter, and there was a horrible dank fug hanging like a shroud over the whole city. It came off the North Sea. It was called haar. It could last for days, sometimes even weeks. It carried with it a smell of stale hops. I swallowed a tot of Lagavulin and crashed into a heavy sleep right through to six in the evening. Then I'd had a large gin and tonic and breakfasted on tins of tomato soup, ravioli, and pears with condensed milk. Then I'd stared at the TV and fallen asleep in the armchair. On Sunday I'd made a brief sojourn to the corner shop for the *Sunday Telegraph* and spent most of the day ploughing through its myriad sections the way an idiot savant might read the phone book. Christmas was round the corner but it never crossed my mind to get a tree, to send anybody a card, buy anybody a gift. I just wanted the season and its bad memories out of the way. What of my hobbies and pastimes? I didn't go flying, I didn't go for a swim, or a run. The bike was rusting quietly in the shed out the back. I didn't play the piano, I didn't read a book. I didn't see anybody. During the entire weekend the phone never rang once. Not even a cold call. I didn't, couldn't, listen to any music. I was in limbo, completely cut off from life's deepest streams. I had no perspective on the extent of my own bewilderment. Yet, when I thought of Caitlin and how badly she had taken it all I became angry and I decided that the game was worth the candle and that we would survive.

Back in Little France I resumed my sullen round, the waiting game of the bereft, 'going forward', as they say in the modern jargon, hopeless and yet not entirely devoid of fortitude, staying on the rails, waiting for the light at the end of the tunnel. There was the daily routine, the patients, the research and audit, the clinical meetings, the M & M meetings, the post mortems, figuratively and literally. In my surgical scrubs with the iconography of the stethoscope round the neck I could assume a personality of equanimity, even of light-heartedness. The merry widower.

Sometimes I would slip into the hospital residency, where there was a snooker table, and shoot a few balls. Mostly on my own. It was just a mindless activity that would pass an hour. Sign of a misspent youth. It became a lunchtime routine. I would shore up those parts of the day when my spirits sank with little rituals – crossword, snooker, G and T. The snooker was anodyne. There was something hypnotic about the gentle tap of cue tip on ball and the click of ball on ball. I began to notice, with indifference, that I could build a break, control the cue ball. I notched up my first century break. Privately. I never told anybody.

I forgot all about Alan Bletchley. Whenever I read, say, a thriller, or a detective story (is that what this is, or is this a confession, a statement?) I often wonder at the protagonists' power of concentration on the matter on hand. Is this acuity of focus a talent of the book's characters, or merely an editorial device of the author? Why are these people not preoccupied, as I am, with unpaid bills and tax returns, office drudgery, dental appointments, commitments various to close kin, extended family, friends, and the community at large? Why do they not even appear to take toilet stops? What about the inner life, the life of the mind? What book is the central character reading, keeping his place by turning down a page corner? Even if the plot has its subplots, there is a kind of monothematic attentiveness that is certainly missing from my life. I am a living exemplar of John Lennon's remark that life is what happens to you while you're busy making other plans. I had no idea that Bletchley was going to turn into a mission. Project Bletchley. He hardly registered with me at all. It took a long time before I realised that I needed to drop everything else and focus on this obsession.

One of the managers grabbed my elbow in the canteen queue at lunch.

'Going to ELSCOMF?'

My heart sank. I suddenly remembered I *was* going to ELS-COMF. The vista of an afternoon's snooker dissolved into the bleak prospect of two hours hunched over a board room table, in committee. ELSCOMF was the 'Emergency Liaison Steering Committee on Moving Forward'. My boss, Forbes Pearson, damn him, had seconded me on board, only to bugger off himself. I whined and bleated, but to no avail. 'You've got to learn to be political, Alastair. Our corner especially needs to be fought for. If we do not survive as a specialty, none of the other specialties will mourn us. Remember that. So, first rule of emergency medicine polemics: be there at the battle.' It sounded like 'presenteeism' to me. Politicians did it. The first hint of a mini-crisis and they would scuttle back from their Mediterranean villas to Westminster, or, for that matter, Holyrood. I couldn't be bothered. Wasn't a political animal. But there it was. I had to go to a ghastly multidisciplinary meeting spearheaded by the managers, with all the paraphernalia of flip charts, breakout groups, delegates 'reporting back', and the group 'going forward'. It had originally been called BPA, this committee. BPA stood for 'Best Practice Activated'. BPA had started as an ethos, expanded into a philosophy, and was now burgeoning exuberantly, one might even say promiscuously, into a multidisciplinary industry. BPA had evolved into ELSCOMF. And here I was, looking at an agenda so long it might well eat into my evening (eating my tin of ravioli, watching the telly). What was more, we had arranged to meet three times that week, prior to an off-site presentation to the acute services, as it so happened, in the Colin Maclaurin Conference Centre at Clerk Maxwell. In the following week we would come together again for a debrief. Meetings generating meetings.

MacTaggart, the Professor of Neurology, chaired. That in itself was anomalous. He was a caricature consultant, big, bluff, flamboyant, and immensely pompous. He wore immaculate Savile Row suits, a buttonhole, stank of cologne, and he drove a Bentley. Once a week he flew down to his rooms in Wimpole Street where City people, government people, and the wives of captains of industry consulted him with their ME. He told them with enormous charm to get over it and he charged them an even more enormous fee. They were on first name terms with him. 'Angus told me to stop taking the thyroxine and join a gymnasium!'

I wondered what my erstwhile colleagues in Melbourne, where I worked as a registrar, would think, of an emergency medicine committee being chaired by a specialist from internal medicine. It would be incomprehensible to them. They wouldn't stand for it. They would tell MacTaggart with imperturbable brash bonhomie to go walkabout. *Nah fuckin' wurries, mate.* Here, the idea of emergency department autonomy had never really taken off. Nobody, physician, surgeon, intensivist, was going to relinquish the levers of power. But why on earth would MacTaggart be bothered with the micromanagement of the front of the hospital? His big research interest was in slow viruses, kuru and scrapie and BSE, infections that could take an epoch to incubate. There was something deeply ironic in the fact that this man should wish to, or even be allowed to, influence policy in the management of emergent conditions. The golden decade. At least, paradoxically, he was brisk.

'Good afternoon ladies and gentlemen. Introductions, down the table if you please. My name is Angus MacTaggart. I am Regius Professor of Neurology and visiting Professor of Neurosciences at the University . . . Dean of Faculty . . . special interest in prehospital management of *status epilepticus* . . .' (Aye, right.) The potted *Who's Who* extract droned on. I could see people further down the table stiffening, hastily rehearsing their own mini-résumés. Nobody was listening. There were a dozen people round the table. Precisely because I'm not very good at this sort of thing, I resolved to attempt to memorise everybody's name by a technique of association. A senior surgeon was on MacTaggart's left, competing in qualification and verbosity. This could take all night. The group had arranged itself instinctively into subsets like sections of an orchestra. Big brass first. I was at the back of the viola section. The lengths of the intros were in proportion to seniority and towards the end became virtually monosyllabic. Let's see: MacTaggart . . . braggart. Mr Hargreaves . . . rolled

21

up sleeves. Leslie Horne blowing his own trumpet, John Worthington worthy, Anne Doctor (Dr Doctor) . . . Helen Gaskell . . . Gaskell . . . gasket . . . fanny mechanic. Eugene Gawkrodger (what a fantastic name) with his bow tie and puce jacket . . . empty chair (Forbes – wily Forbes – sends his apologies) . . . Trish Campbell (tartan skirt – ancient Campbell I think) . . . Phil Clotworthy (overweight – if the cap fits . . .) . . . Henry Bach (gasman, pronounced Baitch, rhymes with aitch, old 'enery). The girl on my right said brightly, 'I'm Tracy one of the nurses.'

I said 'Tracy who?'

She blushed. 'Partridge.'

Ha!

MacTaggart Hargreaves Horne Worthington Doctor Gaskell Gawkrodger Pearson (no show) Campbell Clotworthy Bach Partridge.

I thought of the obscene version of *The Twelve Days of Christmas*. There was a pause.

Chair looked at me enquiringly.

'Alastair Cameron-Strange, emergency physician.'

What would my hat-check description be? Angry young man? Maybe just strange.

'We move to item 1: Mission Statement. Leslie would you talk to this?'

'Thank you chair.' Leslie Horne coloured slightly as he hunched over his brief. 'We're here this afternoon to workshop some of the finer detail of the points we will present in plenary later this week, re the moving forward of A & E services in this hosp–'

'Point of order Mr Chairman.' It was my own forefinger in the air. MacTaggart knitted his brow in annoyance. 'Yes what is it Alastair?'

Everybody round the table had a bottle of water and a glass. I pushed my glass into the centre of the table. I thought of Richard Feynman, the great showman, pulling off a stunt at the Challenger Inquiry.

'Swear box. 20 pence for the A-word. 50p for "A & E". One pound sterling for "Casualty". Two pounds for "Cas".'

22

'What are you talking about Alastair?'

'We are The Department of Emergency Medicine. Or the Emergency Department. Or the ED.'

Mr Hargreaves said, 'I thought ED stood for erectile dysfunction.' Everybody laughed. Except me. I said, 'He who controls the language sets the agenda.' Maybe I was something of a political animal after all. But nobody paid the slightest attention. MacTaggart resumed wearily. 'Leslie?'

'You all got your assignments last week. I hope you've had a chance to do some homework over the weekend.'

Assignments? Homework?

Leslie got up and pulled a flip chart into view. 'We'll just go round the table and jot down your ideas and then workshop them.'

MacTaggart decided to go in reverse order. I have an idea he was trying to catch me on the hop. I shrugged and pouted in a Gallic way, an existentialist sipping absinthe at Fouquets.

'*Primum non nocere.*' It was off the top of my head.

'Pardon me?'

'First do no harm.'

'Yes I know what it means. It doesn't seem terribly ambitious.'

'You'd be surprised. All right. How about, "To cure sometimes, to alleviate often, to care always?"'

'Very homespun. Alastair, I don't think you've quite got the hang of what a mission statement is.'

'I'm sure you're right.'

'It's fine to be pithy, but we also need to be comprehensive. Trish?'

Ms Campbell donned an improbable *pince-nez*. 'I've come up with the following: We pledge to honour and respect our client on his or her journey, protecting his or her autonomy, right to health, freedom to choose, discretion to give or withhold informed consent, offering health care that is timeous, evidence-based, holistic, aligned with best practice, and focused on best quality outcomes.'

'Very good. Succinct. Comprehensive. Alastair – you're pouting again.'

'It's a camel.'

'Camel?'

'You know. A horse designed by a committee. And what are you going to do with it? Put it on a plaque? Perhaps we will form a ring and recite it every morning, like the Cubs and Brownies. We'll dib dib dib.'

MacTaggart took his glasses off and threw them down on the blotter with some impatience. 'Why are you such a wrecker?'

So it went on. The daily round. Who was it said we most of us live lives of quiet desperation? Up, shower, dress, apology for a breakfast, get to work, take the handover, tend the sick and needy, react to other people's agendas, keep a record, snatch a lunch, pot a few balls, attend some ghastly and inconsequential management meeting, take calls, make calls, liaise, keep out of trouble, make an escape. It was dark when I left the flat and it was dark when I got back. I ascended four flights and there, huddled on the landing, sat my sister-in-law.

'Katie.'

'Ally-bally.'

I resisted the temptation to tell her she couldn't smoke on the landing, and I didn't ask her what she was doing 350 odd miles north of Cheltenham. Actually, I wasn't surprised.

'Come in.'

She cast a critical eye around the dull boxlike Victorian foyer, decorated in minimalist style and occupied by my recluse flat mate, a golden carp staring out of the tank at us and solving the mysteries of the universe.

'What's the name of the fish?'

'Tallulah Bankhead.'

'Hi Lulah.' She gave a girlie wave and walked through into my front room and across to the big bay window. She was sixteen, as tall now as Mary had been, and the sisterly similarity of the loping gait caught my breath. She stood with her back to me, staring out across Thirlestane over the roof of Warrender Baths, right elbow resting in left hand, smoking her cigarette. Jeans. Fawn kagool, auburn hair, very long. Great tresses falling to her waist. Might have been Mary. Transfixed.

'Do Eric and Sally know you're here?'

'Nope.' She carried on staring out of the window.

'Mind if I call them?'

'Nope.'

I used the land line and dialled the Stow-on-the-Wold number. Caitlin didn't move. She was listening intently to my side of the conversation.

'Eric it's Alastair . . . Yes she's here . . . No she's fine . . .'

I drew the receiver away from my ear, pointed at it, and glanced interrogatively at Caitlin's reflection in the bay window. She shook her head.

'She'll call you later . . . I'll ask her . . . Yes I'll check on that . . . Don't worry she's perfectly safe . . . Okay . . . Talk to you soon. Love to Sally. Bye.'

She waited until I'd hung up before coming away from the window. She threw the cigarette butt into the grate under the ornate mantel without looking and without bothering to stub it out, slid the kagool off her shoulders and let it fall to the floor. She was wearing a pale lemon halter neck, not, as had been her wont recently, a turtle neck. The thick purple keloid scar which I knew crossed the length of her sternum ascended proximally to leapfrog across her neck just to access her chin, like an inverted exclamation mark. 'Can I stay? I won't be any trouble.' The big brown eyes, set wide apart, gazed at me appraisingly. She was a wild Celt, as her sister had been.

'What about school?'

'End of term.' She sounded a bit vague. 'I can house-sit the gold fish. What was her name again?'

'Thelonious Monk.'

She said accusingly, 'You said she was a girl.'

'He changes her sex constantly.' I wondered what she was running away from. It crossed my mind she was being bullied. Carrot top. Freckle face. Or maybe it was because of the scar. Yet she didn't strike me as somebody who would be prone to bullying. All these posh friends of hers down in Cheltenham had not succeeded in modifying her beautiful soft Dublin accent. 'Where's your luggage?'

'I don't have any.'

'Not even your oboe?'

'What's an oboe?'

How extraordinary. She, too, had taken a vow of silence. Was music cacophony to her now, as it was to me?

'You can stay as long as you like.'

III

After Mary went, I was 'counselled' about my 'grief'. A grim, dumpy bald woman in a tweed suit told me about my 'grief reaction'. Apparently it had four stages. Well what a lot of crap that turned out to be. I was tutored in this stuff. Stage 1 was Shock.

I baulked at that. Shock, madam, is a catastrophic collapse of the circulation leading to irreversible multiple organ failure. Feel my resting pulse – 48 and regular. (I do triathlons.) Take my BP – 110/70. Feel my peripheries – warm, pink, and well perfused. It seems an affront, I know, but I'm not shocked.

She listened to me with the bland complacency of somebody who knows she is right and went on to stage 2: Denial.

Denial? What am I supposed to be denying? She is, after all, dead. She went on to stages 3 and 4 but I'd stopped listening. Besides, anybody can make this stuff up. Stage 3 would be some kind of blunting process of attenuation, an adjustment, and stage 4 would be some kind of resignation achieved on a platonic field. Closure. There's a trendy word.

But I can assure you there will be no closure. Angry? *Moi?* I'm absolutely furious. I never told that counsellor about the devastating effect Mary's departure had on my response to music. It had always occupied such an important part in our lives and suddenly I couldn't bear it. It had just become noise. I was reminded of that Old Testament story about the Tower of Babel, that absurd staircase to heaven, a monument to man's pride. After it collapsed everything became unintelligible, everybody went around talking gibberish. Something like that happened to me with respect to musical language. Music as gibberish. I'm living proof that tone deafness can be an acquired condition. It wasn't that I had lost my musical memory. I was still acquainted with the repertoire. It was just that it had lost its meaning, its emotional substance. It had become an affront.

When does a grief reaction become pathological? I think of myself as a castle under siege. When Mary was killed my enemy pitched a bivouac in sight of my battlements and just watched me, day after day, and in a detached disinterested way, as I strutted about behind the ramparts ranting and raving and gesticulating like Hamlet. *To be or not to be.* The enemy waited patiently; waited for me to go mad. Then when my defences were at their weakest, they would cross the moat, broach the portcullis, and they would be in. And that would be a point of no return. My enemy would have become part of me, like a virus. I could now be destroyed from within. I would destroy myself.

Nowadays psychiatrists tend to view depression as a matter of degree. You're tetchy, you're sad, you're a miserable git, you're a bloody miserable git . . . I've never been convinced by this depiction of wretchedness as a linear progression. Part of the misery of the condition is that you think you are light years and aeons from your destination. But you're not. There's a way out. And it's right there beside you. If only you can find it. It's like a parlour game. A sleight of hand. The trick of life. I was never any good at it.

'Alastair!'

It was MacTaggart, ambushing me as I escaped out the back door of the emergency department and made my way along the medical corridor. It was a chance meeting but I had the odd feeling he had been lying in wait. He smirked at the ED entrance. 'Still down and out among the vagrants I see.'

Ever since I had been his houseman he had been trying to recruit me. He was like a KGB agent, wheedling away. 'Why do you persist in wasting your energy on drunks and vagabonds, stitching up heads and washing out stomachs? I've told you you're better than that. It's all very well doing *pro bono* work but you can't really believe you can make a difference down here. The poor ye will always have. Think ahead. Build a career. You have the makings of a first class physician. There's still time. I need a research fellow. Neurotransmission is an expanding field. Neural networking, neuropharmacology, computer modelling, pain modification. Come on board!'

It was blatant piracy. Forbes would have been furious.

I declined, politely but firmly. 'I am a specialist emergency physician. It may be a Cinderella Specialty, but it too, has its expanding fields.'

MacTaggart smiled thinly and gave a barely audible sniff.

'Perfunctory medicine for perfunctory doctors.'

I had the notion he would never ask me again.

I rather like being in a Cinderella Specialty. My twin sister, MacKenzie, is the viola player in the Arnold Bax Quartet. She has been attracted by a Cinderella instrument. Like bogtrotters, Canucks, and Newfies, viola players are the butt of jokes. I think she and I must be drawn to minorities. We have been born and bred in two viola countries, Scotland and New Zealand. I may have stopped listening to music, and playing music, but I still like to think of MacKenzie as my voice, mellow like Baker, dark like Ferrier. Meanwhile I take my muted, understated viola personality and move about my viola country, my alto clef universe, *sotto voce*.

Caitlin and I fell into an uneasy routine. She had the courtesy to free up the bathroom for me in the morning and let me

get ready for work. She would join me for an even more derisory breakfast than I was taking, wearing a pair of my pyja-
mas, rubbing the sleep from her eyes, crouched sideways on
the chair with both bare feet on the seat. She had intense blue-
black varnish on her toenails, the colour of one's finger nails,
momentarily, as they plunge into the swimming pool, freestyle.
Put your goggles on and look and see if I am not right. She
would chew the edge of a bagel and absently scan *The Herald*,
maybe précis an item that caught her eye. We would have the
Today programme on Radio 4. She would raise her eyes to
the ceiling as the programme's anchors reverted to type – an
intimidating man from Splott, a hectoring badgering female
interrupter, a verbose Scottish windbag who posed politicians
questions so lengthy you had forgotten the drift by the time
he dried up. The first morning, she read me something about
an ex-prime minister who, on leaving office, had kept a low
profile, and was now resurfacing in Uganda to announce that
the future of the continent lay with Broadband. Not with clean
water, sanitation, vaccination, retrovirals, peace, harmony,
and an end to exploitation. Broadband. God help us. I went to
work depressed to my boots.

When I would get back in the evening Caitlin would be
cooking in the kitchen, and have the table set, and would
pour me (and herself) a large glass of ice cold New Zealand
Gewürztraminer. She could be chatty, but inconsequential.
'Thelonious has changed sex again!'

'What's he called now?'

'Vonda Shepard.'

'A fish called Vonda? I don't think so. We just had some
guy talk on the way through. Minnesota Fats and me.' I never
talked about my patients and she never talked about her day.
If I was good at confidential, she was as silent as a tomb.
Sometimes I would tell her about the more outlandish shenanigans of ELSCOMF because it would make her laugh.
Clotworthy and Worthington, for example, tabled this crazy
idea they called 'Opportunistic Intervention'. Down in the ED
we were to 'shoulder tap' all males over the age of forty five

and put them on statins. As if we had nothing better to do. I said, 'Count me out! Do you want to live forever? Nobody gets out of here alive.' A look of mock alarm came over the chairman's face. 'Good heavens, Alastair. For a moment I thought you were going to produce a Kalashnikov.'

Next morning I found myself saying to Caitlin, 'You'll damage your thumbs. Why do you use that rubbish, out-moded, obsolete technology? Why not just make a phone call? Freeze! Look at your *palmaris longus*. Taut as a ship's hawser. You'll get RSI, or de Quervain's.'

'Whazzat?'

'Texter's thumb.'

'Hmph.' She carried on texting, nibbling her bagel.

'I'm thinking of starting a society, opposed to the unfet-tered IT splurge bandwagon. I'm modelling it on the lobby against Muzak. That's called "Pipe Down." My society will be "Log Off!"'

'Don't you mean F–'

'Steady. "Log Off" won't have a web site.'

'I marvel.'

'It's not a close-knit society. We're more of a freemasonry. We all know we're out there. We recognise one another.'

'Do you have a funny handshake?'

'That could be incorporated. Would you like to join?'

'Wild horses, Ally, wild horses.' She finished her bagel and lit a Stuyvesant.

'I wish you wouldn't smoke.'

'You smoke.'

'I've got it down to a pack a year.'

'I've got it down to a pack a day.'

'There. I rest my case.'

You may have guessed that Caitlin was in the car with Mary that night. Front seat passenger, restrained. The airbag deployed to save her life but also split open a section of her integument like an orange peel. In terms of the risk-benefit analysis, it's a small price to pay. There is no therapeutic modality in the world that is not attendant with side effects. Not one.

31

Caitlin. When I started out in medicine, started pacing the wards, started speaking to patients, I only used to ask one question. What is the diagnosis? Now I ask two more. What is it you seek? And, what makes you tick? I wondered about Caitlin. What was the diagnosis? What did she seek? What made her tick? I didn't know. I didn't know enough. There was some vital piece of information concealed from me.

Mr Uprichard's attempt to seduce me was much more subtle than Prof MacTaggart's.

On a Wednesday night the police brought in a nineteen-year-old man they had found in a lane behind a pub on Inverleith Walk. There was a smell of blood, alcohol, vomit, excrement, and death, the latter the more so since as a matter of fact he did die, as he entered the Resus Bay.

'Get him across! Protect the neck! One . . . two . . . three! Trauma arrest.' The nurses cut through the layers of bespattered clothing to expose the torso.

'Start CPR.'

There was a single wound just below the rib cage. I had a hunch the blade of the knife had been directed, expertly, upwards.

'Put the leads on.' I glanced at the trace. It was remarkably normal.

'PEA!' My hands darted across the precordium.

'Borrow your tubes.'

I snatched the Sprague-Bowles. Quick listen. I ticked off the differential diagnosis of electrico-mechanical dissociation.

'He's got a tamponade. Pericardiocentesis needle! Stop CPR. Stop the drips.'

No time for ultrasound guidance. Do it blind. Subxiphoid approach. Aim for the left shoulder. I got back about 15 mls of dark blood.

Somebody with their finger on the pulse called from the head end, 'He's got an output.'

Then we lost it again.

'Thoracotomy set!'

What the hell. He's dead. Nothing to lose. Without bothering to drape up or even cleanse the skin I made a generous incision along the fifth left interspace and got out the Gigli saw, the rib retractors, Metzenbaum scissors and long DeBakey forceps. Don't lacerate the lung! Get the rib spreaders in so you can see what you're doing. Broach the pericardium. Don't prang the phrenic nerve! Too much blood. Suction, swabs. More light please. There was the dark eggplant of the myocardium, flickering in its last throes. Keep away from the coronary arteries. No sign of a wound. Ease the heart forward and have a look at the back. There it is. A hole no bigger than my pinkie nail. I stuck a gloved finger on it, like the Dutch boy at the dykes.

'Foley catheter.' I inserted it and inflated the balloon.

'Open the lines. Get some O neg blood up.'

I gave the heart a few squeezes of massage and glanced at the monitor.

'He's fibrillating. Paddles please.'

A few joules DC countershock were enough. The heart sprang to life.

'Suction.' There was still significant seepage but with the pericardium broached at least he would not tamponade.

'Swabs please. BP?'

'87/52.'

'Slow the drips. Keep it at that.'

It was still pretty precarious. I was still the boy at the dykes. We needed to go to theatre.

And thus it was that Mr Uprichard made his grand entrance, fashionably late.

'Good Lord!' He was in pastel shades, slacks and jumper, incongruously wearing his golfing shoes. Night golf? Had he been on the driving range? I fully expected a tirade of abuse but he seemed vastly amused by the whole scenario. I glanced around. The place looked, and smelled, like an abattoir.

'Theatre I think.' Uprichard gave me a look I might have interpreted. 'You'd better come. You seem very attached to your patient.'

What must our bloodied caravan with its retinue of attendants have looked like in the short transit across the public corridor to the theatre lifts? I skipped along in crablike fashion with my hand still inside the man's chest. We lurched up one floor and along another tiled corridor into the theatre suite. Straight through the anaesthetic room and finally into the inner sanctum, the echoing pristine cathedral.

After the frenetic pandemonium of the emergency department, in here it was entirely peaceful.

'Could somebody relieve the doctor of plughole duty? Mr Cameron-Strange, why don't you see this thing through to the end? Continuity of care and all that. Scrub in!'

The rest of the surgery was perfectly routine. Mr Uprichard liked to work in an atmosphere of calm, to the accompaniment of piped classical music. We closed up to the slow movement of a Mozart Piano Concerto. I couldn't bear it. I wonder if Mr Uprichard sensed my discomfort.

'What sort of music do you like, Mr Cameron-Strange?'

'Arnold Schoenberg.'

'Indeed!'

Tonality . . . atonality . . . it's all the same to me.

'*Verklärte Nacht* is beautiful I grant, but didn't he go off the rails? What about *Erwartung*? What about the violin concerto?'

I shrugged. 'It's a path of wonder.'

'You have very good hands, Mr Cameron-Strange.'

It was only then that I realised I was being interviewed for a job.

I said no.

IV

The swirls of rain caught in the floodlit arc of the department entrance made a drizzle look like a deluge. The place still stank like a brewery. I turned up my collar, and started walking north-east fast along Old Dalkeith Road, keeping an eye on the lanes, the doorways, the passing cars. The haar clung to my skin like radioactive fallout. It had been midnight by the time we had settled our patient in ICU, and the head of the unit had detained me for ten minutes in his office to drink a shot of single Islay malt, Laphroaig, from a paper cup, while he entertained me with crazy anecdotes in colourful language. It was a little ritual we enacted from time to time, as much as anything an act of rebellion against the management who had pronounced the harbouring of alcohol on the hospital premises – let alone the drinking of it – a felony punishable by automatic, and summary, dismissal. It had been a good night. Penetrating trauma arrest, salvaged. I was a bit wired.

Back at Thirlestane I was met with the acrid smell of burnt tealeaves. Caitlin was smoking a joint. I know I ought to have taken it off her, flushed it down the toilet, and confiscated her stash. I am ashamed to say I shared it with her. As with the head of ICU and the Laphroaig, it was really just an act of solidarity. Ill advised, ill conceived I know. I just wanted Caitlin to know that whatever bad place she was inhabiting, I was there with her. (Did I say that to her? How nauseating.) I didn't even like the stuff. It didn't agree with me. I hated that unpredictable flipping between an altered mental state and normality, the sense that one might never 'get back', the struggle with numeracy, the elasticity of time, the munchies . . . I thought I'd left it all behind one night on a deck on Coopers Beach, overlooking Doubtless Bay. But here I was. Idiot. Quite apart from anything else, if I got caught I'd be struck off.

After that it gets a bit fuzzy. Scotch and spliff. A bad mix. Caitlin had disappeared off to bed. I don't remember her going. I was sitting in my front room in a reverie. I hadn't even bothered to take my coat off. It was still wet. Time to lock up and hunker down. I felt in my coat pocket for the house keys.

And there was the crumpled sheet of Alan Bletchley's ED record. I felt a sharp stab of guilt and self-recrimination. I opened it out and smoothed away the wrinkles and stared at it. Apart from the demographics it was a blank sheet. How the hell had I managed that? After that chaotic night shift across the Forth I had sat down in the morning and laboriously written up a log, longhand, of all the patients I had seen. The computers had still been down. Bletchley's had been the only record I had actually taken to the patient, so it wasn't in the pile I had mustered at the reception desk. It just got missed out.

Did it matter? It had been a pretty nebulous presentation and maybe that off-hand psychiatrist at the other end of the line had been right. Was it even worth a cold referral? I glanced again at the crumpled sheet and at the patient's demographics. The patient had filled in his own details in neat, carefully printed capital letters; no sticky label – the computers must have been down even when he had shown up at the desk.

Alan Turing Bletchley dob 23/6/12 . . .

I had to laugh. It was a pseudonym. He had given us an alias. Alan Turing – as everybody now knows – was the mathematical genius who had worked at Bletchley Park in Buckinghamshire during the war deciphering the coded messages the Germans generated with their enigma machine. He had created a primitive computer the size of a warehouse, and he laid down some of the theoretical foundations that would lead to the science of artificial intelligence. And Alan Bletchley – I had no other name to call him – had given a Buckinghamshire address and postcode; I had no doubt if I punched it into my satnav and drove south I would be taken to Bletchley Park. I tried to conjure an image of the man I had briefly and so monosyllabically interviewed in the Gloom Room, but the picture was already fading, like an old sepia photograph. If I went back to the hospital and tried to trace him, nobody would remember him. There was hardly any point in referring him to the community mental health team because he would be untraceable. Lost to follow up.

I smoothed out the crumpled paper of his record and scratched out a brief summary of our interaction, including the failed attempt at referral by telephone. Then I wrote, 'DNW'. Did not wait. And signed it.

For a moment I had the illusion that a corner of the sheet of paper was smouldering. Round its edges there was a heat shimmer of the sort that sits above the hose of a petrol pump in a filling station.

Migraine. I whispered, 'Dammit.' I get about one a year – not frequently enough to take it seriously. I fished around the flat for analgesia, to try to abort, or at least, attenuate the attack. All I could find were a couple of time-expired DF118. Laphroaig then weed then dihydrocodeine. Explain that to the GMC.

The heat shimmer spread out in the shape of a large letter C occupying the left periphery of my visual field. Behind it the world wobbled drunkenly like the tiled floor of a swimming pool. In some ways the aura was more distressing than the subsequent headache and nausea. I lay supine on my bed and patiently waited for it to go away. Twenty minutes later, and quite suddenly, my vision went back to normal. Sometimes I can get away with it, but this time I got the full package. I closed the curtains and undressed and went to bed properly and spent what seemed a few miserable hours trying to doze and intermittently vomiting into a basin. After there was no more to come up I jammed a tiny white tablet of buccal prochlorperazine between my gum and lip, and dozed off. I descended into the abysmal labyrinth of my cannabinoidal night. I got utterly lost. I was back in the dysfunctional emergency department over the bridge, back in the Gloom Room, crouched over the Formica tabletop, solving crossword clues.

Owl specs inside hospital allowed (6) Awful pretty? Quite the opposite (6,5) Astute photo only disrupted tie break (7,8) Poser at Elsinore (2,2,2,3,2,2) First things first: that's beyond excessive. Hot stuff! (6) Heat works out cheaper, for example . . . (9) . . . cooking ling by gas. Weird . . . but a winner! (7,7) New York City under attack? Take what refuge you can (3,4,2,1,5) Liam, I harp on about Beethoven's Fifth Symphony (12) Winston Churchill could murder a pint (5).

Mr Bletchley sat patiently on the plastic chair with his hands clasped on the table, staring unblinking at the opposite wall. His face was concealed behind a balaclava.

I woke myself up with my own startled cry. And I remembered the terrible nightmares of my childhood. Night terrors. My mother would soothe me. 'You're all right now. It was only a dream. It wasn't real.' And I repeated her words to myself.

That was a really bad trip.

The room was completely dark. The digital clock said 03:00. How could it possibly only be 3 am? I had spent an age lying in this bed. My headache was gone, though. As a matter of fact, now my head, my mind, was completely clear. It was the only time I could be absolutely confident that I would not get a migraine – just after I'd had one. I flicked on the bedside lamp, got up, went into the kitchen and made myself a mug of chamomile tea. I said to myself, you are a fool. Never again. Don't *ever* smoke another joint. Not ever.

Why had Mr Bletchley put a balaclava on?

I took the mug of tea back into my bedroom. I'd suddenly had an idea. Mr Bletchley had said he was a crossword compiler, semiprofessional. So Bletchley was not merely an alias, it could be his *nom de plume*. Maybe I could trace him on the Internet. I was awake, but the laptop sitting on the table by the window was still asleep. I nudged the mouse into wakefulness. The screen icons illuminated obediently. I embarked on a search.

'Crosswords. Bletchley.'

The search engine proudly announced that she had scored about 6,500,000 hits in 0.2 seconds. Plenty about crosswords; lots of software packages for compilers. And plenty about Bletchley Park and Enigma, and the response to Enigma, codenamed Ultra. But very little about crosswords *and* Bletchley, apart from a piece of received wisdom that British Intelligence tried to recruit cruciverbalists because lateral thinkers might be good at cryptography. That struck me as a piece of folklore, akin to carrots aiding night vision.

I typed in 'Bletchley cruciverbalist'. I got more of the same. Lights, half lights, the lost mysteries of ancient stenography. I reran the tape in my head of the brief encounter in the Gloom Room but Mr Bletchley had said so little that there was barely anything else I could try. I gave it one last go.

'Bletchley the bottom line'.

And there it was. I clicked on and highlighted '*The Bottom Line* by Bletchley'. I double-clicked and there was the 12 by 12 square grid with its pleasing symmetrical array of bold barricades and below it, clues across, and clues down. I clicked on the tiny print icon and after a pause the printer jumped to attention and began to churn out a single sheet of paper. Then a new window opened on the screen.

Windows has unexpectedly encountered a problem and needs to close . . .

I clicked my tongue in annoyance and clicked on the 'Don't send' box and the window abruptly vanished along with the crossword and I was peremptorily disconnected and left staring at the Cuillin ridge at dusk, my screensaver. Then it too vanished and my laptop went to sleep.

I couldn't be bothered to reboot. I made myself another mug of chamomile, picked up the single sheet that had issued from the printer, sat up on my bed and read the rubric of *The Bottom Line*.

Twelve clues are 'two in one' and code for twin solutions. One solution may be converted to its twin by dropping a letter. The shorter twin should be entered into the grid. The twelve redundant letters, when unjumbled, form The Bottom Line *which is thematically related to and also predicted by four (unclued) lights.*

The legend contained one further line, but it had been redacted, as if by a censor's heavy pencil. Well, I said I was something of an addict myself. In the half-lit, half-conscious other world of the migraineur it was therapeutic to pick up a pen and see if I could fill in some of the lights.

These designer crosswords are so bloody difficult. You read the legend and it doesn't mean a thing. All you can do is solve what clues you can, and hope for a hint from the evolving pattern. I wondered if 'The Bottom Line' referred, literally, to the bottom line of the grid. 41 across. But there was no clue provided for 41 across. The last clue across was 40:

Shrive Elena back (5)

Elena back is 'anele'. What's that Hamlet quote?

Unhousel'd, disappointed, unaneled.

Something to do with confession, or 'extreme unction'.

I wrote 'ANELE' into the grid. One done, 40 to go! Plus the four 'unclued' solutions, plus, presumably 'the bottom line'. That would be a word, or words, of twelve letters, made up of twelve 'redundant' letters from the 'twinned' clues, whatever that was about. 41 across was heavily barricaded off, quarantined. Only five of its twelve letters were deducible from other clues. It could not be solved by serendipity. I would have to identify its twelve letters, and unjumble them. And at the moment nothing gave me a hint as to the nature of the four other unclued solutions and their thematic link. I would just have to fill in as many solutions as possible and hope that the sum of the parts might suggest the whole.

When you start solving a crossword puzzle, the first clue is always the most difficult, because you are operating in limbo. After that, you have a kind of nidus from which to expand. I now knew, for example, that the second last letter of 27 down, Peacekeepers' turn to disclose gradually (6), had to be L.

Peacekeepers . . . the United Nations . . . UN. It's a jaded crossword convention. To turn is to roll. Disclose gradually . . . UNROLL. It's kind of managerial-speak. Anyway it fits. It even gives me the second last letter of the bottom line. L.

Next? 21 down: Ends up in drab mini, topless panto girl; toe curling! (8)

Haven't a clue.

I began to discern that there were a host of clues of the sort that you would come across in any standard daily newspaper cryptic crossword. They were relatively straightforward. But there were a dozen or so clues that seemed absolutely impenetrable. Periodically I would take a step back and look at the half-completed puzzle and take a stab at the unclued lights.

H _ D _ _ E _ T

_ _ _ B _ _ _ E

C _ _ _ _ B _ _ E

A _ A _ _ A _ _

I hadn't the ghost of an idea. For the first one, I got it into my head that I was looking for a superlative adjective. Haddiest heddiest hiddiest hoddiest huddiest hyddiest? Nothing seemed to fit. I didn't fare any better with numbers two and

41

three. Maybe they were proper names. The fourth one looked weirdest of all.

This is ridiculous! It's four o'clock in the morning! Pack it in. You've got to be at work in four hours.

Haddlest heddlest hiddlest hoddlest huddlest hyddlest . . .

V

Now here's the thing about designer crosswords: they are impossibly obscure until you discover the key.

17ac: Muddle sly Lily, and break up first love? Yes, maybe (4)

What on earth is all that about?

Hang on. 17ac is only a three letter word on the grid.

Same goes for 18ac. Princess' rubbish Frisbee record (4)

It's a cock-up.

Or maybe not. They must be examples of the 'two in one' clues with twin solutions. There will be twelve of them. How very considerate of Mr Bletchley to identify them for us in this way.

Odd though. Mr Bletchley is anxious that we solve his puzzle.

Caitlin looked up from her muesli. 'What you doing?'

'Crossword puzzle.'

'Gimme a clue.'

'OK. 19 ac – Mash an ugli, tongue of tongues, with Lagavulin distilled outwith the V & A. Seven letters. Or maybe six. Something I something G something something. Or maybe an extra something.'

'Let me just make sure I've got this straight. You want some drunk weirdo loitering outside a museum to assault some ugly person and do something revolting with his tongue.'

'You've got it exactly.'

'Leave it with me.'

Back at ELSCOMF, the flamboyant peacock Eugene Gawkrodger was flying another outrageous kite. He wanted to reduce the emergency department patient population by 40%. 'An ambitious target I know, but it can be done.' There it was on the PowerPoint spreadsheet. Eugene had done his arithmetic. He had divided up the patients into two groups, deemed 'appropriate' and 'inappropriate'. Rest assured, those deemed 'inappropriate' would not be cast into outer darkness. They would be triaged to a clearing house, run by on site GPs.

I had a sudden vision of a uniformed officer in a great-coat standing under a wrought iron gate at the end of a railway line, watching the huddled masses getting off the trucks clutching their pitiful possessions. He was directing them into the 'appropriate' and 'inappropriate' groups, with a curt nod of the head. His breath was visible in the freezing air. There were dogs barking in the background.

I didn't want anything to do with it.

But I must keep calm. What was it Forbes had said? You must learn to be political. It wasn't enough to badmouth a lunatic idea. You had to argue a case.

'The reason why your model is flawed, Eugene, is that it is based on diagnostic criteria. There, for example, you have deemed patients with "mechanical back pain" as "inappropriate". But how do you know somebody has mechanical back pain unless you afford them the courtesy of a medical consultation? The trouble is, the patients don't come into the department with a diagnostic label printed on their forehead. Some people think they do, but I can assure you, they do not.'

'Is that not the purpose of triage, to wheedle these people out?' This from MacTaggart.

'Triage is a system of patient prioritisation. We don't triage people out. Granted they did so in the Napoleonic wars, but we've moved on a little since then.'

'Nevertheless, we need to get the patient numbers down.'

'Why? If we were in private business, we would welcome customers with open arms. Why do you want to curtail a demand?' Even as I asked, I could tell the committee wasn't interested. Cutting down patient numbers was a given. I was always going to be out of step. I really ought not to be on this committee. I was a spoiler.

'But we are not in private business, Alastair.' MacTaggart was being patient, as if explaining something to a child. 'The NHS is not an inexhaustible well of resource. There are other departments, other specialties. The cake is not infinite. And, to be frank, we can't squander a big slice on an unproven business model.'

MacTaggart had a knack of being simultaneously charming and obnoxious. And I was naïve and ingenuous. I tended only to register an insult retrospectively. It was only later, after we had adjourned, that I twigged, in a slow-witted way, that 'unproven business model' meant the same thing as – what was that comment he had made to me in the medical corridor? – 'peremptory medicine practised by peremptory doctors.'

Peremptory medicine practised by peremptory doctors. Was that what MacTaggart had said to me previously? Something like that but not quite that. Another word like peremptory. More dismissive.

I chided myself that I had not reacted to such a remark. Was MacTaggart just a phenomenally rude man or was he too stupid to notice? I should have punched him on the nose. Peremptory medicine practised by peremptory doctors. My blood boiled. Both rude and stupid. MacTaggart was a very clever man, he was nobody's fool, but he was quite capable of being stupid. Foolishness and stupidity are not the same thing. Fools are ten a penny, but it takes a certain talent to be stupid. And the cleverer you are, the more spectacular your lapses into stupidity are likely to be.

Peremptory medicine practised by peremptory doctors. I would never forget that MacTaggart had said something like this to me. I felt a surge of fury, but with it, a dawning surge of hope. A 'Great Idea' had suddenly occurred to me. I would take the bastards on. I would take on the combined might of the Royal Colleges. Here was something to get my teeth into. Ever since that calamitous night a year ago I had been paralysed, emasculated, incapable of action. Not now. I had rediscovered my *métier*. I was once more on a grand crusade. In a flash of insight it became clear to me why MacTaggart chaired ELSCOMF, why he took pains to be present, to take control of the meetings. It was to make sure we stayed in our place. That was why he chose to adopt archaic language. Cas, casualty, A and E . . . he made our facility sound like a dressing station on the Somme. That was because he wanted it to be so. He wanted the front of the hospital to be trench warfare, chaotic and mangled; a morass of bewildered 'casualties' being treated, maltreated, by a bunch of hapless, and peremptory, juniors. The blind leading the blind. From time to time he would send a lieutenant down to rescue one or two carefully selected individuals worthy of salvage. And when things went wrong he would shake his head. 'Peremptory medicine . . .'

Perfunctory. That was the word.

Bastard.

Cas . . . A and E. Who defines the terminology sets the agenda. Here was a place to start. Don't allow bad language. Don't let it pass. It would be a modest enough start, but a start. I was going to take them on. I would dig in for the long haul, with Churchillian doggedness. 'If necessary, for years . . .'

'If necessary, alone.'

Back at the flat, over the pre-dinner Gewürz, I asked Caitlin, 'How are you getting on with the sleazy guy outside the V & A?'

'Oh that. I decided not to bother. It's beneath me.'

'Not to worry. I've solved it. It's LINGUA. Or LINGUAL.'

'Well which is it?'

'Both actually. Let me explain.'

'Must you?'

'It's two clues in one. The first clue is, "Mash an ugli, tongue." Answer: LINGUA. It's an anagram of "an ugli". Second clue: "Of tongues, with Lagavulin distilled outwith the V & A." Answer: LINGUAL. A distillation of Lagavulin but out with letters V and A. See? I think that's very clever.'

'I think you're the saddest person I've ever met.'

The trouble with smoking pot is that the cannabinoids stay in your frontal lobes for ever. Twenty four hours later I was still having bad dreams. I was dreaming about Edinburgh New Town, and the gracious octagonal elegance of Moray Place, and then I suddenly flitted to the other octagon, the other Moray Place in the other Edinburgh – Dunedin New Zealand. Then I took a flight along the north shore of Otago Harbour. I didn't bother taking an aeroplane. In my dream state, it never struck me as odd that I had the power of flight. I landed at a village opposite Taiaroa Head, close to the harbour entrance, in time to see an armed man emerging from a dilapidated cottage, firing from the hip. Then the film froze, and I woke up.

When you get stuck on a crossword, the thing to do is leave it, do something else, and come back later. For no apparent reason, that which was obscure is suddenly glaringly obvious. I picked up Mr Bletchley's half-complete puzzle and pretty much finished it. After I had done all of the simpler clues I had a look at the four unclued lights.

HOD _ _ E _ T

A _ A _ _ A _ _

_ U _ BLANE

CO _ _ _BI _ E

Then I got stuck into the remainder of the twelve twin clues. Caitlin's 'ugli' clue had been a breakthrough. The redundant letter in this case of course is L. I was beginning to see how these clues worked. Something was beginning to emerge.

HOD _ _E _ T

A _ A _ _A _ _

DU _ BLANE

COLU _ BI _E

That's one solved: DUNBLANE. Nice town, beautiful cathedral, famous sporting son, golden letter box. Does it help with the other three?

HOD _ _ E _ T

A _ A _ _ AN _

COLU _ BI _ E

There comes a *eureka* moment in the unravelling of an enigma. I have to say I didn't think a great deal about it. It just indicated that Mr Bletchley had a mawkish preoccupation with the macabre. Columbine. There it was. The thematic link. What was it?

Notoriety.

And, knowing now what I was looking for, I discovered that I, or at least my unconscious mind, had recognised it already. Maybe a New Zealand background helped. Flickering images salvaged from discarded reels of corrupted celluloid left on the cutting room floor. Something bad had happened deep down in South Island.

ARAMOANA

And something else, across the Tasman.

HODDLEST. Of course.

Hoddle St.

That only left The Bottom Line. I had my twelve assembled letters to unjumble.

ACEEKLLLMRWX

And on the grid – C _ ER _ _ _ _ _ _ LL

I glanced at the clock. 04:00. Not again!

Get some sleep.

Back into Little France, into the blue scrubs, on to the floor, re-enter the world of pain and misery, angst, hope, and despair. Then, worst of all, get along to the Board Room.

'. . . coping strategies for bed blocking . . . Alastair are we keeping you awake?'

'Sorry, Professor. Rough night.'

I could see by his pained expression that MacTaggart really despaired of me. I suppose with all the cumulative late nights I looked like somebody who slept rough out on the streets. I was down and out amongst the vagrants. And I didn't mind. I was like Mr Black, alias Mr Green, one of our recidivist tramps who hung around the entrance and occasionally came in for some respite from the cold. I too was a recidivist tramp. The only difference was I was on the pay roll. I knew MacTaggart thought it was an affectation on my part, pretentious, like Schweitzer heading off to a *léproserie* at Lamberéné. Maybe I had a Messianic Complex, a deeply unhealthy erotic desire to move amongst publicans and sinners in the dark wynds of existence from whence some harlot of low caste would rub nard into my feet with her matted hair. But MacTaggart had dismissed me now, offended by my rebuff. 'Cameron-Strange? He's finished. He blew it.'

Quick visit to the snooker table before going home. I set up the balls, colours only, and rehearsed my routine of potting them from their spots. Twenty seven points on the table. I'd reached the stage that I could sink all six balls on automatic pilot more often than not. Tap . . . click . . . flop . . . two . . . five . . . nine . . . fourteen . . . the chaste kiss of white on pink . . . twenty and, to make twenty seven . . . an exhibition shot on the black.

Click.

It's Clerk Maxwell.

How thick of me not to see it.

The Bottom Line! What did Bletchley say? . . . thematically related to, and also predicted by four (unclued) lights.

Predicted!

Bloody hell.

VI

I laid my cue down on the deserted baize, took out my battered copy of *The Bottom Line* and wrote down the solution to the last clue across, to complete the grid. Then I glanced at my watch. Five to five. If I ran back across to ED I might just catch Forbes in his office.

I felt oddly apprehensive when I banged on his door.

'*In!*'

MacTaggart was there. Forbes, dapper, twinkling, pleased with life, was putting his coat on. I think they were heading out to some Faculty cheese and wine thing.

'Something on your mind Alastair?'

'I've got a problem.'

Forbes glanced at the clock. 'Can it wait? Is it important?'

'I think it could be.'

Forbes's eyes flicked in the direction of MacTaggart and back again. I nodded imperceptibly. This was confidential.

'You go on Angus. I'll be five minutes.'

And I thought, why don't I want MacTaggart to know

about this? Because I definitely don't. Forbes waited for the door to close and then gestured wordlessly at the chair. He was irritated. I felt coy, like a school pupil venturing to show his attempts at verse to his English teacher. I hadn't rehearsed this.

'I saw somebody over at PMH who's planning a Columbine.' I don't know why I felt so reticent about voicing my concerns. I suppose it was fear of ridicule. Only an anorak, a nerd, would have taken the trouble to track the puzzle down, let alone solve it. I laid the paper on the desk. Forbes was frowning. I ploughed on. 'Crossword compiler. I solved one of his puzzles.' I let Forbes read the legend and study the grid. He didn't need many pointers. He was very sharp. I indicated with a pencil.

'Here are the four unclued lights. They predict the bottom line – here.'

Forbes nodded and sniffed to indicate he had taken it in. 'Student prank, most likely. But an ill-advised one. What was he like?'

'Very low key.'

'Well. It's not a crime to set an acrostic, even when it's in bad taste. Let it go. Pass it on. Send it up to the liaison psychiatrists with a covering note. Better copy it to Trubshaw as a courtesy.'

'What if they just file it away?'

Forbes said, with frank exasperation, 'That's their business. You are not a detective. You are not a social worker. You are an emergency physician. Always remember there are more people coming through the front door. You haven't got the time for after-care. It's not your responsibility. Live with it.'

And that was that.

But over the next few days I found it hard to let it go. *The Bottom Line* preoccupied me. I gnawed away at it. I didn't want to, I would have gladly accepted Forbes's advice and let it go. But somehow *it* wouldn't let *me* go. I would set up the jolly coloured balls on the green baize and try to obliterate *The Bottom Line* in the simplified world of Newtonian mechanics. Strike the ball thus; pocket the object ball; position the cue ball for the next shot.

I suppose it was inevitable that, in this frame of mind, I would make a mistake. At least I thought it was a mistake, even if my colleagues were quick to back me and say they would have done exactly the same under the circumstances.

A twenty-one-year-old woman, previously well, presented with a headache. She came in around nine o'clock in the evening looking for some analgesia so that she could get a sleep. She was exhausted because ten days previously she had given birth to a baby boy. The physical examination was entirely normal except for one thing. Her blood pressure was high. Not sky high, but high. Had she had high blood pressure during her pregnancy? No. I was taking it in the noisy environment of the emergency department and at first I didn't get an accurate reading but I registered it was high. I took it a few times and the best I got was 165/90. I recorded this. But why did I record her best BP? Why not the worst? I gave her some codeine and asked her to attend her GP in the morning for a further check of her blood pressure.

She had a bad night with increasing headache and in the morning she chose not to attend her GP but to come back to us, where a colleague recorded a BP of 240/140. She was admitted and treated for hypertensive encephalopathy. She got better. Thank God.

Well, with the benefit of what we call the 'retrospectoscope' I would have admitted her. But would I, should I, really have done something different? I was morose for about 48 hours. The usual thing. Get out of acute medicine and go into research where you can't do any harm. And of course, after a thing like that, you can't just crawl away into a hole and fester. You keep practising medicine. And more acute conundrums present themselves. That is the difficult bit. But I couldn't get the young mother out of my head. What if she had had a catastrophic bleed and died? Or ended up in a semi-vegetative state, lying at the bottom of a remote rehab ward being fed through a tube? And what of me? If I get as upset as this with a near miss, can I really contemplate a career in this environment for the next thirty years?

At length Forbes hauled me into his office and gave me some counselling in typical Forbes fashion: 'You were asked to see a patient. Did you see her? Yes. Did you take a careful history? Yes. Did you undertake a careful physical examination? Yes. Did you reach a rational conclusion? Yes. Did you arrange a suitable disposition? Yes. Did you arrange appropriate follow up? Yes. Would you have done it any differently? No. Toughen up!'

He paused. Then, on another tack: 'I wonder if you're working too hard. I know you've had a rough time, what with Mary . . . Forgive me if I'm speaking out of turn, but do you get out much? I hear you're smoking again. You don't play music any more. You're not getting much exercise. You're not flying.'

And all that was perfectly true. I couldn't stand music. I hadn't flown an aircraft for months. I wasn't current. And after a hard day in the hospital the last thing I wanted to do was go for a run. I'd rather have a large whisky, just to ease my way through that difficult time of day, that time when the day's commitment receded. The awkward twilight hour. The evening yawns at you.

And as I opened the door on my way out he called after me, 'Have you closed the file on Mr Bletchley?'

'No, not yet.'

'Drop it Alastair.'

VII

I fished the business card of my Medical Defence Union out of my wallet and dialled an Edinburgh number.

'Cardwell Walkerburn you are speaking with Vikki how may I direct your call?'

'My name is Dr Cameron-Strange. I am seeking a medico-legal opinion.'

'I'll see if Mr Walkerburn is available putting you on hold.'

Hold was, predictably, Vivaldi, and a blizzard of violins. A pause, and then a clip-clop sleigh ride. I found it completely charmless.

Abruptly the music came to a halt and the line went live, like a cold shower.

'David Walkerburn.'

It was a careful voice.

'I'm phoning about an issue of confidentiality.'

'Yes?'

'It's rather sensitive. Could I call in at your office?'

'Would two o'clock suit?'

So. I had set something in motion. Not yet irrevocably. Mr Walkerburn would protect my confidentiality just as, thus far, I had protected Mr Bletchley's. This thing was still contained.

It was funny how I hadn't wanted to talk over the phone, just as I had not wanted to have MacTaggart present when I confided in Forbes. Perhaps I thought the line to Cardwell Walkerburn wasn't secure. But why would that matter? It wasn't just the confidentiality issue. After all, I could have posted *The Bottom Line* on the Health Board website much like a public health warning, about a nasty epidemic of norovirus in the community, a faulty batch of pharmaceuticals that was being recalled, or a drug addict doing the rounds of various emergency departments under assumed names. '. . . calls herself Felicity Dunlop, Heather McCready, or Sandra Dunn. Five foot three, short red hair . . .' How might I phrase it? 'Police are in receipt –' (I was thinking ahead) '– of a threat to James Clerk Maxwell University College Campus . . . students, staff members, and visitors are asked to be on the highest alert and to report any suspicious . . .' Yet people would want to know the nature of the threat. What? A crossword? You're kidding. That was why I didn't want to fax *The Bottom Line* across to Cardwell Walkerburn. It was just too silly. I almost phoned Walkerburn back to cancel the appointment. I could get myself out of all this. I had woken up that morning full of an intense homesickness for New Zealand. Maybe it was time to go home.

Forbes had pointed out to me how miserable my life was. You don't run, you don't fly . . . You don't get much *fun*. I was anhedonic, as the psychiatrists would say. They always used these daft words that nobody else used. I was *anhedonic* to the extent that I sometimes even entertained suicidal *ideation*.

But when I thought of running, and of flying, I thought of New Zealand. They'd be going into summer now. As I walked northwards through the clinging haar down the hill off Princes Street toward 48 Heriot Row I took off in a Cherokee Archer out of Ardmore, just south of Auckland, and flew all the way up to Cape Reinga. Nice smooth landing on the tiny grass strip. Cut the engine and enjoy the silence after the hours of engine roar. Listen to the little sounds of nature. Make the plane safe and take a stroll down to Waitiki Landing and say hello to the *whanau*. Maybe borrow a ute and take it on to the unsealed road at Te Paki station and take a turn down to the big dunes. Here I will kick off my shoes and slosh down Te Paki stream through the dunes to the great expanse of Ninety Mile Beach and the awesome thunderous silence of the ocean.

'It's very arcane. And rather oblique. Do you think there's much in it?'

We were sitting in a dusky back room in the offices of Cardwell Walkerburn, Writers to the Signet, at the west end of Heriot Row. The haar had even found its way in here, curling its way like trench gas around the dusty bookshelves.

I have a deep distrust of the legal profession. I try to keep away from it at all costs. My view of it is Dickensian. I think of scriveners and proctors toiling away with quills at high desks, of Jarndyce and Jarndyce, of endless litigation, suits buried in a morass of legalese in Latin, Mr Jaggers endlessly washing his hands. But I quite took to David Walkerburn. He was a very tall man – six seven I would guess, with a permanent stoop acquired from the endless interaction with all sorts of humankind. He wasn't a man in a sharp suit. His was a tired three-piece grey pin-stripe which seemed to emphasise his sallow, bookish complexion. He was entirely lacking in razzmatazz. He sat staring at *The Bottom Line* and biting his lip.

'What does Professor Pearson think?'

'That I should pass it on to the psychiatrists and forget about it.'

'You are not inclined to heed his advice?'

'I have the suspicion they will drop it.'

'Because there's not much to it?' He held the paper up like an exhibit.

'Maybe not.'

But I thought of the myriad occasions I had sent a patient to a surgeon, with altered bowel habit, with blood in the urine, with weight loss. The careful assessment and the cautious opinion; 'I reassured Mr X. However, for completeness, I think we should carry out a simple investigation . . .' If you don't have a steady trickle of false positives in the hunt for cancer you are not doing your job.

'So what are you going to do?'

'That's why I'm here, Mr Walkerburn. I need to know, if I inform the police, whether I am vulnerable.'

'In terms of passing the evidence on there is no problem. You found it on the Internet, ergo it was in the public domain already. The problem arises when you identify its originator. And mind, you are making an assumption here. You do not actually know that Mr er, Bletchley, compiled this grid. He may have come across it just as you did.'

'That seems very unlikely.'

'But not impossible. Secondly, he can argue that your going to the police with this information represents a breach of medical confidentiality in that he has neither implied nor explicitly rendered permission for you to do so. The question would then arise whether the information you were divulging was sufficiently weighty, and of sufficient concern to the public interest, that your duty as a citizen overruled your fiduciary responsibility as a doctor.'

But I knew all this. He was like a politician weighing issues on a panel debating programme. On the one hand this, on the other hand that. All very well, you have elaborated the question, now give me an answer.

'So?'

'I would have thought, given the nebulous condition of the evidence, that there might be a case to answer.'

'And would I be liable?'

He spread his hands in a gesture of deliberation. 'You would have to test the case.'

'Yes or no?'

'Possibly.'

I emerged from 48 Heriot Row and walked up to Waterstones on Princes Street and had a coffee on the top floor beside the music section. Once more I spread the crumpled grid out and looked at it.

With respect to Forbes's advice, I had done as I was told. I had appended a copy of the solution to *The Bottom Line* to Bletchley's ED record and mailed it to the liaison psychiatrists at PMH with a copy to Barry Trubshaw, Emergency Department Director. I was absolutely confident that the material would be scanned into the electronic records system and then shredded. And that would be that. Managers were forever sending out memos to the workforce (cascades they were called) under the impression that they were achieving something. But sometimes I thought a delegation of duty was nothing more than a dereliction of duty. If you really wanted something to happen it was useless merely to 'fire and forget'. You needed to hassle people, get back to them, get on their case, irritate them, make yourself a thorough pain in the neck.

Would it be worth it? Or was I just being cranky? Forbes evidently thought the latter. Walkerburn's nebulous response was hardly more encouraging. I should drop it.

Yet what if something dreadful happened? What if somebody hit the ground running on the campus at Clerk Maxwell and stormed through the place strafing the quads with an arsenal of small arms? I might be a witness at a subsequent inquiry. 'Oh yes I knew about that! I saw it coming! It's all here on the medical record.'

'And what action did you take, doctor?'

'Oh I just filed it away.'

There would be silence in court. Perhaps a muffled cough and the embarrassed shuffle of feet. People would keep their eyes down, examining their fingernails.

The thing is, *The Bottom Line* was a test result, like a marker for cancer, PSA or CEA or AFP. Like all these tests, it would have a measurable power, a sensitivity, a specificity, a positive and a negative predictive value. Let's take the positive predictive value: the probability that Bletchley, the man with the positive test (Walkerburn had even questioned that) would develop the disease. Forbes thought not. A student prank, he had called it.

Then again take the negative predictive value. A subtler concept. The probability that if the test were negative, the subject would *not* develop the disease. In other words, if there were no red flags flying, could we reliably trust the subject not to do something crazy? Probably not. A taxi driver in the north-west of England had recently flipped his lid and led the police on a wild goose chase round the back lanes of Cumbria while he had shot a bunch of people, some targeted, some apparently at random. Could it have been prevented? It didn't look promising. The Prime Minister had said that you couldn't legislate against the flick of a switch in somebody's head.

Of course, after the event, there was always somebody ready to say that there had, after all, been red flags. Somebody had heard the jungle drums beating. 'I always knew there was something weird about him . . .' There's none so queer as folk. There's nobody normal, but thee and me. And I'm not so sure about thee.

From time to time you heard of the demise of a child after years of repeated abuse at the hands of dysfunctional parents. It subsequently became apparent that there were numerous occasions (a fantastic number like one hundred and ninety seven would be quoted), opportunities for intervention by social services. Social services would get it in the neck. It seemed to be to be a kind of special British thing, this finger-pointing after the event. It was why people strove to keep a low profile. Keep your head down, don't stick your hand up, don't volunteer. Never admit to anything, never explain, never apologise. Above all else, don't allow yourself to be a scapegoat. Because when the shit hits the fan, rest assured, the authorities will be desperate to find one, so that the whole thing can be tidied up and put to bed. And if you are crazy enough to offer yourself up as a sacrificial lamb, don't imagine for a second that you will get any sympathy. Quite the opposite. They'll be on to you like a pack of wild dogs. I could just imagine the scenario at the inquest (no, not an inquest, a fatal accident inquiry in Scotland) into a dozen wrongful deaths. 'I blame myself,' said Dr Cameron-Strange. 'I alone had access to the information. I should have acted on it.' It would be as if I had been the murderous perpetrator. I would be torn to pieces.

So there we are. I had made up my mind in the lukewarm dregs of a huge cardboard coffee beaker in Waterstones. I would sidestep Walkerburn's vacillations and would blatantly ignore my boss's advice. I was crossing a line. There would be no going back. This thing would no longer be contained.

VIII

When I thought about Caitlin, and my responsibility to
Caitlin, I felt utterly inadequate. My flat was no place for
her. It was empty all day, often all night. It wasn't a home.
It was just a place where occasionally I slept. I had nothing to offer her. No hearth. No circle of friends, no social
milieu, not even the prospect of one. I was a rudderless ship.
Of course, I might argue that this state of affairs was temporary, and no fault of mine. I had suffered a catastrophe,
I needed to pick up the pieces and to start again. But deep
down I had a sense that I would never do this. I would never
achieve any sort of 'life-work balance'. I would cease to try.
I would become one of these confirmed bachelors who were
sometimes a convenience to married people because they
could fill a vacant chair at a dinner party. But I would sel-
dom reciprocate. I would assume an avuncular personality.
I would be 'Uncle Alastair' to children to whom I was not
related. I would join a health club. I would become a clubb-
able man because membership might give a semblance of
integration while at heart I was isolated, in retreat, border-

ing on recluse. No. I wasn't good for Caitlin. I must get her back to Stow-on-the-Wold.

On the way over the Forth I flicked on the car radio and surfed the stations to divert myself from a vague sense of free-floating anxiety and the notion that I really was crossing a bridge. Sometimes I would give music another chance, the way a patient might finger an abscess to see if palpation was still agonising. As I picked each station off my thoughts darted nervously between Caitlin and Bletchley, between Forbes, and MacTaggart, but always back to Caitlin . . . Rach II . . . chill with Classic FM . . . Caitlin in her self-imposed purdah . . . Rap and psychobabble . . . Radio 1 . . . She never called her parents; I did . . . Radio 4's chattering classes . . . I gathered that just before her hasty departure things had been pretty fraught in the Roy household. She was unlivable with, she was giving everybody a hell of a time . . . Prolonged empty silence – Radio 3. Something had happened at school. She was certainly in no hurry to go back. I didn't mind if she wanted to stay over Yuletide, though I could hardly recommend it. I was rostered to work. It would be a grim occasion for her, and a lonely one . . . Convivial banter – Radio 2. Somebody was choosing 'The tracks of their years' on the Ken Bruce show. I liked Ken. He was chirpy and funny and good natured. He was respectful of the stuff he played – of which he had an encyclopaedic knowledge – and I noticed he always identified the artist and the name of the song. Maybe I should dump classical music and go back to all this adolescent emotional roller-coaster love poetry. The Usher Hall on a Friday night is just a museum; music in inverted commas. I surfed on. Unaccompanied Gaelic. BBC Radio Nan Gàidheal. It was a recording of Flora MacNeil, longing for Barra. It was unbearable. I switched off.

In the police station I introduced myself at the desk as 'one of the doctors up at the hospital'. Not quite true. I glanced at the queue behind me. 'This is a bit sensitive.' The policewoman might have been a school prefect, her pen poised over a proforma. 'Do you wish to report a crime?'

'Not exactly.' I was playing a part in an amateur dramatics rehearsal. What a hammy script. I leaned an elbow on the counter and spoke behind a cupped hand, conscious that this, now, was my point of commitment, and of no return. 'I think one of our patients might be planning – well, a shooting, actually.'

She laid her pen down. 'I'll just get my sergeant. Would you take a seat?'

There was a hiatus. I sat between a boy with jangling headphones and a tear-stained girl in a tracksuit, heavily pregnant. Twenty minutes later a door on my left opened abruptly. 'Just come this way, doctor.'

It was another featureless interview room, much like the Gloom Room. I shook hands with Sergeant Matheson, who looked like a retired prop forward with cauliflower ears, fortyish, big, battered, affable. We faced one another across a heavy deal table.

'Fire away, doc!'

I spilled the beans, on the night from hell at PMH, on Bletchley, on the bizarre consultation, the discovery on the web of *The Bottom Line*, its solution, and its implication.

He frowned. 'You've sat on it for a while.'

'The solution took some time.'

Sergeant Matheson took out a thick reporter's notepad and a stubby blunt pencil and we cobbled together a statement. It was good for me. I had to formalise my reasoning. I couldn't toss a crossword puzzle in front of the sergeant's nose as I had done with Forbes Pearson and David Walkerburn with the shorthand headline 'Somebody's going to do a Columbine.' I must not be like one of my patients, vague, inarticulate, the classic 'poor historian'. I must be succinct.

After quarter of an hour we had the first half of a first draft. He read it back to me. 'My name is Dr Alastair Cameron-Strange and I am a Specialist Registrar in Accident and Emergency . . .'

'No. Emergency Medicine.'

'– in Emergency Medicine. My qualifications are MB ChB

Hons, MD, FACEM. On the night of the 7th December I was on duty in Casualty –'

'No. The Department of Emergency Medicine.'

'– in the Department of Emergency Medicine of Princess Margaret Hospital. I was consulted by a man who identified himself as Alan Bletchley, and who gave a Buckinghamshire address. He said that he sought help for an addiction to crossword puzzles. He said that he compiled crosswords on a semi-professional basis. He appeared to be agitated and depressed. During the course of the consultation he absconded. From some remarks he made, I believe I was able to identify a puzzle he had compiled, and posted on the Internet. I was subsequently able to provide a solution to this puzzle. How's that, doctor?'

'So far so good.'

'You'd better talk me through the riddle again. I didn't quite get it.'

The folded sheet of A4 was beginning to have the antiquated look of a Dead Sea Scroll. I spread it out on the table between us, turning it to face Mr Matheson. 'Perhaps you could just read the legend below the grid.'

I took out a pen. I indicated the unclued lights. 'Dunblane, Hoddle St, Columbine, Aramoana. The thematic link is that they are all notorious scenes of mass shootings. Dunblane you will certainly be aware of. A primary school. The perpetrator was a man named Thomas Hamilton. On 13th March 1996, he shot dead Mrs Gwen Mayor and sixteen members of her class. Ten other pupils and three teachers were wounded. Hamilton committed suicide. Hoddle Street – Sunday, 9th August 1987. A nineteen year old Australian army cadet, Julian Knight, shot dead seven people and seriously injured nineteen others in a suburb of Melbourne. He was arrested and sentenced to seven consecutive life terms. Aramoana – a remote South Island settlement in New Zealand. 13th November 1990. David Gray, a thirty-three-year-old unemployed local man. He shot dead thirteen local people, including Sergeant Stewart Guthrie, the local policeman, following a dispute with a neighbour. Gray holed up in a house and was shot dead by police the following day when he emerged, firing from the hip. Columbine, 20th April 1999 – an American High School shooting perpetrated by two disaffected students. Eric Harris and Dylan Klebold. Twelve students and one teacher killed. Twenty four other students were injured. Harris and Klebold committed suicide. Note that the legend tells us these solutions *predict* the bottom line – Clerk Maxwell. In other words, Mr Bletchley is telling us in an oblique way that there is going to be a similar event here on the campus.'

There was a pause. Mr Matheson scratched his chin. 'I'm not sure that I follow you. After all, he hasn't given us any clues for these solutions. You've just filled them in.'

'Yes, but what else could they be? What else would fit, based on the letters supplied by all the other clues?'

Mr Matheson was still stroking his chin. 'Crosswords. I've never really got into them. Sometimes I've had a go at *The Daily Record* when I'm in the dentist's waiting room, but I've never really got the hang of the cryptic stuff. Let's see . . .' He scanned the clues. 'What about this one? 21 down: "Ends up in drab mini, topless panto girl; toe curling!" Eight letters. What would that be?' He covered the grid with a hand. 'No – don't tell me. Mm . . . Strumpet?'

I smiled. 'Not strumpet.'

'What then?'

'Bonspiel.'

There was a protracted silence.

'*Bonspiel?*'

'Bonspiel.'

'How on earth?'

'There are two parts to a cryptic clue. There is the definer – usually a synonym of the solution, and there is a more oblique alternative means of constructing the solution governed by an operator or key. In this case, the definer and the operator happen to be the same word – curling. Curling defines bonspiel, but also instructs you to *curl*, or jumble, the ends, or last letters of 'up in drab mini topless panto girl toe'.

66

During this exposition, Sergeant Matheson studied my face, a barely perceptible smile on his own, trying to maintain a look of polite interest.

'I haven't a clue what you are talking about.'

I had a sudden intuition that we were about to descend from melodrama into farce. Mr Matheson was beginning to have difficulty containing his mirth. I carried on bravely. 'In other words the solution is an anagram of the last letters of these words. It would become more obvious if you were to render the clue thus: *up in drab mini topless panto girl toe: ends . . . curling!* D'you see?'

Now the sergeant was laughing quite openly. His laughter was very infectious.

'But that's just rubbish. That doesn't make any sense at all.'

Now I was like an exhausted cross country athlete who has drifted away from the back of the pack, who is out of the race, but who keeps going just for the moral duty of finishing. Exhaustion was replaced by euphoria. I too began to laugh. I had difficulty getting the rest of my spiel out. 'The fact that *curling* serves as both definer and operator is signified by the exclamation mark. This is a cryptic crossword convention. It signifies a joke.' By now we were both in fits.

Mr Matheson collected himself. He raised his eyebrows. 'Doctor, you need to get out more.'

He made up his mind. He rose. 'Wait here. I'm just going to have a word with the Chief Super.'

I liked Mr Matheson. I thought he was a nice man. I knew he thought I was nuts, but at least he gave me the time of day, and he had prudence enough to refer my case up to a higher authority. I think it was out of deference to my profession. But who knows, maybe I was bringing my profession into disrepute, wasting police time with this nonsense.

The door flew open angrily.

'Yes can I help you?'

The Chief Superintendent didn't bother to enter but stood at the entrance to the room, one hand on the door handle and the other on the jamb, the posture of a man who wasn't going to hang around. I was aware – I was supposed to be aware – of the bustle behind him, the evidence of the real police activity of the day. He was another big man this time with a lot of braid. He stood poised to slam the door behind him as he left. But I decided not to be intimidated. I was quite prepared to say it all again in a prosaic monotone.

'I have explained to Sergeant Matheson that I think some-body might be planning an assault on the university campus.' He might think I'm a crack-pot, but I was going to force him into a decision, one way or the other. If he was going to close the file on this, he was not going to be able to say later on that it hadn't been spelt out clearly for him.

'I see. Who is the man who concerns you?'

'He calls himself Alan Bletchley. But I don't believe that is his real name.'

'Where does he live?'

'I don't know.'

'Did he tell you he had an intention to cause harm?'

'No.'

'Was he a threat to you?'

'No.'

'Did you have any reason to suppose he was armed?'

'No.'

'Are you reporting a crime?'

'No.'

'Have you arranged for Mr Bletchley to see a psychiatrist?'

'Yes, but the psychiatrists aren't interested.'

'No. Well. That speaks volumes. Thank you for your concern doctor. We have taken note of it, and will give it due attention.'

I was being fobbed off. The chief super stepped back. I said, 'This man has left a paper trail, or at least an electronic trail, that clearly alludes to four violent catastrophes, one of which took place not thirty miles from where we now are.'

'Yes, Sergeant Matheson has briefed me on all that. You seem incredibly well informed in the details of these incidents. You take an interest in such material?'

'Not particularly. The details are in the public domain.'

'On the web. You visit these sites often? Perhaps other sites?'

I rose to my feet and gazed levelly at the chief superintendent. 'I didn't catch your name.'

'I didn't give it.' For a moment I thought he was going to give me the speech I am so often tempted to give: *You come in here, with your petty, paltry* . . . But he decided to stay on side with the ever demanding public and he gave me his name through clenched teeth. Chief Superintendent Hoddle. It was as if he was furious to find his name on Bletchley's grid.

IX

'Meant to tell you last night. MacKenzie called.'

'Oh yeah? How is she?'

'She's good. Wanted to know if I was looking after you. She told me to apply for disability living allowance.'

'Where is she?'

'Buenos Aires.'

'What's she doing down there?'

'Dunno. Playing her viola I guess. Oh yes! She mentioned the name of a big opera house.'

'The Colón.'

'That's it. You been to Buenos Aires?'

'Once. Mary and I went.'

'So you did.'

'She loved to tango. I, on the other hand, am two left feet. I cannot boogie. I have no moves. It would be my worst nightmare to be a contestant on *Strictly*. Craig Revel Horwood would make mincemeat of me. Do you suppose he has a card that scores zilch? I can just hear it. "*Fab-u-lous!* A complete dahnce disahster dahling."'

She giggled. 'Darcey would be kind to you.'

'Darcey's kind to everybody.'

'Let's go to Dublin for the weekend.'

'Can't. I'm working.'

'You're always working. Your life is so dull I bet you look forward to dental appointments.'

'As a matter of fact my dentist can be very entertaining. Dry sense of humour.'

'Mine just tells me to floss.'

'I prefer these interdental gizmos. Look like lavvy brushes.'

'That's disgusting.'

When Caitlin finally got round to leaving my flat, as she would, I would miss all this banter. Or jibber-jabber, as Mary called it. I remember in our Buenos Aires hotel room she held up the 'Do not disturb' sign for hanging outside the door. In Spanish, *No molestar*. 'It's official. Don't molest me.' And later, the half-closed lids, the whisper in my ear. 'Put out the non-molestation order.'

Mary could be very profane, in unexpected locations. It could shock, because she didn't look like a coarse individual. MacKenzie said she looked like Maureen O'Hara. One night in Edinburgh we attended a Sick Chicks faculty dinner – a fundraiser for cystic fibrosis research. Black tie, very posh. We were top table. The professor, Sir Michael Whittingdale – very high – led the procession, to a slow handclap, like the Lord Mayor's banquet, with Mary on his arm. I followed, with Lady Whittingdale. As we neared the table, Mary snapped a stiletto heel. She uttered a single, flat expletive, kicked off both shoes, gathered them up very elegantly with a straight back, and carried on. Sir Michael was entirely sanguine, although Lady Whittingdale did raise her eyebrows.

Now that the police had decided I was an utter nutter I faced a bit of a quandary. Was I left without recourse? I had imagined when I took that trip across the Forth that I was crossing a bridge in every sense. The Forth had become my Rubicon. I had automatically assumed that that would be the decisive act for me. The police, the authorities, would take up the alert and explore it and lay down safeguards. For my part I would be able to close the file. My work on it would be done.

But it hadn't worked out that way.

What now?

If I were going to take this any further I really would be crossing a line. I would be freelance. If I got into trouble there would be no help from anybody. I would be absolutely out in the cold.

The trouble with striking out on your own is that there is nobody around to tell you if you are losing the plot. You have no parameters. Where are you on the slippery slope that leads from insight through uncertainty to eccentricity and finally to madness? This is why single-handed practice is such a bad thing in medicine. But who could share this burden with me? I thought of telling Caitlin but it wouldn't be fair. Caitlin didn't need it. What about MacKenzie? But she was so far away. For the moment she was far away from me in every sense. I don't mean she wasn't sympathetic. When Mary went she sent me a card from New York that said 'My heart is breaking for you' and she had meant it. She came over for the funeral. She even played at it. Unaccompanied Bach. Even though I had suddenly become tone deaf I could sense she had discovered a new depth of musical expression. She had discovered a tone of voice and she found herself able to express something through it by which, along with her colleagues in the quartet, she could tap into something very deep. If it was just a noise to me at least I knew the fault was mine. I didn't want to disturb her, to upset her concentration.

MacKenzie has pitch. I think of it as a kind of equanimity. I never had pitch. Certainly not now. Coincidentally, Caitlin has pitch. I remember how it came to light. MacKenzie had asked her if she knew Vaughan Williams's *Flos Campi*, for viola, wordless choir, and small orchestra. It starts with an unaccompanied oboe solo. MacKenzie had sung it to her. Caitlin didn't know it but when they next met, a month later,

Caitlin recalled that rather dark, brooding theme, and sang it back. It was in the right key. MacKenzie had smiled broadly. 'You've got pitch.'

I had another option, the one that had occurred to me on the way down to Heriot Row. Drop the whole thing. Not just Bletchley, but Blighty. Go into Little France and put a letter of resignation on Forbes's desk. Clear the flat of my meagre belongings and load up the car. Get Caitlin back to school in Gloucestershire. Say hello, and goodbye, to Eric and Sally. Have a car boot sale and then sell the car. Buy a one way ticket to Auckland.

What was keeping me here? MacKenzie lived in the States. Certainly I was close to Mary's people but I was probably just a liability there, a constant reminder of a terrible event. Time to move on. Get out. Go home.

But not quite yet. For a little while I would become an amateur sleuth. It amused me to think of my new-found role. A private dick. A shamus. It occurred to me to indulge in a spot of 'profiling'. Didn't the police employ psychologists to construct a kind of identikit of the minds of serial killers? (The police would enlist anybody if they got desperate enough – clairvoyants, mediums, psychics, water diviners, reflexologists, and other assorted crazies, you name it.) And the perpetrator of a mass shooting was a kind of serial killer; it was just that he (or she? – surely vanishingly rare) committed his serial acts within an incredibly compressed time frame. It was a grotesque obverse of 'the golden hour', that window of opportunity that allowed emergency physicians to save lives rather than destroy them. What element would I select from the periodic table to characterise the rampage of a mass shooter? The plutonium hour. It would be a kind of thermonuclear event.

In the hospital residency I set up the balls on the green baize and pocketed them on automatic pilot while I constructed my Bletchley profile.

First of all, he'd be around. He wouldn't be hidden away. The best way to become invisible is not to absent yourself, but on the contrary to merge with your surroundings. Create an atmosphere, play a part, *be* a part, chime in, harmonious, like a viola player. Thus, you disappear.

What can I surmise about the compiler of *The Bottom Line*? I assembled my identikit picture to the accompaniment of the taps and clicks and kisses of the balls. Clearly, he would be intelligent. Articulate but not verbose; precise, fastidious. A little smug, yet, deep down, dithering. Lots of bravado but no self-confidence. An eye for detail. Very angry, but in a suppressed way. Smouldering. Invisible in society. Not one to make a splash. Perhaps irritated that he is not noticed, undervalued. Lives alone. Poor Billy No Mates. Individual pursuits. A bit schizoid. Sexual orientation? Either-or but, in any case, jilted. Might harbour a grudge. Certainly not one to forget a slight. Prickly as hell.

That's him.

I sank the black.

It's me.

I asked Forbes over coffee, in an offhand way, 'What's the story with Trubshaw? Is he in trouble? Alcoholic? Is he suspended?'

'Yes. No. And not yet. Why do you ask?'

'Just curious.'

I'm a poor dissembler. Forbes raised his eyebrows. 'The trouble with Trubshaw is that he is a prehistoric monster. And his trouble started a long time ago. He is a hepatobiliary surgeon who has been passed over. About fifteen years ago when they all had to learn the new laparoscopic techniques, I think he just found the learning curve too steep. He did an Anthony Eden on somebody at the Grange.'

'Anthony Eden?'

'He mistook the common bile duct for the cystic duct and cut it. That's what happened to Eden. Some people think that caused the disaster of the Suez crisis and the collapse of the British Empire. It must be hard to make good decisions when you are plagued with colicky abdominal pain all the time. Trubshaw's patient was a high flier too. A banker, I think. There was the hell of a stink. The surgeons tried to close ranks but the papers got hold of it and they had to let Trubshaw go. But the surgeons took pity on him and found him his job across the Forth. Cynical move really. It just puts the trouble on to somebody else. What does a surgeon know about emergency medicine?'

'I see. Dear me. But that's all history. Something else must have happened.'

Forbes sipped his coffee ruminatively. 'That's true.' But he clearly wasn't disposed to elaborate. He told me a little more about Trubshaw's CV, but I could sense the secrecy of the confessional descending like a shutter. As far as anything scandalous was concerned, all Forbes would say was, 'Barry Trubshaw's coat's on a very shoogly peg.'

It's a rum old place if you ask me, the UK, with the unfathomable involutions and convolutions of its freemasonries. It's not a place for the individual. People hunt in packs. Trubshaw had been isolated. He had the mark of the outcast upon him. He was a leper. A pariah. He had been blackballed. He was no longer a member of an exclusive club. He might even have been handed a pistol with a single round in the magazine. Rum place.

Why is it so weird? It's the legacy of the empire. The people who are running the show now were brought up at a time when the map on the wall in the primary school classroom was still predominantly pink. The Mercator projection served to accentuate the pinkness. Pole to pole, great swathes of shocking pink. With all this power and influence, surely it must be the greatest stroke of good fortune on earth to be born an Englishman. (A Scot can be an honorary Englishman as long as he observes the club rules. Formidable chaps, these Jocks. Fight like dervishes, y'know. Very excitable, highly stressed individuals. Berserkers.)

From my own point of view, I found the low-down on Trubshaw encouraging as far as it went. I knew I would have to go back to PMH if I wanted to find Bletchley and I just couldn't see my way in. People might have a vague recollection of me, and of the shift I put in, but I would have no right to inspect the records and any attempt to follow up a patient at this distance would be bizarre. I would be an outsider and my temporary password to the computer screens would have expired.

But I had this notion that Trubshaw might be a way in. A man who is down, and being kicked, looks for allies. So on my next afternoon off I went to see him. I telephoned his secretary and booked an appointment. I deliberately rehearsed my first journey, missing my stop and retracing my steps through the campus of Clerk Maxwell.

How very odd to be back. Everything was just as it had been. I walked past the same security barrier and over the same trim pathways through the landscaped lawns with their scattering of leafless trees silhouetted against a dull grey sky. The same sense of precognition. I might even have passed the same students. Why is it that a young woman going for a walk can't seem to detach herself from her smart phone? It's like a baby's dummy or an old man's pipe, a comforter. Maybe it's a way of sending out a message to passing males: don't bother me.

The haar hadn't shifted.

Odd, too, to be back inside PMH ED, a department I had not thought to revisit. There wasn't much going on. The waiting area was almost empty. There was a cleaning lady moving among the chairs with a broom. The place was like a deserted film set in the back lot of an abandoned studio. I announced myself at reception and the clerk swipe-carded me through into the administrative warren and the suite of offices along the back corridor. We reached a stout oak door bearing a name plate which had lost a screw and a couple of letters and was hanging at a perilous angle. The legend read 'Mr B. Tr bshaw, Dire tor'. It was as if he was vanishing in front of everybody's eyes. Maybe there was no point in carrying out a simple repair. The clerk knocked and went ahead of me, announcing me in a low voice, and ushering me through. She left us and closed the door softly behind her.

'Ah! Cameron-Strange!' A squat jowlish man rose from behind a desk and raised a hand in cheery salute. I was momentarily distracted by the desk top. It was the most untidy I had ever set eyes on. It was overflowing with bizarre knick-knackery. There were ancient medical museum pieces – a first edition Bailey and Love, a microscope Pasteur might have used, a plethysmograph with a rotating drum covered in soot, and ancient surgical instruments doubling as paperclips, paperknives, and other elements of office detritus. The Sellotape dispenser held a roll of zinc oxide surgical tape. Behind it sat a pathological specimen preserved in a bottle which I didn't care to examine. I could imagine an irate Matron periodically shooing Trubshaw out of his domain and conducting a radical deep clean. But it would be futile. It would all reaccumulate. I forced my gaze away from the morass and fixed on the heavy man in the buttoned-up white coat. I had the odd notion that moments ago he had donned the heavy accoutrement of his sluggish professional personality. It had been an enormous effort but he was seasoned to it. We shook hands. The grey face quivered. I found myself saying, incongruously, 'Are you okay?'

'Fine! Fine!' The words exploded like shots from a starter pistol, one for the off, one for a false start. He grabbed the initiative back. 'Sit down, please. The nurses told me all about you. You made a great impression I must say. I suppose it is a young man's game, being a Cas Officer. Sorry! Emergency Physician. I must get the style or title right. We'd be pleased to have you back. Just take it easy with all these central lines and rapid sequence inductions. Don't be a cowboy. Don't be gung-ho.' He reminded me of a deposed prime minister, who seeks obscure platforms from which to make pronouncements, under the delusion that he can still influence world affairs. 'Now let's check the roster.' He took a tiny diary out and frowned at it, chewing his lip. 'Cover for January. You don't mind nights?' The monologue was running away.

'Mr Trubshaw, I'm not looking for work. I'm actually here about a patient.'

'Oh!'

'His name's Alan Bletchley. At least, that's the name he used...'
I recounted the story for the umpteenth time. It was all news
to him. Any material I had copied to him, if it had crossed his
desk, certainly hadn't crossed his mind. I had lost my reticence.
I was getting quite blasé about the daftness of it all. I'd an
instinct that Trubshaw would try to help without looking for
a hidden agenda; it would just be such a relief to him to be of
use, to be needed. My instinct proved right. I let him think out
loud, blundering his way through all the blind alleys I'd previously explored. Now that I was seated I could see the framed
family photograph which for him at least obscured the view
of the pathological specimen. There was a pretty woman with
a smile which seemed to withhold some painful knowledge;
and two teenage children, boy and girl, in smart school uni-
form, grinning oafishly at the camera. Next to the picture there
was another framed artefact; it was a piece of verse printed in
rather elaborate uncial script. I recognised Kipling's *If*.

If you can keep your head, when all about you
Are losing theirs and blaming it on you . . .

If . . . *if* . . . *if* . . . All these preconditions. Did Trubshaw
use them as a primer to teach his son how to be a man? More
likely they were his own *vade mecum,* providing him with a
compass through the rough seas of life. Trubshaw struck me
as an iffy man. A man who lived his life in the subjunctive
mood. An *if only* man. Somehow, somewhere, sometime, he
had taken a wrong turning in his life, and he had never been
able to find his way back.

Yet here he was, musing on my behalf. 'Pity the computers crashed that night. But there might be a trace of a record
somewhere. Maybe he's a frequent attender. A revolving door
patient. Maybe he's on CCTV. How long do we keep the film
for? I haven't the foggiest. Shall we check? Let's go through.'

Perfect.

Now, with Trubshaw, I was official. His own coat might
be on a shoogly peg, but it was still hanging up. Together
we went back out to the front desk and accessed the compu-

ter screens and hunted through the ancient A4 records and even some mildewed dog-eared Lloyd George envelopes. And we called Security to find that the CCTV footage was erased every week. But Trubshaw wasn't for giving up. Who was on that night? Who would remember? Who was the triage nurse? Somebody called Connie. Yes, by a stroke of luck, Connie was on just now. Where's she working? She's in Recovery. Could she spare five minutes?

A slim, sharp-featured woman with cropped black hair emerged from the back of the department with the hunted, haunted look – a peculiarly British look – of someone who has fallen foul of authority.

'Ah! Connie!' I had the impression that Trubshaw, despite the familiarity, wouldn't have recognised her from Adam. 'We wonder if you remember a patient named Bletchley. You triaged him a couple of weeks ago.'

She coloured deeply and shook her head. Clever girl. When you are about to be accused of something and you don't know what it is, default to denial. Especially in this country. Never explain. Never apologise. Don't put your hand up.

'You put him in the Gloom Room.'

She shook her head.

I nudged her memory. 'He was an addict. You triaged him category 6.'

The blush was rapidly filched away to be replaced by a deathly pallor. I sympathised with Connie. Now she could see where this one was going. She had passed a snide remark on paper and it was coming back to haunt her. Bletchley was dead and she had triaged him 6 as a joke.

'It's okay.' Put her out of her misery. 'We just want to follow him up and don't know who he is or where he lives. We think he gave a false name. That's all.'

It was hard to know whether Connie was reassured. She had clammed up. Yes, she remembered the guy now, but she didn't know him. Had never seen him before and hadn't seen him since. It was another dead end. Could she get back to Recovery now?

And that was that. Trubshaw spread his hands in a gesture of apology. 'Is there anything else I can help you with today?' He was courteously withdrawing his sponsorship. It was time to go.

'Come and work for us! The offer stands! You'd be most welcome.' The cheery salute again. We shook hands and he made his way back through the security door. I found myself once more speculating about the nature of his impairment. He had been dubbed an 'impaired professional'. Substance abuse? A mental health issue? Professional misconduct? Sheer incompetence?

Impairment. It had become the ultimate stigma in the profession.

Well. We're all impaired.

X

'Get your shoes on. We're going flying.'

Caitlin tossed her *Hello* magazine aside. 'Cool!'

Thank heaven I caught her mood. Anything to get out of this dank, cloying mist. But first, I had to endure a meeting in the west end of Glasgow. This is what I meant about a lack of monothematic attentiveness in my life. Forbes sent me to Glasgow and there it is. I dropped Caitlin off on Byres Road where she was happy to mosey around the shops, parked on Church Street, and passed under a frowning gothic archway that might have been familiar to Lord Lister. The hospital site was a great higgledy-piggledy mishmash of more or less newly erected buildings crammed inside the original quadrangle of black sandstone which must hardly have changed in a century. I found the emergency department with some difficulty. An inconspicuous notice above a small doorway in a gloomy recess bore the legend 'Accident and Emergency'. Was this really the front door of the hospital? And what did that say about the attitude of the hospital towards its clientele?

I can't remember the substance of the meeting. Something about drugs. There was some anti-Edinburgh vitriol that I first mistook for joshing, for banter, but swiftly came to realise was unalloyed contempt. I might have been in Timbuktu for an hour. A Patient Advocate whined nasally, 'Parachute me anywhere into Glasgow and I'll find you a dealer within fifty yards.'

On my way back to the car I was accosted by an emaciated cadaver, shoving a tatty magazine in my face.

'Gishoo?'

'Gesundheit.'

'Have a nice day.' He looked so crestfallen that I changed my mind and handed him two pounds fifty.

Later I asked people back in Edinburgh what *The Big Issue* was. They weren't very sure. Something to do with poverty and deprivation. Unemployment, maybe. Or alcoholism. Or drug addiction. Or homelessness. Or maybe the whole shebang. The poor ye will always have. And I remembered, that was what MacTaggart said, gesturing at the emergency department. The poor ye will always have.

Why is this so? I used to think that it was because some people are temperamentally suited to poverty. They cling to it as a child clings to a woolly toy for comfort. But I've changed my mind. It's simpler than that. The poor will always be there because the rich will always rip them off. The other stuff is just a piece of propaganda. It suits the rich to peddle it, because it justifies them in their wealth. This is why Glasgow is such a travesty. For decades, for generations, the city fathers who should have fixed it have maintained the status quo. And the City Chambers sit smugly and grandly east of George Square like a Kremlin.

People are absurdly sentimental about Glasgow. They buy coffee table picture books of cosy couthie folk grinning toothlessly against a crumbling backdrop of tarnished municipal pride. They would not be out of place in a Brueghel. Urchins play in the dust in tenement back lots. It could be the Warsaw ghetto. Everyone is cheerful. Salt of the earth.

And yet, d'you know, I prefer Glasgow to Edinburgh. All of life is there on Buchanan Street. Glasgow is simultaneously magnificent and terrifying. Edinburgh looks nice but there is something impenetrable about its society. There is something repulsive about the self-satisfied smugness of Edinburgh's elite. I could spend a lifetime there and I would never fit. I would always be colonial. Get out, before you become completely dissociated and displaced. Get back to Auckland. Go home.

Back on the western periphery of Edinburgh, at the aero club, the aviators were hanging about as aviators do, waiting for the weather, waiting for an engine part, quipping, gossiping. There's a lot of waiting in aviation. I might have been a commercial pilot but for the waiting. You wait for clearance and you take off and climb and establish the cruise and then you wait for top of descent. The guys at Edinburgh Airport momentarily shifted their attention to Caitlin, radiant as a French impressionist painting in the cusp of her loveliness. We escaped airside through the security doors, and donned fluorescent yellow windcheaters to cross the apron. I had chosen a Slingsby Firefly, and there she sat, sleek and low slung, waiting, wondering why we'd taken so long.

In the fog we barely achieved the minima for a legal take-off, but out to the north-west there was a promise of finer weather. We took off on runway 24, turned right, climbed and headed out over the south bank of the Forth. The rail and road bridges, and the half-constructed stanchions of the third bridge, emerged surreally out of the great blanket of haar, and slipped behind the trailing edge of the starboard wing. Ahead, the oil refinery at Grangemouth with its flaming cauldrons was sparkling in sunlight. Here were the broads of Skinflats; Kincardine Bridge and Clackmannan Bridge formed a V across the river. On the north side of the Forth stood the bulky chimney of the Longannet Power Station which was a useful marker for the extended downwind leg of the runway 24 circuit at Cumbernauld. Now that we were clear of that, we had the skies to ourselves. It was very quiet up here, no traffic around, and at last this blessed eagle-eye visibility. I stayed on the Edinburgh frequency and they let us operate between Stirling Castle and the Kincardine Bridge, up to 7000 feet over the flatlands.

When you fly an aeroplane you really don't feel inclined to think about much else. I wondered why I hadn't done this earlier. All these months sitting around in a dank Marchmont apartment when all I needed to do was give myself a shake and come up here! What a blessed relief to get out of the mist into this delicious air, to gaze through the sparkling orb of the prop at Dumyat Hill to the west of the Ochils, and to pan further west to the first of the great Scottish mountains, Vorlich, Stuc a' Chroin, Ledi, Lomond. Flying a plane is like climbing a mountain; you rise above all your petty preoccupations and attain a new perspective. For a time, you escape. And Caitlin was enjoying herself. On the right hand seat she looked very chic with her headphones on. 'Can we turn some tricks?'

'There's a turn of phrase. You mean aerobat? Sure. You have control.'

'I have control.' She put her hands confidently on the dual controls, stick and throttle. We had done this before, in New Zealand. She was a natural. I told her what to do and she just did it. HASELL checks: height, airframe, security, engine, location, and lookout. I called Edinburgh again. Still happy. They had us on radar.

We started with a loop. 'Moderate dive . . . 130 knots, pull back on the stick . . . keep the wings level . . . there goes the horizon, keep the back pressure. . . . there's the other horizon, power off into the dive . . . pull the nose up past the horizon, power on gently . . . very good!'

'Hey-hey!' Caitlin's eyes were shining. A breakthrough. 'Can we do a roll?'

Temperatures and pressures ok, quick lookout . . .

'120 knots, pull back to forty five degrees . . . check the stick . . . full left aileron . . .' (I felt the joystick push against my knee.) 'Whoa! Where you off to?' We regained straight and level in a sickly way.

'Terrible roll, not a bad barrel roll.' She laughed. I said, 'Stall turn?' She nodded.

'110 knots . . . pull back to the vertical . . . hold it there . . . speed coming back . . .' The Slingsby reached for the sky and almost came to a halt in the vertical climb. 'Full right rudder now . . .' The nose yawed around in perfect slow motion. 'And . . . into the dive . . . power off . . . centralise the rudders.' The ground was comfortably far away. 'And . . . gently pull back . . . back up to the horizon . . . power on . . . straight and level . . . perfect!'

She was giggling now. Not a care in the world.

Then Edinburgh called. 'Golf Echo Charlie Kilo Oscar descend to below 3000 feet expedite.'

I guess there must have been some incoming jet traffic. I read it back and then said to Caitlin, 'Let's show them expedite. Spin?'

She nodded.

'Power off, straight and level, speed coming back . . . bring the nose right up . . . stall warning buzzer . . . there's the buffet . . . full left rudder . . . stick right back . . .'

Then the world went crazy. Always the combined yaw and roll and pitch is a welter of confusion. We were spiralling down to earth in a maelstrom. I counted the revolutions of the sun.

Three . . . four . . . five . . . six . . .

'Recover!'

'Recover, Caitlin.'

Her feet were jammed solid on the rudder pedals in full left deflexion.

Seven . . . eight . . .

'Get your feet off the rudders, Caitlin.'

Nine . . . ten . . . eleven . . .

'Caitlin!'

Twelve . . . thirteen . . .

I slammed my right elbow into her midriff. The buckle of the five point harness took most of the force but it was enough. She jack-knifed forward and suddenly the rudder pedals were free and I pushed full right rudder, paused, and deliberately began to push the stick forward.

And nothing happened. The sky and the sun had vanished and we had slipped under the horizon and there was nothing but a great whooshing spinning screaming helter-skelter grey-black kaleidoscopic blur of solid earth tumbling all around us.

Suddenly the rotation came to halt.

Centralise rudders, pull back on the stick, bring the nose up . . . up . . . up . . .

There was the horizon. We were out of it. I glanced at the altimeter.

650 feet.

Christ!

'Caitlin?'

She threw up all over the instrument panel and the bubble canopy.

Three times before I had felt Death sit with me in the cockpit, once coming out of a short strip at Coromandel, once descending into Queenstown, once trying to find Paraparaumu in a howling gale. Here he is again, crouched unceremoniously in the back for the rumble seat ride, rather a droll figure, with his white face and his black cape, like that chess player in Ingmar Bergman's *The Seventh Seal*. His visitations come upon you very quickly. You go through the motions as an aviator, but really, it is *he* who decides whether to remain with you, or depart and leave you for a future assignation.

'The broom's in blossom in late December! You can even smell its scent. Like marzipan. It's incredible. I don't remember anything like this. It's like living in a green house.' David Walkerburn gazed meditatively out of the window towards Heriot Row's private gardens.

'I think that's the general idea.'

'Quite.' He turned back into the room's gloomy interior. 'So you decided to tell the police after all? What was their reaction?'

'They weren't remotely interested.'

'Indeed!'

'I did try to take it a little further. I went back to PMH to try and find contact details for Bletchley.'

'Above and beyond, surely?'

'Maybe. Anyway he's lost to follow up. I can't think what else to do.'

'Did you keep Professor Pearson apprised?'

'No. Do you think I should have?'

He raised his eyebrows and bounced the question back at me. In the Maori culture, raising your eyebrows is like nodding your head. It signifies a yes. That was the closest Mr Walkerburn ever got to giving me his own opinion.

Back out in the car parked outside No 48, Caitlin had shifted across into the driver's seat. 'Can I drive?'

'Sure.' I handed her the keys. 'All yours. I'm going for a walk.' I headed east. She caught up with me a minute later and handed the keys back.

'Incidentally, why do you need a lawyer?'

'It's something to do with work.'

'Is somebody suing you?'

'Not yet. Look! There's No 17. RLS stayed here.'

'RLS?'

'Robert Louis Stevenson. You know . . . *Kidnapped*?'

'Haven't read it. We did *Catriona* at school. I liked Miss Grant.'

'You've got to be joking. She's just so *Edinburgh*!'

We wandered up on to Princes Street. Caitlin still looked a bit green about the gills. To tell you the truth I wasn't feeling that chipper myself. I wanted to feel the earth under my feet. I don't think Caitlin had any notion just what a close-run thing that spin had been. The Slingsby's instruments had recorded 5G coming out of it. I still had butterflies in my stomach. I'd experienced a sharp pain in my right ear during the plummet towards earth and now I had a strange clicking sensation that I first thought was my traumatised drum settling down, but then it seemed to morph into a tic, an auditory hallucination.

For a moment I was a quivering mouse, trying to find a way out of the horrific labyrinth of my own limbic system. *Wee sleekit, cow'rin, tim'rous beastie* . . . An electronic mouse. Click click.

The aerobatics, and a near disaster, exerted further curious effects. Three things. I was thinking about the man in the cockpit with the white face and the black cape, the man who had cuckolded me. I suddenly realised after all this time that I was very angry with Mary, for having wandered away with him. Meanwhile, I was aroused from nigh on twelve months of libidinous hibernation. Mortal danger – it is the last aphrodisiac. Up on Princes Street we headed east along the broad crowded pavement. Christmas shopping! It didn't mean a thing to me; I was living in a parallel universe. In my memory I am alone, yet I know Caitlin was there. Maybe she was lagging behind, looking in the shop windows. I kept glancing back, but it wasn't to look for Caitlin. I had considered myself – in a self-indulgent Walter Mittyish fashion – a single-handed vigilante looking for a lone psychopath. Now it suddenly occurred to me that there was a third party involved, that the compiler of *The Bottom Line* would not himself perpetrate the act to fulfil its dark prediction. He would not sully his hands; he would be a 'grey eminence' working invisibly in the background, quietly pulling the levers like a pilot flying a drone by remote control and from a great distance.

Meanwhile, I was distracted. I was subjected after all these months, once more, to the appalling tyranny of being male. I call them *The Nubility*. Here were two posh types, arm in arm, both loaded with designer bags and designer labels, jaunty with youth, mistresses of the universe. Then a tall black girl in a tight oil black shirt and the palest blue jeans, loping, thoughts miles away. Now a corporate executive type, pin-striped skirt and jacket, rather elaborate white blouse open to a deep tanned cleavage, slim legs, heels, moving forward, on a mission. Click click click. Beneath the New Club, a waif, short blond hair, the most beautiful face, frowning, biting her lip, texting. At Jenners, the sullen hauteur of a *señorita,*

Hispanic, no – Argentinean – I swear I have seen this girl on the Avenue July the 9th. And at Waverley Bridge, a group of goddesses emerging from the train station and crossing the road, in animated conversation. Stop perving! You'll end up on some sort of register! Look at this fair apparition, effortlessly beautiful in jeans and T-shirt, as we move to pass one another opposite the Balmoral. I held her eyes momentarily and she did not avert her gaze but gave me a shy, appraising smile. The earth moved. I felt rather than heard a muffled buffet followed by a sharp cacophonous report and I instinctively ducked. I stopped dead in my tracks. Something had happened above and behind my right shoulder. Everything dissolved into slow motion. I looked up at the battlements of the Castle. There was a wisp of smoke. I ran my eyes along the Old Town Skyline and back to the solid and substantial stonework of the Balmoral. The clock said five minutes past one. It would. I looked back at my pretty girl. She too had stopped dead and the smile had frozen on her face. Her mouth had opened in an exaggerated O of surprise and she was taking a deep breath and lifting a hand to cover her mouth. It had happened to me again. I'm a sucker for it. Every time, lunchtime Princes Street, I forget. These damned efficient adrenals squirt their adrenaline and noradrenaline into the circulation before my brain can tell them to stop. I gave my pretty girl a smile and a brief shake of the head in reassurance. It's only the one o'clock gun. Its reverberations still rattled along the windows of the Princes Street frontages. Here's Caitlin again. She's rushing towards me. She's as white as a sheet! She's pushing me towards a shop doorway. It's not that bad! I should have warned her about this ridiculous daily ritual up on the castle battlements, while the Balmoral's clock runs fast as an aid for late train commuters. There was a brief rumble and a grumble above my head and a sharp crack in the ground beneath me. Something stung my right shin. A tonne of masonry had calved itself off from high up on the Princes Street frontage and joined us on the pavement.

XI

Caitlin said abruptly, 'Tell me a goodnight story.'

'What sort? Detective? Thriller? Love story? Horror?'

'Mm . . . all of the above. Only it has to be a musical.'

'OK. I'm going to bore you to sleep. When your eyelids close, don't fight it. And don't complain about my singing.'

She snuggled down, gave her pillow a punch, and turned on her side. 'Begin.'

'This is the story about the inception of a musical virus, the provenance of a pathogenic theme.'

'Oh.'

'Once upon a time there was a famous Russian virtuoso pianist named Yevgeny Poporoffskiovich.' She giggled. 'He came from a background of faded gentility in Vladivostok where his father was a retired captain of the Russian navy, and his mother was a music teacher. You might think a naval captain married to a woman of some cultivation and artistic refinement would run a splendid household, but the fact is that Captain Poporoffskiovich's old submarine, The Professor Multinowski, was a rusting hulk listing in the shallow waters of the harbour at Vla, quietly exuding plutonium 238 into the bay. He had not received his naval pension for six years and Captain and Mrs P struggled to feed, clothe, and shoe their nine children, of whom Yevgeny was the youngest. Their sole income came from the meagre fees Mrs P charged a handful of local families who sent their children for piano lessons. Mrs P taught on an old Broadwood upright which was the P family's only cherished material possession. They were caught in a terrible poverty trap, the more so as they, along with everybody else, had to pay protection money to the head of the local mafia, a man with a hair lip named Schplizki who chewed tobacco, played backgammon, and was, incidentally, tone deaf.'

'Why do I get the feeling you are making this up as you go along?'

'In this self-evidently desperate situation, the Poporoff-skiovichs' sole consolation and only hope lay in the glittering talent of the young Yevgeny. Mrs P knew her last child had an unusually penetrating musical sensibility. Yevgeny had breast-fed so placidly to the sound of the Broadwood even when played by her more modestly talented pupils. From the age of twelve months, the child would sit on his mother's lap and tap out ancient Russian folk melodies with a chubby finger.'

'Bollocks.'

'In no time at all he was playing a Ravel concerto with one hand tied behind his back.'

Caitlin blew a sleepy raspberry.

'Mrs P was obsessively protective of her son's prodigious talent. She wished it to be unsullied. In this regard she was rather precious. The equivalent in our culture would be a woman of the middle classes who strives so hard to keep her child away from germs that he ends up with milk intolerance, food allergies, and then asthma. She kept music that she considered second rate from his ears. Folk melody was all right, but nothing that could be considered anarchic. Nothing for which the pianist might forsake a straight back in favour of a slouch. Nothing with *attitude*. She was particularly frightened of Bill Evans. Look what happened to him.

'Meanwhile, the economic situation in Vladivostok was getting out of hand. All of Mrs P's students had quit piano and were working for the town's Mafiosi as drug peddlers, gun runners, and pimps. Yevgeny's oldest sister was working in the local brothel.'

'I don't think this is a very nice bedtime story.'

'There was no alternative but to pack the young Yevgeny up and send him to Moscow and then to the Paris Conservatoire to earn his fortune. So they deposited him in a 3rd class carriage of the Orient Express with nothing but an old samovar, a live chicken, a dog-eared Urtext edition of Debussy's *Images – première série,* and a letter of introduction to Nadia Boulanger.'

'Nadia Boulanger? Thought you said there was plutonium in the water at Vladivostok.'

'Madame Boulanger lived to a ripe old age. In Paris, the young Yevgeny was lionised. With his long wavy hair and dark brooding looks his was a commanding platform presence. He was soon the darling of the concert-going public with his dazzling interpretations of Scriabin and Rachmaninoff. Soon, Yevgeny found he was able to command appearance fees of the sort enjoyed by film stars, international icons, and a handful of superstar operatic tenors. He married a diva, bought a villa in Lucerne and a *pied-à-terre* in Chelsea, signed a recording contract with EMI, and founded a dynasty.'

'What about poor Mrs P?'

'Yevgeny never forgot his family. He sent monthly sums back home. He offered to rehouse them in Switzerland. You can solve any immigration problem in Switzerland with a fat bank account. But Mrs P would not budge. She had become chairperson of a local self-help group in Vladivostok and had decided to take on the protection racketeers. Would Yevgeny come home and play just once for the community? No he would not. He would not go back east, to remember what it was like. Instead, he appeared with his wife the diva at an Aids charity event in some posh hotel in Los Angeles. Rich men in tuxedos, ladies in glittering gowns, $3000 a ticket, you know the sort of thing. The diva was going to sing something from a Broadway musical. Yevgeny was to accompany. Thanks to his upbringing, he had never heard of the song, the musical it came from, nor its renowned and eminently successful composer. You must understand that Yevgeny was like a man who had never seen a television set. You might pass a remark about *Coronation Street* or *EastEnders,* and he would look at you as if you were a Martian. At the back of his mind he had the nagging suspicion that his mother would not approve. "You play this pap for these bourgeois, yet you will not play music here, for your people, uh? Is that it?" Yet he consoled himself that the song they were to perform was based on some poems by a great American poet. And after all, Aids research was a noble cause. They gave the performance.

'And nothing happened. At least, not for a while. Then a trivial and amusing incident occurred during a rehearsal with the Cleveland at Tanglewood. They were having a run through the last movement of the Beethoven first concerto and as he embarked on the second subject, Yevgeny broke into that piece Gustavo Dudamel sometimes does as an encore with the Simón Bolívar, or the Teresa Carreño. *El Sistema.* They all put on gaudy jackets and look like Wall Street traders. *Tico-Tico* by Zequinha Abreu. Yevgeny stopped dead and stared, aghast, at his hands. There was a momentary stunned silence from the orchestra, a raucous belly laugh, and a spontaneous burst of applause. Well well! The Great Scowl had a sense of humour after all.'

Caitlin said, 'I suppose you know you're as mad as a snake?'

'Later, seated alone in his hotel bedroom, he stared at his wayward, sinewy fingers. They had betrayed him. Nothing like this must ever be allowed to happen again. He made some heavy pencil jottings in the score.

'But it was already too late. The virus he had picked up in LA expressed itself again in Carnegie Hall during the slow movement of Rachmaninoff's fourth concerto. You've guessed it. Three blind mice. The mental aberration, the syncope of the musical memory, lasted barely an instant. Yet, barely audible, there had been a titter in the stalls. Next day he feverishly grabbed the review pages of the *New York Times*. Five stars. He had gotten away with it.

'But the third time, there could be no cover-up. Complete calamity at the Wigmore. Beethoven again. The Opus 106. The pianist's Nemesis. The slow movement of the Hammerklavier. *Una corda, mezzo voce, appassionato e con molto sentimento.*

'Beautiful dreamer.'

'Bonkers.'

'He had become a musical vandal. An absurd Hoffnung figure. He immediately retired from the concert halls of Europe and, following an anguished sabbatical spent with a team of Viennese psychoanalysts in an Alpine sanatorium, he took to the conductor's podium. His own technique, his unparalleled facility and execution, might have been permanently destroyed by the "gremlins of the trivial" – his own expression (or, as his analysts put it, *gremsprechstimmeschaftge-schrottkitschgrübler*) – yet surely he could wield a baton?'

'Barking.'

'Not so. Merely, his anguish was internalised. The angelic sounds produced by the orchestra were not the ghastly, strident, screeching, and above all hideously chirpy tunes that now besieged his musical psyche and threatened to push him over the edge. Rachmaninoff's Symphonic Variations became a Highland jig – "Petronella". Shostakovich's Easter Festival Overture, "Hold that Tiger". The cadenza of the Elgar violin concerto – "It ain't necessarily so". The overture to Rossini's early melodrama, *Tancredi*, "Lily the Pink". And the final ecstatic movement of Ravel's *Ma Mère l'Oye* . . .

'"My Way".

'Yevgeny put away his baton. At first, people were kind. That was before Yevgeny became disinhibited. He attended concerts, struggling with the taunts of his internal, hallucinogenic Furies. He would cover his ears and accompany the orchestra with his own tuneless plaint that would inevitably degenerate into a popular song of the day. One night he was ejected from the Musikverein singing "Old Man River". A trespass order was slapped on him. His wife had left him, he was bankrupt, his creditors had picked his carcass dry. He drifted to Paris and disappeared among the beggars on the left bank. He was in the gutter. His sole confidant was a penny-whistle-playing dwarf who led a subterranean existence in the sewers underneath Pigalle on the border between the ninth and the eighteenth *arrondissements*. He had reached rock bottom.

'Then, one night, he had a terrible dream. His mother, old and white haired now, was singing a duet with the tobacco-chewing, backgammon-playing tone-deaf Vladivostok mafioso. It was unutterably kitsch.

'"Mamma mia".

'Next day Yevgeny started busking with a mouth organ in the Paris Metro. A few commuters, putting him down as a pitiful psychotic, tossed a few centimes into a dilapidated cap. In about three months, he had enough to buy a train ticket to the east, to the ocean, as far as the line would go.'

You will know that Yevgeny and I are one and the same. I had committed the cardinal sin of any trafficker in *reportage*; I had become part of the story. Alastair Cameron-Strange glanced down at the figure under the white sheet and at the auburn hair splayed across the pillow. Caitlin's breathing was even. He eased himself quietly out of the room.

. . . and slipped into the front room and for the first time in nearly a year, put a CD on. It was *Cantos Sagrados*, choral music by James MacMillan. The third track, *A Child's Prayer,* some four minutes long, commemorates Dunblane. If this memoir, this confession of mine, has a sound track, then this is it.

All our young lives, MacKenzie and I, we had lived and breathed music. It seems to me that we were borne along in a tide of music. Music was nothing less than life itself, or an ultimate expression of it. And therefore the eschewing of music has to be a kind of death.

Sad music is an indulgence to the young. It is only later that some sadnesses acquire a particularity. There are irreversible sadnesses. I had wanted numbness, not, specifically, numbness against grief. Not even numbness against joy. It was numbness against loss.

15dn: Light music for pinball (9)

XII

We were all on a retreat. Management had spent a huge amount of money getting cover so that the acute services could come off the floor and, indeed, off site, to indulge in something called 'team building'. The deliberations of ELSCOMF were being rolled out. I had wanted to give my apologies and was prepared to offer any fabrication of an excuse no matter how outlandish – my twin sister had been in a plane crash, my sister-in-law was having a termination, I was having chemotherapy . . . but then I remembered we were convening in the Colin Maclaurin Conference Centre at Clerk Maxwell, so I put my hand up and got on the agenda.

The previous evening, I'd caught the late night news on TV and seen a brief clip – I'd often seen similar clips – of a white security van shooting out from a High Court underpass. Women bystanders were shrieking venom at the monster handcuffed within, while the press scrambled along beside the accelerating vehicle, cameras held up to tiny barred windows, snapping multiple exposures like machine guns. Click click click click click. A man was on trial somewhere in the north of England for the murder of a string of prostitutes. It happened periodically. Sharon Blakemore, Diane Penderton, and Seonaid MacAndrew. The names, the names! I always noticed the euphony of the names. And I thought, I might be in a position to thwart the activities of another monster. I need to go back over to Clerk Maxwell.

'Dr Cameron-Strange–' MacTaggart made no attempt to suppress a cavernous yawn. He adjusted his half-moons and read from the agenda, his voice heavy with the quotation marks of infinite condescension. '*A new way of working.* Your fifteen minutes await you.'

I took to the dais. I attempted to embrace the audience with a smile.

'A new way of working indeed.'

There was a kerfuffle at the back. The techs couldn't find my disc for PowerPoint. I called back reassuringly, 'It's okay. I'm not using visual aids.' This did not relieve the consternation. They just didn't believe me. My talk was disrupted by a totally irrelevant slide show cast mostly across my face as the techs flicked through the subsequent speakers' material. I had the dawning suspicion that I wasn't going to make a connection.

'All over the world, people associate emergency departments with delay. If you have the misfortune to spend a Saturday evening in ED with a sprained ankle, it's six hours out of your life. That's just a fact of life. Gentlemen, I don't have slides!

'Those of us who aspire to run a state-of-the-art facility may look down our noses at more chaotic institutions. But you know, it's *schadenfreude*. There isn't an institution in the world has solved this problem. Not one. Would it be possible to turn that off?'

There was another distraction – the photographers. Always they take over. MacTaggart had organised them. There was going to be an abstract of the proceedings in the form of a glossy. It would be a plush job, extremely professional, and it would come out quickly. MacTaggart wanted visual impact.

He'd given the snappers free rein. They went mad. They do the same at a wedding, monopolising the bride and groom and putting them through all sorts of improbable scenarios, chasing one another round trees, while the wedding guests gather at the bar, hungry and disgruntled.

'I want to propose a model of working practice, a *modus operandi*, whereby, particularly when the department is pressured by sheer numbers, we can keep up. It involves a strict adherence of each individual member of the team to his or her specific role, and it is predicated on absolute trust among the team members.'

Two photographers had advanced down the aisle and were encircling me at close quarters, like big cats on the Serengeti isolating their quarry.

'I can best describe the method in practice by following, if I may use that hideous expression, the patient journey.'

I could sense I'd lost the audience already. They were distracted. I glanced behind. There was a large ulcerating chancre on screen. I think a wrinkled penis was sprawled across my forehead and nose. I thought of having a tantrum, or walking out. No. Head down, get to the end.

'We start with triage. Triage is not a consultation. Triage is not history and examination.' I was lecturing them in a hectoring way I had not intended. 'Triage is merely a snapshot.' This, to the accompaniment of a firework display from the paparazzi. I heard a titter.

'We must not be afraid of a mis-triage. Rather we must have systems down the line robust enough to up-triage, or down-triage, in a timely way.'

Now the sound system began to play up. I was getting feedback. An echo was reverberating around the hall like an air raid tocsin.

'Next, a word on nursing care. Duplication of activity is the death-watch beetle of emergency medicine. In a specialty whose whole *raison d'être* is the race against time, don't indulge in an activity which is better done by somebody else.' I was dazzled by a flash at point blank range and

I think it was maybe this that caused me to speak unwisely. 'The nurses need to rediscover their traditional values, of kindliness and care. They shouldn't be indulging in amateur doctoring. If they want to take histories and perform examinations, fine – go to Med School. Nurses need to rediscover how to nurse.'

I'd just lost half my audience.

'As for the doctors, what we need, what I need, is to be freed up. I need to be able to move from patient to patient. The emergency physician is primarily a diagnostician. Indeed, he is primarily a history taker. The history is fantastically potent. Let a competent emergency physician take a history and 99 times out of a 100 he will accurately predict an outcome on that data alone.

'History and examination are the bread and butter. I need to be able to perform these two tasks at the bedside and, on their basis, say to someone at my elbow, "Do this, this, this, and this." And move on to the next patient. That way I can get round large numbers. When I return to patient A, like a grandmaster playing a simultaneous chess competition, this, this, this, and this are done. The position on the board has changed. I am able to make a revaluation, perhaps on the basis of test results. Treat, admit, discharge. This is what I do. On no account should I get bogged down with what the North Americans call "scut" work, taking bloods, putting up drips, filling in forms.

'A word about the atmosphere in which we work. Emergency departments are traditionally seen as centres of chaos. People pour through the entrance, paramedics swoop through double doors yelling vital signs over patients expiring on gurneys, phones ring incessantly, bleeps are bleeping, pages are paging, the Tannoy system never stops.'

There was a tremendous crack as the sound system packed up and simultaneously the lights went out, leaving only the background illumination of gummata on PowerPoint. The last flurry of activity from the photographers resembled the Blitz. I tried to get my closing comments in but they were pretty well drowned out in a gale of laughter followed by the steady rumble of an audience conversing amongst itself just prior to a coffee break.

I had a paragraph to go, but I gave up. The IT may have ended with a bang, but I ended with a whimper. 'We need to work in quietude.'

I resumed my seat. There was no applause.

'Questions? No?' MacTaggart didn't even afford me the courtesy of casting one up himself. 'Well, there's a first. We break for coffee. Plenary again at eleven sharp, thank you.'

In retrospect, I think it was from this point that my behaviour became slightly erratic. I date it from that terrible sinking feeling of emptiness.

I skipped coffee. I went for an aimless walk amid the stands of the conference trade exhibition. A girl from AstraZeneca in a smart blue pin-striped trouser suit collared me and gave me her five minute spiel about why Nexium was the best proton pump inhibitor and why Crestor was the best statin, while I gazed at her blankly and thought about that moment between the twelfth and the thirteenth revolution of the spin in the Slingsby, when – I forced myself to admit – it had crossed my mind not to release the rudder pedals from their full left deflection.

'Thank you, Conference.' (Fancy addressing the conference with the vocative 'Conference'. I felt as if I was attending a party political event, at Brighton or Bournemouth.) 'Break out groups! Pass these around please.' Trish Campbell the facilitator was a slim blond woman, late forties, underweight and overexposed to the sun. She might have been an aerobics instructor. In a way she was, putting us through our paces. 'Groups of six. Elect a spokesperson. Delegates report back at –' she glanced at her wrist watch '– 11.30 sharp.'

Kerry Donaldson, an anaesthetist on my left, muttered 'Jolly hockey sticks.' I glanced at the handout. It was to be an exercise in communal decision making. The scenario depicted a disparate group of people, trapped at the foot of a mine

103

shaft that was rapidly flooding. Rescue was hazardous and only one person per hour could be retrieved. The mine would be totally flooded within six hours.

It seemed a highly unlikely situation. What were all these people doing down there? Was it a day trip for Rotarians? The group demographics were odd, in a Chaucerian way. There was a Nobel laureate, an MP, an ophthalmologist who had worked for peanuts in the developing world, a home help, a drug addict, a man with a criminal record, a child with severe developmental delay . . . There was even a paedophile who also happened to be morbidly obese. Donaldson said, 'Well let's drown the fat-arse nonce for a start!' He addressed the chair.

'Have you ever been trapped underground, Ms Campbell?'

'No, thank goodness.'

He sniffed. 'I have.' I remembered Donaldson was in the TA. He had done a couple of tours in Afghanistan. 'One thing I can assure you. Decisions like this are not made in committee.'

Somebody else from the floor was making the laborious point, in a rather heavy weathered way, that moral judgments had never impinged on medical decision making. (Was that really true?) It sounded pompous and Hippocratic. For me, it all rested on the integrity of the rope and the bucket.

We broke out. I said to Kerry, 'This is rubbish. I'm gonna split. See you tomorrow.'

'It cost a grand a head to get us out of hospital. That's before you factor in the conference rooms and the catering. You'll be in trouble.'

'I couldn't care less.'

I emerged into the haar and took a deep breath of harsh saturated air. It had occurred to me that I would pay a call on the Vice-Chancellor. It was a short walk to the administrative offices in the Joseph Black Building. I got directions at the front desk and took the lift to the eighth floor. The plush Axminster beneath my feet verified that I had identified the right level. And here was the double door to the imperial suite. The plaque said, 'Professor Sir Douglas Horton, Vice-Chancellor.' I knocked and went in.

This was an anteroom to the inner sanctum. The secretary glared at me severely over her gold rimmed spectacles.

'Yes?'

I adopted the pose of one who is habituated to getting his own way. 'My name is Dr Alastair Cameron-Strange. May I see Professor Horton.' I kept the question mark, the Antipodean up-speak, out of my voice.

'You're late.'

'I beg your pardon?'

She lifted the phone and tapped in a four digit extension number without diverting her fixed gaze of disapproval.

'Brian. The external's here . . . Yes I know. Horton'll go ballistic. Where are they holding the exam board? Will you? Thanks.' She hung up.

'The reader is coming to collect you. Take a seat Professor Strang.'

She thought I was somebody else. A little devil sitting on my shoulder holding a trident whispered, 'What the hell! Run with it.'

Brian came in all in a lather, breathing heavily from his sprint up the stairs, a flurry of navy jumper, jeans, and suede shoes. He grabbed me by the wrist.

'Quick!'

We pelted along the corridor. He glanced back at me to make sure I was keeping up. 'Train trouble I suppose? You might just get away with it. They've got a ton of special factors to wade through.'

The reader was on tenterhooks. I thought about Professor Horton. What sort of man is so intimidating that the messengers think they are going to be shot? Brian tapped nervously on the board room door and led me into the middle of a conference.

'. . . felt he needed more time because of his dyslexia.'

'Is there a doctor's certificate?'

The conspicuously handsome man at the head of the grand

boardroom table gave me a pained expression and waved me exasperatedly into the one vacant chair. If I hadn't the courtesy to be on time, he wasn't about to interrupt the proceedings to effect the introductions. I would just have to wait.

'Here it is.' Somebody produced the chit.

'Can I see that?'

It was passed round.

'It's from the Consulate. Dr Duncan. MB Cantab. I can't read his writing.' There was laughter.

'Look. Irrespective' – I recognised a Melbourne accent – 'of whether or not the guy can read, he's got 37%. He hasn't exactly covered himself in glory.'

'He's only three marks off a pass.'

'Yeah, well –'

'Are there any more marks to be garnered, here and there?' This from Horton. He rested his elbows on the table, formed a Norman arch with his opposing fingertips and rested them against his pursed lips. 'If we can get him up to 38, 39 . . .'

'Great, but what about the people sitting on 37 who *haven't* put in a special factors form?'

'If you don't ask, you don't get.'

'I guess it helps if you've got a letter from His Excellency the ambassador.'

'Be careful. That's prejudicial language. Don't minute that Ms Foye. It might do in Wagga Wagga land but not here.'

The unobtrusive secretary at the corner of the room stopped writing. Her face was expressionless. She was an attractive woman, sexy in a severe way, slipping imperceptibly into middle age. I thought, funny how an indelible impression can be struck on a single utterance, even a single word. It was the Wagga Wagga remark that did it for me.

'We'd better hear from the external.'

All eyes turned on me.

'Professor Strang? We haven't met.'

I know I ought to have owned up at this point. But the little demon with the trident was still whispering in my ear. And besides, I had an opinion.

'I think that if the candidate only managed 37% in the exam, then he has failed it.'

The man from Melbourne stared at me, wide eyed. He hadn't expected this. I went on. 'You're offering him a poisoned chalice. It may be convenient for him now, and for you, but it will undo him in the end, and you, and us all. What sort of a society will we have if its leaders have received a pat in the back for achieving 37%? Would you like your surgeon to have got 37%? Your airline pilot? Your teacher? Your banker, God help us! Tell him the truth. Tell him he's failed. It's not the end of the world. Nobody died. He can take the next diet.'

There was a stunned silence.

The board room door opened and Professor Strang, the external examiner from Manchester, hurried in. 'Professor Horton I am *so* sorry. Points jammed at Berwick.'

Later on, I had to ask myself why I had been crazy enough to walk into a room full of academics who were perfect strangers and impersonate a visiting VIP. It was just a chain of adverse circumstances. Being on retreat at Clerk Maxwell was like being back at school. I was fed up to the back teeth with ELSCOMF, I had just given a disastrous presentation, I took an instant dislike to Professor Horton, and frankly I was just pissing around. It was the sort of thing I used to do at school through sheer boredom.

I didn't like Professor Horton one little bit. I had a sense about him, a sense of a steel fist concealed inside a velvet glove. He reminded me of a type of senior consultant I occasionally come across in medicine. I call them 'The Incandescent Lights of Medicine'. No doubt such incandescences rise to the top in every profession. These men are extraordinarily focused. They are single minded; they are driven. They are totally inconsiderate. They cut a swathe through the minor inconveniences of daily life. They live like Pashas. They tend to organise their affairs the way they want them without noticing the zone of disruption that surrounds them as they plough on remorselessly like a Dreadnought through the rough seas of life. They take pains to have at their side a lieu-tenant who can deal with the tiresome minutiae of business so that they can concentrate on The Big Picture. They will drive on regardless and leave the lieutenant to clear up the mess they leave behind them. They have no idea of the trouble they cause other people. Horton was such an Incandescent Light. I had rather that our respective universes never impinged, but I had a sinking suspicion – more, I was absolutely convinced – that I would have to deal with him, would have to con-front him. There was no point in trying to wheedle out of it. I might pray, 'Heavenly Father, let this cup pass from me . . .' but it would be no bloody good. I'd better get on with it. I'd better blag my way into his office.

Two hours later I was on a mission. I was going to leave no stone unturned. I was encouraged by the fact that, although I had been exposed as an impostor, miraculously, I had gotten away with it. It might have been a crushingly embarrassing exposé, me floundering at the boardroom table trying to explain myself. He might have summoned security, had me detained, even got the police. But I was saved by Horton's abiding self-confidence. He had me sussed. I was a media man. Some sort of investigative reporter. A paparazzo. That I should wish to infiltrate his meeting he regarded as *de rigueur*. He almost treated me with indulgence, raising his eyes to the ceiling.

'Good try, but no dice. Off you go! Any recording equip-ment, mikes, cameras, leave them at the door please.' Hence I had brass neck enough to have another go. Back up to the eighth floor. Another walk with destiny on the seductive shag pile.

'You have an appointment?'

Here was another stroke of luck. She was a different receptionist.

'No I do not. This concerns a health and safety matter relating to the University.' I smeared on the pomposity with a trowel. I could feel a crazy mirthfulness churning away in my bowels. Health and Safety. I'd pressed the right button.

'One moment.'

She slipped silently into the inner sanctum. The connecting door had frosted glass and I was vaguely aware of a blur of human shapes behind. I glanced around idly at the accoutrements of the outer office, the desk top VDUs and the telephones and the fax machines. Would I be stone-walled? Perhaps asked to make an appointment, put it in writing.

'Sir Douglas will see you.' At that moment the Vice-Chancellor himself appeared, ushering out a black man and a black woman of striking appearance. The secretary, Ms Foye, who had been present at the exam board, stood discreetly behind them. The black man was of slim build and had aquiline features. He was very cultivated. As he emerged into the anteroom he was addressing the Vice-Chancellor and I caught the tail end of his conversation. It had a slightly anachronistic idiomatic flavour. Empire English. 'It's all grist to the mill, manna from heaven, and what have you.' Damn sight better than saying it was 'win win', whatever it was. He was dressed in an expensively tailored three-piece suit of exquisite fit. The shirt and the flashing teeth were of dazzling white. The woman was incredibly beautiful. High cheek bones, shoulder length dark ringlets, another expensive suit, camel, tight fitting and mid-calf length. Taupe patent leather courts. She carried a gunpowder Mulberry bag, Alexa Hobo, over her shoulder. They seemed to be sharing a joke as they said their farewells. Horton was being gallant, exuding boundless charm. The men shook hands.

'So sorry you can't make *Conversazione* on the 24th.'

'Perhaps next year.' The voice was silken.

Horton took the woman's beautifully manicured hand and raised it to his lips. The atmosphere was thick with sycophantic, meretricious concupiscence. The woman walked past me with the feline gait of a supermodel. The man gazed at me with cold eyes. I had the odd sensation that I was having my photograph taken. Then they were gone, to the airport I presumed. In two hours they would be back in cream stucco land – diplomat territory in Belgravia.

I studied Sir Douglas with curiosity. Early fifties, tall with short fair hair and no trace of grey. He carried himself with a certain stiffness. He too was superbly and immaculately dressed in a beautifully tailored suit of old-fashioned cut, light grey, with a pattern I think called Urquhart. (I began to feel quite shabby.) He was vaguely reminiscent of somebody. I couldn't decide whether it was the Duke of Windsor or Douglas Fairbanks Junior. I recognised him. Hadn't there been a picture of him last week in the papers, emerging from No. 10 with the PM? I didn't know the first thing about him, beyond the fact that he was a man on the up, a mover and shaker, with the ear of government. But I had no idea what his own academic discipline was, far less what inner lights propelled him. I had a vague recollection of Jeremy Paxman interviewing him in an aggressive way. Horton had been totally unfazed. Hard as nails. But I couldn't remember anything about it.

One thing. Just a sound bite. 'Jeremy – there are two sorts of people, there are winners, and there are losers . . .'

Anyway here he was. He cast a vaguely curious glance in my direction. It was another stroke of luck no doubt thanks to his crammed agenda and punishing schedule – he had forgotten all about me.

'I only need five minutes of your time, professor. Literally five. It's very important.'

'To you or to me? Enter.' He addressed Ms Foye without looking at her. 'Come back in with us, Muir.' Whatever this was about, he wanted a witness.

We entered the inner sanctum. I was taken aback by its spaciousness. This was a reception room, resembling more a lounge than an office. It was decorated in rich reds and golds. In the foreground was a long, low glass coffee table surrounded by deep red-brown, studded leather armchairs. Round the room's periphery, the furniture was in dark oak. There were gilt-framed paintings by the Glasgow boys, and the Scottish colourists, liberally festooned all around the walls. Guthrie and Hornel and Lavery; Fergusson, Cadell,

110

and Peploe. I don't think they were reproductions. I found it all a bit much. Beyond, a desk of Bismarckian proportions sat before a huge triptych picture window occupying the entire south-facing wall and substantial segments of the east and west walls. When the haar lifted this would surely afford stunning near 360 views of the Firth. Just to the left of the triptych window stood a finely preserved old grandfather clock, with its quiet, somnolent, bradycardic tick.

'Sit.' He indicated a severe high-backed chair. Charles Rennie Mackintosh. He took his own seat behind the desk. Muir Foye took her backstage seat with her notepad in the corner of the room, and crossed her legs demurely. She was considerably older than I was. I found her very attractive. I had a notion she had abjured passion, a husband, and family, to devote herself to being Douglas Horton's secretary. She had not yet left it too late. I was contemplating her page-boy dark hair, for the moment tied back, the intelligent eyes, the rather strong chin, when my attention was diverted back to the huge desk top by a small piece of theatricality. Professor Horton had produced from his top drawer a small sandglass perhaps slightly larger than an egg timer. He placed it between us on the expanse of the dark red leather and inverted it. The shocking pink sands of time began to trickle away. He made a rather discouraging open-handed gesture. I thought, I bet the sophisticated African couple didn't get the egg timer treatment.

'Thank you very much for fitting me in. I happened to be attending a meeting in the Maclaurin Conference Centre this morning –'

'Ah! You are with Forbes Pearson's group! Splendid chap. Sutured my daughter when she took a tumble out riding. Cut forehead. Lovely job.'

'He's very neat.'

'I trust the conference venue is fit for purpose?'

'It is an excellent facility.' I didn't tell him about the lousy sound system.

'But you wish to draw my attention to something?'

'Yes. Nothing to do with Conference.'

111

He frowned.

I took out my piece of paper and went through my well-rehearsed routine. He resumed his Norman arch pose with his elbows resting on the arms of his chair, fingertips resting against pursed lips. He stared at me without blinking as I droned on. His eyes reminded me of Tallulah my reclusive flat mate. Half way through he had frozen solid. He had suddenly recognised me from our previous encounter. I detected the change in atmosphere. I was a madman. Somehow once again a crazy guy had infiltrated his domain. In a moment he would reach stealthily for the panic button beneath his desk and summon security.

After I had finished my pitch there was a protracted silence punctuated only by the tick of the grandfather clock. He continued to stare at me icily. He might have bombarded me with questions but I could see him pitching them up and then discarding them. He was a very clever man. He kept his enquiries to a minimum.

'You've told the police.'

'Yes.'

'Whom else have you told?'

'My colleagues, the psychiatrists, my medical defence union.'

'And now you have told me.'

'Indeed.'

'May I see your . . . doodlings.'

'Take a copy.' I pushed *The Bottom Line* across the desk top. It sat beside the sandglass. I had about two minutes to run.

He picked up the wrinkled sheet without diverting his gaze. He held it just off the desk so that his view of me was unobstructed. Then, briefly, he dropped the direction of his gaze and scrutinised the grid. I had the impression of a computerised brain scanning an image. Then the cold watchful eyes settled back on me.

'May I have note of your General Medical Council registration number.'

I gave it. I could see no reason not to. He jotted it down. He need not have troubled. Ms Foye was taking minutes. He pondered for a few moments longer. I could sense he was evaluating risks. I had a sudden apprehension that we were not singing from the same hymn sheet. I was scared of a lunatic rampaging through the campus with a submachine gun. He was scared of a lunatic going public with a hair-brained piece of adverse publicity that was going to upset his Business Plan. I could hardly blame him. I was the anarchist who had nearly wrecked his exam board.

Then he made up his mind. Still without diverting his gaze from my face, he crumpled the A4 sheet into a tight ball within the grip of a single powerful fist. Then he leaned across the desk and pushed the litter into the lapel pocket of my jacket. It sat there, bulging out, like a rosette.

'Listen to me very carefully. I don't know what your game is, but I will not allow you to expose the students and staff of this university to fear and anxiety as a result of a piece of arrant nonsense. If you persist in taking this further I will take steps to ensure that you never practise medicine in this country again. Don't think I can't. In short, I will break you. Let's be clear.'

He swatted me, like a fly. I grinned at him. 'Gin clear. Crystal.'

Back outside in the haar, there was a brief Shakespearian tag nagging away at the back of my mind.

The proud man's contumely.

Funny word, contumely. It looks like an adverb, but it's actually a noun. It means contempt.

I wasn't quite done with Clerk Maxwell that day. After my meeting with Professor Horton I wanted to bathe. I wanted to rid myself of the pungent miasma that had emanated from him and was now clinging to my clothes, my skin, like something poisonous out of Porton Down. So I walked over to the sports complex and bought a casual visitor's ticket to the pool. The accommodation was Spartan enough. I slipped into my togs and crammed my outdoor gear into a tiny locker and went for a swim. I kept it brief. I didn't have goggles and there was too much chlorine in the water. There was a women's water polo team practising, and only one lane roped off for swimming. Twenty lengths, a shower, and back to change.

There was a football team in the locker room, mud bespattered and voluble. Is there anything more tiresome than the conversation of men without women? Effing this and effing that. The whole sad business of the desperate bravado of being male is summed up in post-match locker room banter. I stood it for as long as I could but in the end I lost patience.

'Put a sock in it.'

The conversation came to a dead halt.

'What did you say?'

'I said save it for the pitch. Just tone your language down.'

There was a big boy standing with his back to the changing-room entrance. He said to me, 'Are you talking to me pal?'

'Well I'm not chewing a half-brick, *pal*.' It was a statement of provocation tantamount to an act of self-harm.

My interlocutor turned pale. He was genuinely affronted. He said, 'Why don't you mind your own fucking business?'

'And why don't you step aside?'

And I thought to myself, you are an idiot. You stick your nose into somebody else's affairs and now it is going to be broken. I don't know what would have happened; but abruptly the door behind him was pushed open and a tiny girl, maybe three years old, with a pink dress and blond ringlets appeared, followed by her father. She marched into the company of a dozen naked men with complete aplomb. A generation ago such a scenario would have been unthinkable. I suppose it is the inevitable consequence of collapsed marriages. This afternoon must have been the father's precious time of access. There was no more profanity. A little

114

girl succeeded where I had failed, and she didn't even have to try.

My putative assailant moved to one side and as I passed him he hissed.

'Wanker. Ass-hole.'

Maybe he's right.

XIII

Back on the other side of the bridge, I told Caitlin to grab her kagool and we would go out for something to eat. We went to an Indian restaurant in Stockbridge. We walked. I remember pacing quickly across the Meadows with my hands in my pockets, deeply preoccupied. Caitlin clutched my arm and scampered along beside me. With extraordinary facility she texted ahead and booked the table. And did I want to order? Yes I'll take a bhuna lamb with pilau rice and a chapati, onion bhajis on the side, and a pint of lager. Her thumb darted across the tiny console. 'Sorted. Result.'

It was very quiet in the restaurant. Even the canned Bollywood chanteuse with her backing combo of violins seemed subdued. There were only two other tables occupied. A lone diner sat quietly in a corner reading a book. And then the Hortons were dining *en famille*. Table for four. I tried to rationalise it. Edinburgh is only a village. They were a very good-looking family, all blond and blue eyed, terribly Aryan. It crossed my mind the name Horton had rather a Norse ring to it. Professor Sir Douglas had his back to the door, which was maybe just as well. I chose the table furthest from him, where I could hide behind the great drooping fronds of a climbing vine. My attempts to stay under cover were nearly scuppered when I managed to spill my pint, with a crash, all across our table. But the waiter unfussily cleared up the mess, put down a fresh tablecloth, and even brought me a fresh pint, gratis. Caitlin said to him apologetically, 'I'm his carer.'

The food came. I can't remember what Caitlin had. It seemed little more than a piece of water cress. I don't think she had an eating disorder; more like disordered eating. She said she'd have some pudding. She sipped a glass of dry white Sicilian Catarratto so pale it looked like water. She played with her water cress and occasionally reached her fork across and stole from my plate.

'So what's on your mind?'

I had decided to tell her.

'I met a man, a patient. He's thinking about harming a lot of people. He doesn't necessarily have a plan. But he's thinking about it.'

'What's he going to do?'

'Go on a rampage with a gun.'

'Like Hungerford?'

She lived in Cheltenham. It would be natural for her to choose Hungerford rather than Dunblane.

'Yes.'

'Tell the police.'

'I have.'

'What are they going to do?'

'Nothing.'

Caitlin frowned. 'That's bad. So what now?'

'They think we should leave it to the trick cyclists.'

'The who?'

'Shrinks.'

'Sorry?'

'The psychiatrists.'

I was trying to keep my voice down but we were getting competition.

'The standard of debate – well, Frances – it's really quite embarrassing.'

'I *know*, I *know*.'

Professor Sir Douglas had a remarkably penetrating voice. It was a deep baritone with an edge to it, as if it were amplified through a megaphone. I wondered if Lady Horton might be deaf. Or was Horton just the sort of man who couldn't care less that the other diners in a restaurant should know his business?

'And in that frightful accent.'

'Ugh! Don't mention it.'

'It reminds me of the former Mr Speaker.'

'Not a speaker. They have a presiding officer.'

'No no. I mean, *dine scythe*. Westminster. What was his name?' Horton snapped his fingers impatiently. 'Played the bagpipes.'

'Alastair Campbell?'

'Lord no, dear. The speaker from Springburn. Gorbals Mick!' bawled Horton. 'Dumyat does a brilliant impersonation.'

'Uhrder! Uhrder!' said Horton's son, dutifully.

Caitlin caught my eye, suppressed a conspiratorial giggle, and silently mouthed, 'Dumyat?'

The Hortons were chortling away. Not the girl. She was staring expressionlessly at her plate. I had an idea she had a long experience of silently enduring her parents in public places. She said something in a low voice.

'Not snobbish at all. I think, Whangie, we have a right to expect that our leaders not be parochial.'

This time Caitlin only managed to suppress a yelp of laughter by slapping a hand across her mouth. She composed herself, removed her hand, and mouthed at me again.

'*Whangie?*'

'But really–' Horton resumed his public address, now speaking through a mouthful of vindaloo. 'To return to the foot of the Royal Mile –' He made a vague gesture south-east. 'Just suppose our noxious rotund little first minister – and his

118

charmless thin-lipped deputy – just suppose they *had* gained their precious independence, would we really have wanted them to represent us on the world stage? Do they really think they could cope, outside of their Holyrood high school debating society –'

'A pretendy parliament.' This from Dumyat, still in role as the ex-speaker from Springburn.

'Little Alex.' Horton was shaking his head. 'Such a nimby. Scrap Trident, can you imagine? Doesn't he realise we have enemies? We could be obliterated.'

The girl named Whangie got up abruptly, tossed her napkin on to the table, and went to the loo. She was six feet tall and had a voluptuous body. Caitlin saw me look at her and gave me a kick under the table. 'You were saying?'

'What?'

'You went to the police.' Now Caitlin was deliberately speaking in an overloud conversational tone. 'They didn't want to know. So what now?'

'I've been freelancing. It's like playing a game for three players. The good guy, the bad guy, and the authorities. You play the game for sport, and then you suddenly realise it isn't a game. It comes at a cost.' I thought of the falling masonry on Princes Street. 'Then you don't know who to trust. It's a kind of fatal triangle. It's like the Monty Hall problem.'

'What's the Monty Hall problem?'

'You're a contestant on a game show. The compere shows you three doors.'

'What's a compere?'

'The emcee. The host of the show.' I was hopelessly obsolete. 'He says, "Behind one of these doors is a BMW. Behind each of the other two is a goat. Choose a door and I will open it and gift you what is behind."'

Caitlin wrinkled her nose. 'I don't like BMWs. Too kraut.'

'As for Scottish Conservatism,' Horton droned on remorselessly, 'We really are in a sorry pickle.'

119

'On the other hand,' Caitlin was saying, 'I'd quite like a nanny-goat. Very good for keeping the grass short.'

'Anyway, you choose a door. Call it Door A. "Before I open it," says the compere –'

'The emcee.'

'"Before I open it, I'm going to show you what is behind one of the other doors." And he opens another door, Door B, to reveal a goat. Then he offers you the choice of changing your mind. So you can either stick with door A, or you can change and choose Door C.'

'And this affects you how? What's it got to do with your predicament?'

'I thought I was on the side of the forces of law and order, but I'm beginning to change my mind. It's as if Richard Hannay lost his faith in the Empire.'

'Who's Richard Hannay?'

'Character in a shilling shocker. Imagine if he stopped trusting Sir Walter and Mr MacGillivray.'

Caitlin opened her eyes wide. 'What the *hell* are you talking about?'

'Mr Cameron. He's still frightfully young.' Frances Horton was being rueful. I wondered if she was a party activist. All that door-stepping and leafletting. Who could bear it?

'But frightfully good, Frances. A safe pair of hands. And he has that ability to connect, I honestly believe it. Think what we tried and discarded during the wilderness years. Hague always looked like a sixteen year old at the party conference. Sledging in a peaked cap wasn't a photo opportunity. It was a big mistake. Howard – remember "something of the night"? As for Duncan Smith – Well – he's a nice chap but hardly leadership quality. "The quiet man has turned up the volume." D'you remember? Where on earth do they dig up their speech writers?'

'I *know*, I *know*.'

'So the question is – do you stick with your original decision, or change your mind?'

'What?'

'The goats.'

'Sorry. I was listening to –' She tilted her head in the direction of the Hortons.

'You're supposed to be helping me out with my dilemma.'

'I'm on to it. Stick with your original decision.'

'Why?'

'Because it's a fifty-fifty chance. Car versus goat. No point in changing.'

'You're wrong.'

'You can take a horse to water.' Lady Horton was despairing of the Scottish nation. 'You can't make it drink.'

'I suppose,' I mused, 'we could ask *le patron* to turn up the Bollywood muzak.'

'*Le patron?*'

'The *maitre d'*.' Whangie was walking back to the table. Caitlin gave me another kick.

XIV

'Tea?' asked Forbes. 'This Darjeeling is very good.' Blue rimmed Minton crockery. Gracious.

'Well, that was a very interesting talk you gave. But if you don't mind my saying so, you haven't the foggiest notion how to present a case.'

Another gut-wrenching assault.

'Oh, I don't mean a clinical case. You can do that with your eyes shut. I mean a political one. It doesn't matter how original and insightful your ideas are – and I do think some of them have weight – if your audience stop listening to you. Granted you had bad luck with the visual aids and the mic. But even so, if you tell the nurses they don't know how to nurse, how on earth are you going to get them to put the drips up for you? It's a question of pragmatism. Yes, you can present your case in an honest and direct way, and then go off in a huff when nobody pays any attention. Or you can use strategies to get people on board. I thought your chess grandmaster simile was very ill chosen. I had this image of you lording it around the department being cerebral while everybody else formed a team of servants running after you. You're probably too young to remember a common variety act in which a juggler kept about a dozen plates spinning on poles across the stage. He would run from plate to plate giving them a burl. By the time he'd spun the last plate the first one's spin had decayed badly and the plate was flopping around at a dangerous angle. He would rush across the stage to refresh the spin. The plates would run down at unpredictable rates and the audience took a kind of sadistic pleasure in watching the juggler run himself to exhaustion reacting to each impending disaster. I have the sense that you could be that juggler. You're just the man to do it. You're all heart, Alastair. You would run yourself ragged. Throttle back. It's either that, or you will be burnt out inside ten years.'

'I expect you're right Forbes. But I'm not a political animal. Maybe I should just stick to seeing patients.'

'Nonsense. What are you, a martyr? I've said it before. Learn to be political. And one other thing. Stop picking fights with people. Or at least, be a bit more selective. Choose the fights you can win, and the fights that matter. At the moment, you're looking for a fight the way other people look for their dinner.'

It was perfectly true. People would say to me, by way of light passing conversation, 'I hear New Zealand's a lot like Scotland.' And I would snap back, 'That's rubbish! Yeah, right, it's got lakes and mountains. But believe me, New Zealand is nothing like Scotland! New Zealand like Scotland? Pah! Nothing could be further from the truth!' And they would look startled and take a step back. I wondered if I was turning into an absurd caricature, a kind of swaggering braggadocio. MacKenzie said I was like Don Quixote, tilting at windmills. I went around assaulting thoughts, ideas, and people entirely devoid of sinister malice. I was like one of these punch drunk individuals you sometimes saw shadowboxing their way down Leith Walk. Or like somebody with Tourette's, hurling obscenities randomly at startled passersby. I was particularly fond of taking up forlorn, lost causes. I might march with a body of men, but I would insist I was the only one who was in step. MacKenzie would sometimes catch sight of me across a room, filing another minority report. She would catch my eye, shake her head and whisper urgently.

'Tilting! Tilting!'

Back on the floor, I took part in what risk managers would term a Significant Event, perhaps even a Critical Incident. Stroppy patients are a bit like medical mishaps – they come out of left field; you don't see them coming. You plan for the last strop but the next one is totally different. He was just another addict with a long convoluted and tiresome saga of lost prescriptions, missed appointments (through no fault of his), needy dependents, and irate probation officers. Basically he was looking for his medication. He told me in very reasonable tones that he was very concerned about my safety, and the integrity of the treatment room we were occupying, because experience had taught him that if he didn't get his way, an inner demon, over which he had no control, might emerge from deep within his subconscious, and there was no telling what might then happen. Now I can't stand that. I told him he had better visit his GP and get a referral to an anger management class. Goodbye. As I made my way past him I just caught the glint of the switchblade out of the corner of my eye. It all happened so quickly that I could hardly say my reaction was premeditated. In fact you might say that an inner demon, over which I had no control, emerged from deep within my subconscious, and before I knew it I had picked up a rather cumbersome desk top computer terminal and used it as a battering ram, driving it hard against his right forearm. The knife dropped to the floor and the addict fell backwards beneath the devouring octopus of the visual display unit with its tangled tentacles of wire, mice, mouse pads, memory sticks, extension tables, adaptor plugs, CD ROMS, and other assorted IT accoutrements. It gave me enough time to reach the panic button on the wall. Security were impressively quick, and that was pretty much the end of it. The man went off to x-ray ('night stick' fracture of the ulna, big deal) and then away in a stookie (personally I wouldn't have bothered) in police custody. A manager came round to get some details from me. He surveyed the wreckage of the written-off computer terminal, and asked me if my reaction had not been rather OTT. I very nearly launched another computer at him. Forbes dropped by. He looked a bit harassed, as if I were becoming too high maintenance. I could only shrug. I'm not accident prone. I'm not a walking disaster zone. Nobody seemed much bothered that somebody had attacked me with a knife. It was only later that it crossed my mind that I might have become vulnerable. Was somebody sending a man with a knife and a grudge in my direction, was somebody hurling bits of masonry at me? Paranoiac.

I visited the MP for the Clerk Maxwell constituency. No stone unturned, you see. I have to admit I did so pretty much as a box-ticking exercise. I had stopped believing in the possibility of getting anywhere. I wonder if my motivation hadn't changed. I believe I had started with a genuine wish to do the right thing as a citizen. Now I felt thoroughly disillusioned. I was going through the motions so that after the balloon went up I'd be able to say to an authoritarian hierarchy I'd grown to despise, 'I told you so.' Part of me even wanted to be ignored so that I might relish such a *dénouement*. Childish I grant.

Westminster or Holyrood? The member at Westminster was currently at his London domicile. I wrote to him at the House of Commons. I will tell you now that by the time I got a very polite reply, well, things had moved on considerably. The Holyrood member was doing constituency work. I was in luck. I booked an appointment at her evening surgery. I had always thought the use of the term 'surgery' for the business of constituents consulting their democratically elected representative was a bit of an indulgence. But, sitting in the cramped waiting room of that Dunfermline High Street lock-out, I sensed the word's appropriateness. I might indeed have been in a GP surgery. I suspected the clientele were probably the same, and the presenting complaints not far removed from one another, certainly manifestations of the same underlying misery. I've never much cared for the political class. A bit like lawyers, I suppose. Of course many of them *are* lawyers. Why do people go into politics? Is it, as they say, 'to make a difference', or is it the lure of power? If you want to make a difference, be a nurse, be a home help, mend the roads, sweep the streets. The only honourable reason that I can see for getting elected is to stop the bad guys from getting in. (You can see why Forbes thought I was politically naïve.)

I wondered if MPs regarded this side of their work, their surgeries, as purgatory. I had a hunch it could be the most important thing they did, if they only knew it. I began to formulate an idea, sitting there, that the more exalted we all were in our professions, the more ineffectual we became. Everything that matters to humanity happens at close quarters. The really important transactions are one on one. My MP might sit in the House and draw up grandiose plans, but what did it matter if they weren't put into effect in the doctor's surgery, in the classroom, on the beat, in the care home, at the check-out counter. Men would strive for high office, devote a lifetime to struggling up the greasy pole, maybe attain their goal, only to find they were powerless.

I was the last patient, and the Honourable Member was running late. Her name was Angela MacVicar. Mrs MacVicar had a party activist sitting in with her. I had the impression of a capable and driven woman trying to juggle her commitments as wife, mother, MSP, junior minister, and non-executive board member, and nearly succeeding, so long as she didn't have to spend too much time with needy constituents. The party worker looked like a bouncer. I noticed there was CCTV, a tiny camera at the corner of the ceiling. Only two months before, a member had been attacked by somebody with a mental health issue, and a machete.

Mrs MacVicar stared at me. 'You're not a constituent.'

She'd had advanced warning. I had a notion that Horton must have made a few calls.

'No, but it is a constituency matter.' I got out *The Bottom Line* and prepared to launch into my laborious pitch.

'Yes I already know about this.'

I wasn't going to be stonewalled. She would hear me out. I trundled through it, the way a cold caller reads an offer of a new kitchen to you over the phone at six in the evening. We are going to be in your area . . .

She listened with an unmoved expression. I was one of these revolving-door patients who turn up in the waiting room, once, twice a week. It doesn't matter how comprehensive your last consultation was, there they are again. Before I knew it I was being ushered out. Thank you very much for your concern. Yes, everything that should be done, is being done. Rest assured. Everybody has been briefed, the police, the university authorities, it's all in hand. Thank you and goodnight. As I left the consulting room I just caught the exchange of glances between the MSP and the party activist and I realised with a flash of insight that now I came with a government health warning; I was one of these heart-sink drug-seeking Munchausensy people on a list, with a personality disorder and a dark hidden agenda, somebody you needed to get out of your department before they made a scene and wrecked the joint.

I even phoned the office of the Ombudsman. Actually the Ombudsman turned out to be an Ombudswoman, Lady Barbara Wylie. I spoke to her secretary who it seemed to me was short with me even before I had started. I had an image of a sharp-featured woman wearing extravagantly rimmed glasses held round her neck by a cord.

'I should try the Independent Police Complaints Commission. This does not fall within Lady Wylie's remit.'

'But surely . . .' I persisted doggedly. 'But surely if I have exhausted all other avenues . . .'

'I can tell you quite categorically that this is not germane to Lady Wylie's ombudswomanship.'

Ombudswomanship!

Was that in the dictionary? I recognised it instantly, in my idiot savant fashion, as a fifteener. It could occupy an entire row of the *Herald* crossword.

Now I was almost left without recourse. I had one option remaining; I could go public, I could become a whistle blower.

Whistle blowing occupies a special place in the UK and especially in the NHS. It is beyond the last ditch; it's really an act of self-sacrifice. Even if it's effective and has the desired result, the establishment will never forgive you for showing them up. They will rewrite history to obliterate your part in it. Whistle blowing – it's *kamikaze*. You would think I would have thought long and hard before going down this route but by this time I was past caring, maybe because I had a premonition it wasn't going to work anyway. My ultimate pitch was like something out of Theatre of the Absurd. I called the local rag's news desk. This time I went for sensation.

'Yes?'

'There's going to be a mass casualty incident at Clerk Maxwell.'

'Uh-huh?'

'Twenty, maybe thirty killed.'

'Putting you on hold.' They were so blasé about it that I was convinced they, like the MP, had seen me coming, with my 'special note' attached. They knew there was a loony doing the rounds.

Pachelbel. The canon.

'Yes?'

'As I was saying to your colleague, there is going to be an incident.'

'Is this a bomb threat?'

'Not a bomb. A shooting.'

'How much warning time are you giving?' I had the impression somebody was filling in a template on a computer screen. They were trudging through a menu. Threat: bomb, firearm, chemical, biological, other. Maybe they were inundated with calls like this every day from a great army of hoaxers.

'It's not me. And I don't know the time frame.' The person

at the other end of the line took a deep breath and gave out a sigh.

'D'you want to run it by one of our reporters? Let's see who's available. Hang on a sec. Where are you? Do you know the Dog's Bollux on Rose Street? Ask for a Mr McAveety.'

Mr McAveety was drunk. He couldn't take in the detail of *The Bottom Line*. He listened to my blurb with a low chuckle full of cynicism. 'I thought I'd heard everything . . .' Then he gave me an indulgent clap on the shoulder and wobbled out of the pub. I sat on, staring into my pint, reminiscing on the day, my thoughts darting about chaotically in disjointed jack-in-the-box jerks.

That morning, Caitlin had taken her usual picky breakfast and scanned *The Herald*.

'Some doc's been done for downloading child porn off the internet. It's all over the front page. Works in Fife. Trubshaw's his name.'

So. The last piece of that particular jigsaw.

'He's been told to expect a substantial custodial sentence. Do you know him?'

'I've met him. Once. He was very courteous to me.'

And meanwhile, tucked away at the back of the international section was the briefest report, barely a column inch, of an incident in an already forgotten war that had occurred somewhere on the Pakistan–Afghanistan border. The Americans had received intelligence that a high profile Taliban militant was to be present at a wedding ceremony, and had sent in a remote-controlled drone with a payload. Thirty people had been killed, including the bride. It turned out that the target, the Taliban militant, wasn't actually there.

After the pissed hack had meandered out of the Dog's Bollux, I became lugubrious. I sat staring into my beer glass. I was entering *un vin triste. Une bière morose, peut-être.* All these people I've pestered – maybe they're right. Maybe I've lost the plot. There's only a certain amount of 'contumely' a man can sustain before he assumes that he must after all be contemptible. I really am like Hamlet. Was Hamlet crazy or was he just putting it on? Is the distinction worth making? You know, I learned Hamlet's 'To be or not to be' soliloquy at school, verbatim, without actually realising it was a suicide note. None of Hamlet's 'fardels' much bothered me. I was yet to experience the pangs of disprized love. It's only later on that you gradually begin to piece it all together.

I had been so precious about my Hippocratic Oath, the vow of silence, the secrecy of the confessional. It seemed rather quaint now to think that when I went to the police I imagined I was crossing a line. I could have put up a soap box on Princes Street and bawled at passers-by with a megaphone and nobody would have paid the slightest attention. The fact is that I was inherently not newsworthy. The thesis that I was peddling was geekish, nerdy. I was a dweeb, born into the wrong century. If I had set up my stall to broadcast, people would have given me barely a moment before turning away to get on with their lives. I was a deserted freak show on the fringes of a tatty, down-at-heel funfair. It was just as well that I had gone into medicine. I was harmless there. Medicine doesn't need attitude. People rather resent it if their doctors are flamboyant. They want them to be low key, entirely lacking in chutzpah, invisible. At least I had something to fall back on. The fact is, in the lights of the modern world, I am a complete nonentity.

I began to appreciate what it must be like to feel that you are disenfranchised. You have a corner to fight, and nobody will take up the cudgels for you. What do you do?

I swallowed my drink. The dregs tasted bitter. I could feel that familiar quiet fury settling again in the pit of my stomach. Settling down for the long haul. Well, I tell you what. I'm not going to go quietly. I'm not going to take this lying down. Quite the contrary. I'm going to create the hell of a stink. Just you wait.

XV

Then my sister MacKenzie breezed into town and presented me with a *fait accompli*. She'd tried to track me down at Little France and had got through to Forbes, and the upshot was that she had left four tickets for Forbes and Dorothy Pearson, Caitlin and me at the box office at the Queen's Hall. The Arnold Bax Quartet was playing.

My heart sank. It wasn't that I didn't want to see my twin sister. It's just that, if I have to work on Saturday, I never schedule anything social for the evening. It's a sure fire recipe for disaster. Every time I do it, my Saturday afternoons go pear-shaped. Suddenly everybody wants to crash their car, take an overdose, have a heart attack, chop a few fingers off. Somebody would come in at five to six on the brink of doing themselves in. I would have to spend an hour persuading them that life was after all worth the candle, all the time with my eye on the clock wondering if I am going to make it for the overture. There is no more uncomfortable experience in medicine.

As it turned out, it wasn't the clientele that conspired against me, it was the IT. The computers went on a go-slow. *Zareba-*

131

abattis is conducting a background task. All of a sudden I was trying to crawl through sludge, like a channel swimmer who has encountered an oil slick. *Zareba-abattis firewall is dealing with an incoming threat.* I suppose I just had to take *Zareba-abattis'* word for it. Sometimes I suspected *Zareba-abattis* of manufacturing the viruses it purported to protect us from. They were in fact a bunch of protection racketeers. *Windows has encountered a problem and needs to shut down.* Oh for God's sake!

I rebooted. It took forever. Endless menus, endless requests for user names and passwords. God I hate these bloody contraptions. Click bloody click.

And we were going paper light. In a few months all the A4 folders sitting behind the reception area would be scanned and then incinerated. I had no faith in the robustness of the systems. If nerdy teenagers could hack into the Pentagon they would have no difficulty with the NHS. All that confidential information would leak out of the flimsy porous envelope of security. A virus, a helical strand of RNA would slither through a crack under the firewall, insinuate itself into a deep recess of the system's nuclear bunker, and reproduce itself with promiscuous abandon. Next step, lysis. The tenuous membrane of defence would be breached from within, and billions of little replicas, clones of nasty information, would spill out into the world, searching for other tiny defects in other systems.

I didn't really want to go to the Queen's Hall, and it occurred to me to succumb to the turgid recalcitrance of the cyber systems, and stay on late. But in the end I cut myself loose. I could hardly whinge about my failure to entertain Caitlin and then turn the invitation down. Even supposing I had stopped listening to music. I don't think Caitlin was any more enthusiastic than me but at any rate we fronted up. Nothing could have been more redolent of our shared plight than the sense of detachment, distraction, and sheer alienation we both experienced, and surely made evident, as we arrived at the door. The usher visibly started. She clearly thought we'd come to the wrong venue. Should she ring for security? Caitlin was all in black, and pallid, like a punk Goth. I must have had a wild, frazzled, dishevelled look. I actually had to blag our way in. Yes we did have friends waiting in the foyer with our tickets. There were Forbes and Dorothy. Forbes was looking at his watch. We only just made it, to take our seats in a packed hall.

The Baxes. Rafael Preller, Dominique Moulin, Anne Strange (she used her viola name), Malcolm Broadsword. It was a programme with an American theme. They started with the Samuel Barber quartet. Its adagio is, of course, *the* Adagio. The five star crit that appeared in *The Scotsman* the following Monday spoke of the sustained intensity of each line, and of the unity and power as a whole of this, a quartet emerging as one of the great chamber music voices of the modern world. I was entirely unmoved. I sat and solved *The Bottom Line* again in my head.

Next, the three Pieces for String Quartet by Stravinsky. There was still an albeit tenuous American theme. Igor was to relocate to Beverly Hills. MacKenzie held a sustained minor ninth, *sul ponticello*, while the first violin iterated a coarse and hypnotic gypsy song against the cellist's pizzicato osti-nato, and a kind of guerrilla attack, in chopping down bows, from the second violin. It petered out, to leave MacKenzie holding her dissonant double-stop. The second movement was funny and zany and weird. I had the conviction that if I had been at all receptive that night I would have liked it. It seemed a suitable accompaniment to my preoccupation with *The Bottom Line* and its rubric. Under the censor's pencil, something had been concealed from me. Cruciverbalists are economic with their guidance; whatever was concealed could not be redundant; yet I had succeeded in filling in the grid. What was I missing?

The last movement reminded me of the Symphonies of Wind Instruments. It seemed to me to be music of planet Earth millions of years ago, cold, disinterested, devoid of humanity. And yet, and yet, what was the meaning of that intense unresolved Stravinskian chord, leaving behind it only the faint echo of MacKenzie's last, barely audible cadence?

Now we had the interval to endure. How odd to be out and about with people who were living a life. MacKenzie emerged briefly and caught up with us at the bar. I noticed the way people gave her space. I reflected my sister was, after all, a celebrity. To me, MacKenzie was just MacKenzie, the tall girl in the long black robe, with long black hair, the dazzling cobalt eyes, the broad, full candlepower smile. Difficult to have any real interchange in the artificial surroundings of a crush bar. As I struggled to pick up the drinks I could hear the great and the good haw-hawing behind me and I recognised all too easily the rich gravelly baritone.

'Sublime.'

Horton stared right through me.

Dorothy asked us all back to Moray Place for supper, but no, MacKenzie had to shoot through. They had a shuttle to catch. They had it all to do again at the Wigmore. What about Alastair and Caitlin? Caitlin muttered that she had a headache, and I said we'd better have an early night. Couple of wet blankets. Anyway, MacKenzie said she would be back for the Festival and would see everybody then. Meantime, best go back and tune up for the Dvořák F major, the American. I accompanied her to the door backstage. I suddenly wished I hadn't come. I realised I badly needed to talk to my sister and here she was, surrounded by the impenetrable aura of artistic performance. She was 'on'. And there was no time.

'How do we sound?'

'Wonderful.'

'You're not even listening. What's up?'

But how could I possibly tell her? How could I burden her when in a few minutes she and her viola would have to announce that F major folk melody that would transport Bohemia to Appalachia? It was her night. I couldn't possibly intrude. And it was being recorded, going out on Radio 3 later in the week.

'I'm fine.'

She gave me an uncertain smile. 'We're doing all six Bartoks in September. You'll come?'

'Of course.'

'Catch you.' She gave me a swift peck on the cheek and pushed open the door. She had an afterthought.

'Oh! Had a funny dream about you. You were on a beach.'

'Chance would be a fine thing.'

'Not a Hawaiian beach. Black sand, lots of jetsam. Old rope and empty containers. Big rock basilisk like a carious tooth. Oh, and a waterfall down a cliff face. Only it was flowing backwards. Caitlin was there too.'

'Surreal.' Caitlin entertains this kind of New Age mumbo jumbo that MacKenzie and I, being twins, are telepathic. This sort of notion just irritates me. If MacKenzie has the power, I don't. Maybe the telepathy gene comes along with the pitch gene. Me, I have absolutely no interest in ESP, ghosts, media, spectres, or any other manifestation of the paranormal. I do not wish to have my tea leaves read. I do not wish to have my entrails deciphered. I do not wish to be in the vicinity of any crystal balls, Delphic oracles, Cassandras, or Sybils.

'Enjoy the Dvořák!' MacKenzie gave a brief wave and vanished.

I didn't much. And I berated myself. Dvořák didn't have an easy life. And he kept smiling. I really ought to take a leaf out of his book.

Caitlin was unusually quiet on the way home. Maybe she really did have a headache. She disappeared into the kitchen to make us a cup of tea while I slouched in an armchair staring vacantly at the BMJ and wondering if Project Bletchley was all washed up. She brought the tea in and I absentmindedly took it without looking up. She sat still on the settee. After a minute I became aware of her immobility. She was staring at me intently as if trying to make up her mind about something. I put the journal down.

'You okay?'

135

'Not really.'

I didn't press her. I just waited. Doctor's trick.

'Can I tell you why I'm here?'

'I'd like that.'

So, that night, Caitlin told me why she was on the run.

Basically, she had tried to kill somebody. She was keeping her head down, maintaining a low profile, in order to avoid a charge of attempted murder.

The girl she had tried to kill was named Francesca Moncoeur. Mademoiselle Moncoeur had a buddy yclept Cassandra Tilde-Broughton. You wouldn't make it up. I could see them, arm in arm strutting their stuff down the streets colour-coded green on the Monopoly board, loaded with bags and designer labels – Topshop and Zara and Jigsaw and Miss Selfridge and Russell and Bromley. Cassandra in her cream frill top and dusky blue wool cardigan, a grey chiffon layered skirt and her taupe suede peep-toe espadrille wedges. Francesca in an ivory sundress and a putty linen sheer cardigan. Cream leather flats. Fran and Cass. (Cass yes, or even Cassie, but, as Caitlin pointed out to me, nobody ever shortened Francesca's name.)

They all had fancy phones and had Twitter and Facebook and SMS and used all sorts of engines and websites I'd never heard of. According to Pear Analytics, a San Antonio-based market research firm, 41% of the traffic on Twitter is 'pointless babble'. Surely an underestimate. Of course, the champions of these sorts of communications leap to a defence. Danah Boyd, a social-networking researcher responded to the Pear survey by saying that Pear's 'pointless babble' was better characterised as 'social grooming' and/or 'peripheral awareness'. Personally I don't want to be aware – not even peripherally – of what my friend is about to have for her dinner, of which train station she is about to pull out of.

Anyway . . .

Caitlin started getting these tweets appearing on her mobile. They were kind of view-halloes in Spanish. Initially she didn't think much about them. Spanish was one of nine subjects she carried.

'¡Huy dia!'

'¡Ole Hobo!'

(Hobo was Caitlin's school nickname, because she was a waif, a gamine, and she played the oboe.)

'¡Hautbois!'

It was some sort of adolescent craze that would have expired by lunchtime. At first she replied with a cheery 'Hello 2 U 2!' then because of the sheer volume of messaging she gave up. She was aware of a vague unease but she couldn't quite identify its source. Then the messages became short and terse. No words. Only punctuation.

'¡!'

And finally, only the Spanish orthographic convention of the inverted exclamation mark at the beginning of a sentence.

'¡'

Reiterated.

'¡¡¡¡¡¡¡'

Messages were coming from elsewhere. Not just Francesca. Cassie had joined in. And other friends. Or 'followers', to use the technical term. She was being picked on. It was her scar. They were ridiculing her scar.

Ignore it, she told herself. They'll get bored. She went to bed and switched her phone off.

So. That's how you get bullied in a girl's school. Why couldn't they do something straightforward like stick your head down the toilet? Trust them to dream up something far more excruciating.

The next morning she reluctantly switched her phone on to be deluged by a twitpocalypse. Each inverted exclamation mark had somehow intensified its virulence. A gibe had become a physical blow. And not a word was spoken. Nobody came near her. She had been sent to Coventry. Little cliques would see her coming and divert away, giggling. She ran after Cass in the street one day and put a hand on her shoulder and Cass shook her off and quickened her pace and muttered over her shoulder, 'Eff off.' Suddenly she was in agony, and she was utterly alone.

The cyber bombardment continued, night after night, like the Blitz. In a moment of insight, she realised it was not going to abate. There were four weeks of term left. What could she do? She could suffer it. Actually she didn't think she could; it was never an option. She could run away. She thought seriously about that. But that seemed to her to be a kind of cowardice, and she didn't want her tormentors to win. She could tell her teachers. But that seemed cowardly too, and it wouldn't work. Francesca would merely shift the goalposts, alter the ground rules, torment her from a different angle, and with doubled intensity.

Or she could force a confrontation.

She settled on the latter. When Caitlin told me this I told her I admired her for it but she shook her head without emotion and told me that it had not been an admirable thing to do. She had had no choice. Her back was to the wall.

Actually it wasn't all inverted exclamation marks. She got other stuff, more explicit. She didn't want to talk much about that, but she did show me a message on her phone that she had saved.

Go back to your Irish bogs, scarface. Wish the airbag had ripped you apart with your sis, loser.

The Irish taunt was kind of interesting. Most of the time the English just pretend the Irish aren't there. You rarely hear any Irish news on the BBC. Even on the weather forecast, they sometimes just erase Eire from the map and leave the six counties looking forlorn and embarrassed floating around in the Atlantic.

I didn't ask Caitlin this, but I thought, why not just switch the phone off? Or get a new sim card? Why allow yourself to be screwed up by the rantings of people who are clearly screwed up themselves? Of course, in the thick of it, it's not as simple as that. Digital pile-on. The whole world is watching. Most of us are more thin-skinned than we think. In New Zealand I once got a letter of complaint from a patient's rela-

138

tive that I knew to be unjust and way over the top. So what did I do? I framed it and stuck it up above the loo. Caitlin was much braver than me. She was going to take them on. She was going to face them down.

After class one day, Spanish as it happened, Caitlin picked up her books and crossed the room to where Francesca and her entourage were congregated. She had a memory of the clique catching sight of her approach, of the circle opening to reveal Francesca, and of the conversational buzz dying to absolute silence. They all looked at her with amused, quizzical expressions.

'Francesca we need to talk.'

'No we don't. Don't talk. Send me a text. If you like.'

These were the ground rules. All right. She would play by them.

She thought long and hard about the text she would send. She dismissed the idea that she might simply ask Francesca to desist. She wasn't going to express her anguish because she knew the sadistic pleasure of the bully resided in the sight of the victim suffering. She most certainly wasn't going to beg. What else? Threats? 'I'm going to tell on you.' Pathetic. No. She needed to hit back. What were Francesca's weaknesses? She didn't have many. Popular, clever, posh, well connected, rich, beautiful.

One thing. She was scared of heights.

How did Caitlin know this? It had just been a chance remark she had overheard during spring term. Cassie got an exotic present for her sixteenth birthday – a balloon trip, for Cassie and five pals. Caitlin, experienced aviator, had jumped at it. But Francesca didn't want to go. 'Oh God no,' she had laughed. 'Sweaty palms!' Caitlin thought little of it. But she had filed the tiny snippet of information away. And now she had retrieved it from the filing cabinet of memory and she sat down and without pausing to compose or edit a script she let her thumbs dance across the key pad.

'Francesca, meet me on the high board at the pool, Thursday, 5pm. No show – you are a coward. Caitlin.'

She copied it to the entire body of exclamatory correspondents and pressed send. So within a few seconds the entire school knew about it. She had no sense of exultation, but there was a sense of release. She had no clear plan, merely a hunch that, whatever happened, things would come to a head and there would be some sort of resolution. She began to sympathise with suicide bombers. She had heard on the news about young Palestinian and Iraqi and Afghan boys and girls walking into crowded supermarkets with explosives tied round their waists, and it had been incomprehensible to her. She had despised them. Surely they were brainwashed. They were savages. Now she wasn't so sure. She was muddled.

She had chosen the time and the venue for the showdown carefully. Thursday afternoon was swimming practice, for the serious swimmers. Mr Foubister took the session. Stamina work. 100 metre fartleks, freestyle, 70% effort. Poolside, he sauntered up and down in his fawn polo neck and slacks, impervious to the drenching he was getting, yelling technical advice and encouragement through cupped hands. By quarter to five they were warming down. Then Foubister usually let them skylark around for ten minutes before calling it a day. Caitlin was banking on it. At five to five she went back to the dressing room and took off her swimming cap and let her gorgeous red hair fall down her back. Then she slipped out of her one-piece Lycra racing costume and put on a flesh-coloured bikini so exiguous that at first glance you might think she was completely naked. The broad purple keloid stripe from epigastrium to throat was almost completely exposed. She wanted them to know that she didn't give a damn. Now if only she could get to the board without running into Foubister. She was in luck. He had his back turned, stuffing coins into a coffee machine. Nobody had left the pool. There was a higher turn-out than usual, and nobody seemed in a hurry to get dressed. Francesca and her entourage had already congregated on the 12 metre diving platform. Caitlin began to ascend the narrow stairway, no more than a ladder, to the top. She took her time because she did not wish to be out of breath, and she did not wish her heart to be hammering, when she got to the summit.

Caitlin's recall of the group was vague. Was Cass there? Five or six girls, maybe. Some in swimming gear, others casually dressed. There was a kind of sarcastic 'Oooooh' when she came up level with them. The group drew back. Francesca had positioned herself well away from the business end of the platform. She wore a cream cotton playsuit with a ruched brown jumper. Pale tomato sandals. The two girls faced one another. Caitlin had her back to the pool. She wondered what was going to happen next. She hadn't written a script. Francesca was watching her carefully.

'Yes?'

'Come here.'

Francesca gave an indifferent shrug and took two paces forward so that they stood with their faces only inches apart.

'What do you want?'

'I need you to stop sending me texts. You are to stop. Now. Do you understand that?'

Francesca searched Caitlin's eyes with curiosity, looking for a hidden agenda, an ultimatum, a strategy, a plan B. She realised that Caitlin had none of these things. She had come to the table empty handed. All she had was this pitiful plea. Leave me alone. Francesca smirked. 'Go back down, Caitlin. You are a waste of space.'

There was a pause. Bit of an anticlimax. Caitlin looked round vaguely for the stair rail.

'Oy!'

Foubister's yell ricocheted around the piscine, batting off the vaulted ceiling. He had just spotted a naked girl on his high board. There was a diversion. Caitlin felt rather than saw the company turn their attention to the man poolside. Without any premeditation she hugged Francesca as if she were bidding her farewell and then she took a step back off the diving board. But she didn't let go of Francesca. There was a second of freefall and then a terrific smack as the embracing couple hit the water and sank. Caitlin had instinctively taken a breath but Francesca had been so taken by surprise that the impact released whatever air was in her lungs and she immediately began to drown. And as they hit the bottom Caitlin tightened her grip and rolled over on top and thought savagely, stay under, keep a tight grip, wait till she stops struggling. Now Francesca had gone limp and bubbles were escaping passively out of her nose and mouth and her eyes were open and unseeing. And Caitlin thought, keep hold, just stay here until your own lungs are ready to burst.

There was a crash by her side as of a depth-charge and she felt Mr Foubister's strong arms come round her from behind and scythe away her grip around Francesca's body. Then Caitlin was propelled to the surface. She took a gasp of air. Foubister took one frenetic glance at her and then jack-knifed below the surface again. Seconds later he was struggling to the pool edge in a clumsy backstroke, one hand cupped round Francesca's limp chin. In a well-practised manoeuvre he placed Francesca's hands on the pool edge and then leapt from the water without letting go of her hands. Then he dragged her out and laid her supine pool side and commenced CPR.

The next 24 hours were a blur. Caitlin seemed to spend most of them in bed, for no very good reason. She was perfectly well. A doctor came to see her, and a matron, and various teachers with various mentoring and counselling roles. She heard with indifference accounts of Francesca's progress from the pool via ambulance to Cheltenham General Hospital's Emergency Department, to ICU, to HDU, to a stepdown ward, to a normal ward. The word was that the respiratory injury would be shortlived and that, largely thanks to Mr Foubister's skill and speed, Francesca would be 'neurologically intact'. The focus of attention began to shift from the immediate clinical issues to one of critical incident monitoring and significant event analysis. What the hell had happened? Sir Ronald Moncoeur, Francesca's father, came up from London. Cabinet minister. He started to throw his weight, which was considerable, around. What did Gordon Foubister think he was playing at? Was it his idea of supervision, to have a cluster of excitable girls on the high board? The school would have to let him go. He'd be lucky if Sir Ronald didn't take matters further. Some of the girls said Foubister looked at them in a funny way.

Caitlin had the sense to play the amnestic card. 'I remember we were fooling around on the high board. I think I slipped. Then it's all a blur. I remember Mr Foubister pulling me to the surface . . .'

But she told one person. She told her oboe teacher, Nicholas Shakespear.

'What on earth were you thinking of?'

'I was trying to kill her. I wanted her dead.' And she told him all about the incessant cyber bullying that wore her down and finally took her to breaking point. Mr Shakespear listened to all of this with compassion and a mounting sense of fury, because he had endured five years, fifteen terms, of nonstop bullying at an English public school, twenty years before. He let her tell her story out in full, and then he got up and made sure the door to the music room was closed. He glanced at the windows and around the room as if to make sure they weren't being bugged. Then he sat down beside her.

'Listen, Caitlin. A lot of this will have to come out. Tell them all about the bullying. Tell them about your proposed assignation. Perhaps there was a tussle, I don't know. You pushed somebody into a swimming pool and then it all went pear-shaped. Things got out of hand. Yes you were angry, maybe you were so tormented that you didn't quite know what was happening. All of that. But . . . but . . . what you said just now. Don't say that. Do your hear? Francesca's going to be all right. We can manage this whole thing in-house.'

Caitlin didn't say anything.

'One other thing. You are wrong about these texts they sent you. You think the upside down exclamation mark is your scar. But it isn't. It's your oboe. These girls you hang out with – they are afraid of your oboe, and of your talent as an oboist. They are afraid because it is the thing that marks you out, that separates you from them. They seem to have everything, these so-called friends of yours. Money, background, connections, prospects. But in reality, they have nothing. They are utterly dull. They are utterly wretched in their poverty. In a few years they will all be married to utterly dull young men who work in the City and together they will fuck up some utterly dull progeny who will come back to this school and start the cycle all over again. They aren't even pretty. They are pug ugly. Already you can see them laying down the lines of smug complacency, condescension, vanity, self-centredness, and bitchiness. They are pug ugly, and they know it. And they are frightened of you, because when you play your oboe, you express something utterly alien to them.'

Caitlin said in a remote voice, 'I was thinking of giving it up.'

'Then they will have won. And they will have destroyed you.'

The day Francesca came back to school, Caitlin was excluded.

There were no more texts.

XVI

On Sunday I went for a run; but it was no good. Spottis-
woode, The Meadows, Middle Meadow Walk past the old
Edinburgh Royal Infirmary and into university land. You
know that archetypal recurring dream where you are being
pursued by something and you can't get your limbs to co-
ordinate . . . I lurched down George IV Bridge, disarticu-
lated, and thought, I've forgotten how to run! I'll take it
as far as The Royal Mile and if I can't get my scampering
thoughts to settle down into a rhythm I'll go back. Well,
Forbes, I went flying and nearly got wiped out, I've endured
all that scraping and scrunching in the Queen's Hall, and I
can't say I'm enjoying this much either. I'll hang a right into
the High Street, right again at South Bridge and go back
past Old College.

I pulled up 100 metres behind the unmistakable figure of
Whangie Horton. She was wearing a rather severe dark blue
belted Burberry trench coat and a matching beret. I felt as if
I were tailing somebody in the French Resistance. She went
into St Giles. I followed.

I was just in time for a very early morning family service taking place in a sequestered south-west corner of the cathedral. The meeters and greeters were men in their middle forties casually dressed in open-necked shirts and chinos. The shirts weren't tucked in. At least I didn't completely stand out like a sore thumb in my tracksuit, but I sat in an obscure corner at the back, under the frowning pilasters, beside a substantial plaque on the black stone with a relief of Robert Louis Stevenson, and a grace, which I could only scan, piecemeal, in the gloom. '. . . grace . . . courage . . . the quiet mind . . . strength . . . peril . . . tribulation . . . wrath . . . down to the gates of death . . .'

The men with the shirts outside their trousers (why did I find that so irritating?) began to construct a screen that obscured the communion table. I suddenly realised I had come to church, here in this last chance saloon, to ask what Jesus would do.

The first hymn was of a happy-clappy nature. The purpose of the screen up front became clear. The words of the hymn were on PowerPoint. No hymn books. Even the High Kirk had gone paper light. I had a notion I had stumbled into a special service, that this was not the normal bill of fare for St Giles. If you don't have a hymn book, you can clap. Some of the men with shirts outside trousers were even making extravagant gestures with their arms.

Next, a children's address. I always hated them as a child. I hated being patronised. But the presenter was Whangie. I sat up. Oh God. Once more, like Dickens' Monsieur Manette, *Recalled to Life*. The agony of the ice breaking up after the long Russian winter. With the trench coat and beret gone she was wearing a rather ecclesiastical long brown gown secured at the waist by a rope. It might have afforded her a dowdy, even a frumpish look, but the effect was quite the opposite. Novitiate chic. The bells of golden hair danced about her shoulders. And she had a way with the kids. There was plenty of audience participation, a bit of origami, and a guitar. Whangie had everybody's rapt attention, for one reason or

146

another. The kids were mesmerised; the men were entranced; the women sat up stiffly with pursed lips. The origami was all to do with a topological mystery – the Möbius strip. I should have paid more attention but I found myself wondering if the Hortons were churchgoing. Surely not. Sir Douglas would be rational – deeply secular. This would be Whangie's private passion, her means of escape, her assertion of her own identity. 'So you take the end – you join it to the beginning and hey presto – a false bottom.' Meanwhile the mummy fascists let their babies yell but no-one seemed to mind.

The lessons were both from the New Testament. Something about Zacchaeus, skulking up a tree. And Nicodemus, visiting Our Lord by night. I had a kind of fellow feeling for Zacchaeus and Nicodemus. They were shadowy figures. They blended in. They lurked on the periphery of life. They were viola people.

The sermon rather took me aback. It was a hand-wringing exercise about homosexual clergy. The minister, following a short preamble, announced that he was going to make three points, and he headlined them. They were alliterative. Actually they were doubly alliterative. I had the suspicion that he used this format week in week out, and that the Kirk Session moaned about him behind his back.

The promise of redemption. The perplexity of rancour. The peace of resolution.

Fancy having to refit this straitjacket every week. He would be in a lather on a Saturday night, hunting for synonyms like a crossword compiler working to a deadline. The burden would always have the same shape. It would essentially be the same sermon. A beatific vision, some sort of fly in the ointment necessitating suffering and a journey, and finally a destination. If you rehearsed it often enough, it would become more and more meaningless. I started counting stone flags. Then I started making up my own alliterations.

The perpetuity of reductiveness. The peregrination of relativism. The pedestrianisation of Ravelston Dykes.

After twenty-five minutes I could sense he was beginning

to wind it up. It's a common failing, this inability to stop. Indeed, it's almost hardwired into the mistaken notion of how to teach. First you tell 'em what you're gonna say, then you tell 'em, then you tell 'em what you've said . . .

The predestination of razzmatazz . . . the pontification of Rumpelstiltskin . . . (I'd lost it.)

And so on. Closing hymn. The computer crashed and the screen went blank and we were left to clap and lip-sync. Surely you go to church to absent yourself for a while from the ghastly apparatus of modern life. Personally I blame the men with the shirts outside their trousers.

Bit of a disaster? Not entirely. What would Jesus do? He would invite himself to dinner at Zacchaeus' place. He would drop down off the High Street through some dark narrow stair-well into another realm of existence.

I was back in Thirlestane by midday and switched the radio on. *Private Passions* with Michael Barclay on Radio 3.

And there he was again. The familiar voice set my teeth on edge. Why did he keep turning up in my life like a bad penny? It was all I could do to keep the radio on. In fact periodically I switched it off. Then I would switch it on again, responding to an itch, challenging myself to identify some gobbet of the repertoire. For somebody self-professed as tone deaf, I didn't do too badly. Here was the Aria from Bach's Goldberg Variations. I knew it was played by Glen Gould (I could hear him crooning away in the background), I knew it was the 1981 and not the 1955 recording, and I even knew it was the *da capo* rendition that closed, rather than opened, the performance. Horton was lecturing the country on 'the sublime'. It gave rise to a discussion on religious feeling, and Barclay ventured the suggestion that music *was* religion. If that were so, then I was truly lost. I was Job, covered in boils, cursing God. Horton droned on. Everything was 'sublime'. Well, maybe it was. But did we need Professor Sir Douglas Horton to tell us so? He was at pains to point out that, although both opening and closing arias match one another note for note, the experience is not the same. After everything we have been through, the culminating rendition seems to carry an extra dimension of meaning that is truly sublime. (Horton was really fond of the word sublime.) He didn't seem to realise that what he was saying was cliché. It might have been true; but it was truism. You can get away with any piece of turgid pomposity on air if your accent is posh enough.

Next, Britten's *Lachrymae*. I was unreasonably affronted that Horton should have chosen MacKenzie's Naxos recording. He got off sublime and got on to something he called 'pellucid limpidity.' It was the most precious tosh you've ever heard.

Bit of Mahler, bit of Strauss (Richard), bit of Schubert. Then Shostakovich. (I have to say Horton never managed to surprise me.) The scorching second movement of the tenth symphony.

And finally opera. I just *knew* he'd be an opera buff. It was *Das Rheingold*, a bleeding chunk from Act II – The Nibelungen and their anvils. I suddenly felt I had an insight into the character of Professor Sir Douglas Horton. It was the Herbert von Karajan recording. *DA-da-ra DA DA DA DA!* An unalloyed expression of sheer naked power.

I looked up Douglas Horton in the phone book. It was a New Town address. Ann Street. I decided to go over. I wasn't going to be pushed around.

I got there at dusk. It was a beautiful town house on four levels undivided and entirely unspoiled. With many period features, the Savills brochure would say. Or perhaps Retties. It would easily command a seven figure sum. Parking was a nightmare. The elegant Georgian Street was littered with Mercedes and BMWs. I gave up and dumped mine on the pavement and marched up to the big slug-black door and banged the knocker without preamble. There was a tremendous commotion inside as the dogs went mad. I could hear Lady Horton reasoning with them.

'Baxter! Eustace!' I waited patiently. 'Take the dogs, you two.' Now the jangle of the door chain being released, and the door opened.

'Yes?'

'Lady Horton?'

'Yes?'

I grinned at her. 'I'm Dr Cameron-Strange. Is the Professor at home?'

'He should be back any moment. Is he expecting you?'

'Yes.' I took a piece of paper from my inside pocket and waved it vaguely in the air. 'Just a piece of college business. Shouldn't take five minutes.'

'You'd better come in.'

I looked dubiously past her at the dogs. They were being restrained by the Horton progeny.

'Put the dogs in the rumpus room. Whangie, show Dr Cameron-Strange into the drawing room.' She didn't stumble over my name. I suspect access had been so easy precisely because I have a double-barrelled name.

We foregathered in the gracious high-ceilinged living room, delicately and exquisitely furnished. There were logs blazing merrily in the open fire. Beside it, the Christmas tree was substantial and heavily bedecked with decoration. Even so, there was no sense of clutter. In the deep recess of the bay window there was a grand piano, a Blüthner. A diminutive television was showing Fiona Bruce anchoring *Antiques Road Show*. It was an old set. Big flat screen TVs are the iconography of the lower classes. An expert was examining a figurine off somebody's mantelpiece. It looked like a piece of junk to me.

'Do you like it? No? If I were to tell you it's worth fifteen thousand pounds, do you like it now?'

Politely, Lady Horton switched the programme off. 'We were just having a cocktail. Will you join us?'

'That would be very nice.'

'What would you like?'

'Would you have a gin and tonic?'

'Of course. Dumyat, there's a bottle of Tanqueray . . . Oh by the way, the twins . . . my son Dumyat –'

I gave him a brief gesture of salute. He waved back.

'My daughter Whangie.'

Fancy saddling your children and burdening them all their lives with fantastic names. Had it been her idea? Probably Sir Douglas'. Two gentle Scottish lowland walks. If he had been a Munro-bagger he could have made it more unobtrusive. Ben and Hope. Whangie held her hand out to me and gazed at me levelly as if challenging me to laugh at her name. Maybe she was Susan Whangie Horton. Surely her father would have had pity enough to offer her that get-out clause. She was tall like her mother but whereas Lady Horton was thin, Whangie had one of these luscious exuberant bodies so curvaceous that it is difficult to stop staring. She was wearing a shapeless caramel-brown single-piece dress which ended about four inches above the knee – maybe Sunday was her brown day – and, so far as I could see, very little else. I wondered if she continually dressed down in a vain attempt to divert attention from her shape. No jewellery, no tights, nothing on her feet, apart from dark blue nail varnish. Caitlin uses the same – must be a trend. I held her gaze, smiled directly into her eyes and shook her hand.

'G'day.'

Blue eyes, candid and challenging.

'Australian?'

'New Zealand.'

'Oops! Sorry.'

'Actually only half Kiwi. Thanks.' I took the gin and tonic from Dumyat. We all raised our glasses. Lady Horton was on Harvey's Bristol Cream, Whangie had a glass of white wine, Dumyat a pint of lager.

'Cheers!'

'*Slàinte.*' The G and T was ice cold and had ice and lemon. It was very strong. I had the car. I would just take a few sips.

We all sat down. I poured the rest of the Fever Tree tonic from its small bottle into my glass. I began to develop a strong sense of the ridiculous. We would have to indulge in small talk. My cover would begin to run. Better take the initiative.

'Are you at university?'

Whangie nodded. 'Dum's at Cambridge, I'm at Oxford.'

'Really? Which college?'

'Gonville and Caius, and Brasenose.'

'What do you read?'

'Maths and English.' Whangie smiled. 'Respectively.'

'You're the mathematician?'

'Oh God no. I'm allergic to numbers.'

'That's all right sis. I can't read.' Dumyat took a pull at his lager and nestled the pint glass under his chin. 'What's your field, doctor?'

'Medicine. I bet you, though, Whangie can do maths perfectly well. It's like men not multi-tasking and women not map-reading, a kind of role-play.'

Whangie laughed. 'I can assure you –'

Lady Horton frowned. 'We don't have a medical faculty at Clerk Maxwell . . .' The doorbell rang in a ferocious and insistent manner. She raised her eyes to the Georgian frieze. 'Your father's forgotten his keys again.' Dumyat went to the door. The dogs had started up from the bowels of the rumpus room. I took a more generous pull at my G and T, and sat it out.

'You must be with PAMs.' Lady Horton furrowed her brow. She suddenly found she couldn't place me.

'PAMs?'

'Professions Allied to Medicine.'

'Oh yes. PAMs. PAMs indeed. Yes indeed.'

The living room door flew open and the great paterfamilias force entered.

'*You!*'

I rose from the deep recess of the sofa.

'Frances, phone for the police.'

'Is anything wrong my dear?'

Horton took four strides across the room to the blazing open fire and clasped in his right hand a stout poker from the brass companion set on the hearth.

'Douglas – what is it?'

'I warned you. I told you, you snivelling little nobody, that if you persisted in your madcap charade, I would break you. Not only have you persisted, you have the audacity to enter my house on some grotesque pretence at an errand. Not only will I break you, I will *destroy* you. You dare sully, you dare defile my hearth and home . . .'

I took the copy of *The Bottom Line* and extended it to him.

'But it is not a pretence, Professor. It is real. See for yourself. Evaluate the evidence.'

He blinked. I just don't think he had ever had the experience of somebody arguing with him. I don't believe I have ever seen a man as angry in my life. I wondered if he was going to take a stroke. He was absolutely incandescent with rage. Frances and Dumyat looked suitably alarmed. Whangie was flushed; her mouth was open and her breathing was a little rapid.

He did his one-handed crumpling act again – I thought he looked a bit absurd with a ball in one hand and a poker in the other. He looked like the exponent of some kind of bizarre racquets game out of Imperial Rome. This time he threw *The Bottom Line* in my face. I caught it automatically and pocketed it. It crossed my mind I might be in immediate physical danger. The pitch of his voice had escalated through several levels. He sounded like a Dalek in falsetto.

'Get out of my house! Get out! Or I'll set the dogs on you.'

The big black door got slammed abruptly behind me. I stepped back out into the dark street. It was raining, the sort of very fine rain that soaks you through in a minute. Why did I resist the temptation to run back to the car? I was trying to maintain a dignified nonchalance for any audience I might have. I stopped and turned and glanced back down Ann Street. There was nobody there. The street smirked at me. I heard it pass a barely audible derisory remark. Why did I keep thinking somebody was walking right behind me?

Here's the car left where I abandoned it on the pavement. I got in behind the wheel and closed the door behind me. I sat for a few minutes and stared blankly at the little rivulets of water running down the windscreen.

Ever since the man with the white face and the black cape had sat briefly behind me in the Slingsby, for the rumble seat ride, I was being watched. I had this vague awareness of a third party, mixed up with a jumble of disparate images – Christ's walk to Emmaus, Shackleton's trek across a frozen southern wasteland, something to do with an ordeal, a supreme trial of strength and endurance. Men on a forced march, men at the end of their tether, begin to hallucinate the presence of an extra individual.

The passenger door opened abruptly and Whangie Horton slid into the seat beside me. She had put on a pair of sandals but hadn't bothered with a coat or jacket. She must have slipped out of the back door and come round by the side lane. She paused to get her breath back.

'What the hell was all *that* about?'

'I just wanted to let your father know something he doesn't want to hear.'

'Hah!' She raised her eyes heavenwards and then shook her head to indicate the futility of my expedition. The golden hair danced again about her shoulders and I wondered if this was really why I'd come to Ann Street. She had that gregarious openness and ease of communication which for her boyfriends would be a lure and an enchantment and then, when they realised she remained open to the world, a heartache.

'I've seen you before. You were in the restaurant in Stockbridge, with your girlfriend. She's very cute.'

'She's not my girlfriend. She's my PA.'

'I suppose that's better than saying she's your niece. She didn't seem that interested in the Monty Hall problem.'

'You must have excellent hearing.'

'I've never got it, myself. Dumyat has tried to explain it.'

'Did you get the Möbius strip idea from him too?'

'You're stalking me.' The idea amused her.

Extraordinary, the way somebody can explode into your life. A silhouette at another table, a name, a low voice, a gait, a public persona, a few words of casual conversation . . . at what point do you realise that something is happening, has already happened? We spoke as if we had taken up a conversation that we had left off before. I could see it was a powerful weapon of hers, this sudden intimacy. Look, let us be done with the social niceties. These piercing blue eyes stared intently at me. Perhaps she used them chiefly as a means of defence. Most men would evade them, would avert their gaze and indulge in small talk and imagine they would not have a faint heart on the next occasion.

'I have to say, you were great with the kids. You reminded me of somebody I used to know. And incidentally, when you smile, you have beautiful dimples.' I reached over and caressed her cheek. I dropped my eyes to the deep cleavage of her breasts and then to the tanned thighs where the brown dress had ridden high above her knees. It was just impossible for her to disguise her body. I wondered what it must be like to live within such a frame, to walk through life forever conscious of the evasive hunger in men's eyes, and the cold flat appraising look of other women. What a curse to be blessed with such a body. Never to be able to get away from it, to turn it off, to shut it down. Maybe that was why she needed the sanctuary of a church, to escape from the gauche advances, the awkward fumbling. Yet it might prove a heady brew for some, this clash of the spiritual and the carnal. Whatever turmoil she might cause in others, she had a quiet serenity, the inner certainty of someone who knows she will never walk alone.

And yet even now a part of me remained immune. Maybe that was why she felt comfortable to sit with me in the car. She probably guessed I was in love with a ghost. She could feel perfectly safe. It crossed my mind to start a relationship with her solely in order to torment her father.

But I decided not to hit on Whangie. Quite the opposite. I would kill the notion stone dead. I would do this by explaining the Monty Hall problem to her. Can you imagine any less flirtatious exposition? Winston – hardly the world's greatest flirt – used to go to dinner parties and totally ignore pretty young women seated at his elbow. One of them gave him a nudge when he was lost in abstraction and said, 'What are you thinking about?'

'I am thinking of a diagram.'

There's a chat-up line for you.

'The thing about Monty Hall – it's basically an exercise in Bayesian statistics. Think Game Theory. Think Johnnie Von Neumann. What's the other guy gonna do?'

Abruptly Whangie swung round and pushed herself between me and the steering wheel.

'Push your seat back.'

I scrabbled for the levers. The seat shot back and tilted into the reclined position. The hot breath and the weight of her body were on top of me. She grabbed my hand and pulled it between her legs.

'Quick.'

Afterwards – (after what? I'm not even quite sure what) – I wondered what on earth had prompted such a brazen advance. Was I irresistible? More likely she was turned on by the unprecedented sight of somebody antagonising her father. Or did she just crave the excitement of having relations in a public place?

After we had resumed our seats and readjusted our clothing, she gave a smile, a sigh, and then a mirthful giggle.

'You're not quite the anorak you purport to be.'

And then, rather shyly, 'Are you Anne Strange's twin?'

So that's it! She fancies my sister. Fame by association. The female sex – they like to think they are free agents. But there always seems to be some other item on the agenda that has nothing to do with the wind that bloweth as it listeth, and everything to do with society, status, fame, power, and wealth. But it was strange to me, the way she enquired about MacKenzie. Clearly my sister's fame extended well beyond the rather closeted confines of chamber music. It was perhaps the first time in my life that I sensed that I might be related to a superstar.

XVII

At the reconvening of ELSCOMF, I finally lost the plot. It started when a girl from upstairs began her PowerPoint presentation with an algorithm illegible from the front let alone the back of the room.

'I apologise for this busy slide . . .'

'Well bloody *don't*! Just get it off.'

That was me. I bit my lip. She carried on. The ghastly plot unfolded. Upstairs wanted to introduce a system of electronic communication between the emergency department and the in-patient services. It was called LIAISON. LIAISON stood for Live Intranet Access into Strategic Online Nexus. Oh, a phone call was fine. It's good to chat. But apparently we needed something a bit more hard-wired. It left an audit trail. Performance would therefore be measurable. Effective interfacing could therefore be evidence-based. LIAISON was integral, going forward. LIAISON was patient-focused. LIAISON was indispensable to patient safety. LIAISON was a KPI.

So. It was happening, before our very eyes. We had gone paper light and there had been no resistance. No *Fahrenheit*

451. Who was it that said that after you burned books, you would burn people? I had been naïve to suppose that these people were merely opposed to the destruction of trees. It wasn't paper these people wanted to ban. It was language.

The girl from upstairs wittered on. It was scary the extent to which this project had already advanced. It was naïve – again – to suppose that think tanks like this composed their LIAISONs, their clumsy acronyms, as an academic exercise. LIAISON was fast becoming a reality even before its diabolic machinations had been unfolded. Here it was – the what the who the how the when the which the whence the wherefore . . . it was being rolled out. Stakeholders had to be kept in the loop.

The deadly dull minutiae of the system's working were paraded before us. Click here . . . select from the drop-down menu . . . tick the box . . . fill in this compulsory field otherwise you can't proceed . . . marvel at the way the patient's data, the complete life history, is automatically retrieved . . . free text here for those who want it (not compulsory) . . . and . . . double-click to submit! She signed off with a triumphant gesture.

Any questions?

I found myself on my feet. I hadn't rehearsed my question. It was an odd, out-of-body experience, like hearing another member of the audience.

'You have mentioned the what, the who, the when, etc, but what you haven't done is mention the *why*.'

She blinked at me superciliously.

'My question is, why bother? Why liaison? Why would you want to displace a conversation in favour of a drop-down menu? We have this marvellous gift. I mean language. It has evolved with us over millennia. In English it has found one of its most expressive forms. English is capable of great subtlety, great differentiation, niceness of meaning, and of course great expressive power. Why on earth would you want to replace all that with a form and a series of tick boxes? What on earth is the point?'

Her answer was a regurgitation of the earlier part of her talk. I must admit I wasn't really listening. Audit trail . . . evidence-base . . . patient-focus . . . patient safety . . . KPI . . . measurable targets . . .

'Oh for God's sake! We don't need to put up with this. Why are we allowing management to dictate the way in which we practise? The managers don't know the first thing about medicine – and why should they? It's time the medical profession put its foot down. We need to take a stand. We could start right here. Right now.' My forefinger, unbidden, was making stabbing gestures in the air. I hadn't planned to do this. It just ran away with me.

'Why are we all so infatuated with IT? Why is it that, just because a technology exists, we feel compelled to utilise it? I'm not opposed to computer technology. It can be very useful. It has a place. But it needs to subserve our core business, not supplant it. But look what's happened. Everybody's spending their entire day hunched over a computer screen. Clickety clackety click! We have neglected our craft. People who peddle IT in medicine are always going on about patient focus. The best way in my experience to focus on the patient is to turn the desktop off. We need simplicity. We need a return to basics. We need to restore the sanctity of the consultation. History and examination. That is what we do, in the emergency department, more than anywhere. We consult. And when we need the help and expertise of our colleagues, we talk to them. I propose that LIAISON be nipped in the bud right now. Drop it. Bin it.'

I sat down. There was an awkward silence. No applause. No 'hear hear'. I heard the restrained sound of somebody coughing into a fist.

MacTaggart said, 'Thus spake the Tolpuddle martyr.' There was a burst of loud laughter as if a pressure valve had been released. MacTaggart let it die down and then addressed me confidentially across the table, with pained indulgence.

'It's coming, Alastair. No point in trying to turn back a

tidal wave. Not unless you want to keep Casualty in the dark ages.'

'What the hell do you mean by that?'

I felt a hush descend upon the board room.

MacTaggart turned down the corners of his mouth. 'I only mean what I say, Alastair. It's hardly rocket science. Moving along . . .'

'Maybe I'm too stupid. Spell it out for me.'

'Very well. We are merely trying to get you and your colleagues down at the coal face where, let's face it, you're struggling, to move into the twenty-first century. You should be grateful. We're trying to help you.'

'Well if you really want to help, give us more doctors and nurses – "down at the coal face", as you put it. At the end of the day it's perfectly simple. Patients turn up at the front door, and we should be there to care for them. Invest in that – not this . . . sterile nonsense.'

'Alastair, we've been over this before. If ELSCOMF achieved one thing at the Maclaurin Conference Centre last week, it was the consensus that we need to drive 40% of the patient load back into General Practice. Compassion is very commendable, but a tertiary institution like ours, with an international reputation in research, in state-of-the-art technology, cannot afford to mire itself in the daily grind of the needy and inadequate. I've seen it all before; open the doors and you will be inundated. It doesn't matter how many doctors you have down there – it's a bottomless pit. I told you – the poor ye will always have. You might spend the next thirty years down there – I have a horrible feeling you are going to – and at the end of it, everything will be exactly the same. Keep it as a training ground for the juniors.'

'That says it all. You're not the solution. You're the problem.'

'I beg your pardon?'

'How dare you impugn the Emergency Department with a charge of backwardness? You have taken pains to ensure that the department is disempowered, disenfranchised,

160

understaffed, underfunded, the fiefdom of a bunch of absentee landlords who wouldn't be seen dead in the place and who haven't dealt with an emergency for twenty years. You have no idea what goes on in a modern emergency department.'

Then it got personal.

'You come in here, with your airs and graces and your insufferable pomposity and you dare to talk to me about "Dark Ages"? If anybody's obsolete round here it's you! *Casualty!* What the hell is that? Have you any idea how pre-historic you sound? Spew up this garbage in any other part of the English-speaking world and you would be a laughing stock! You're ridiculous anyway. You smug, *effete*, bloody Regency fop! You're irrelevant, and you don't even know it. And look at your idea of help. Look at this junk, this hap-less rubbish! What do you people know about medicine, and humanity, with your useless, sterile, clunky, tick-boxy, drop-downy, crappy, cruddy . . .'

The red mist had descended. I welcomed it. I believe I was hoarse and weeping. What a blessed relief. Forbes had slipped in and quietly appeared at my side and had an arm round my shoulder.

'Let's go for a cup of tea, old chap. Come on.'

He led me out of the boardroom. My exit came straight out of Opera Buffa. As he pushed the door open somebody heckled from the committee.

'Luddite.'

I yelled back. 'I am not a Ludd–'

The door slammed.

That night, I had a blazing row with Caitlin. Back in the des-olate flat with its dank subliminal aroma of inoccupation, I poured myself another glass of Lagavulin.

'What did you think of the Bax Quartet the other night? Did you enjoy the concert?'

'No. Can I have one of these?'

'Wouldn't you rather have some cocoa?'

She ignored the question and poured herself about three fingers.

'Steady. Put some water in that.'

She didn't. She sipped it appreciatively. 'Nice drop.'

'I thought maybe the music would inspire you to get out your oboe.'

'Yeah. Well I tell you what, I'll get out my oboe when you take that layer of dust off your piano lid.' She was always merciless in the counterattack. I should have let it go, and to be honest I didn't really have the heart to pursue it. I was just being dogged.

'Caitlin. You're going to have to make plans. What are you going to do? What are you going to be?'

'I thought I might get pregnant then I could get a council house in Pilton.'

'Attagirl. Don't let anybody piss on your dreams.'

'Tread softly.' She threw the rest of the Lagavulin back in one gulp.

'Caitlin get a grip. You've got your problems. Don't you think I know that? But you can't solve them hiding away in a flat in Marchmont. I can help you, but not like this. Go home. Go back to school. Get back to a semblance of normality, even if you don't feel like it.'

'Smile though your heart is breaking?'

'Something like that. Because if you don't, I tell you what, it'll destroy you. It all seems a helluva blast to you just now, the cigarettes and the whisky and the attitude, but trust me, in no time at all you'll turn into an ugly middle-aged alcoholic slag.'

She laughed at me incredulously. 'So throw me out.'

'Go to bed.'

Caitlin took three steps up to me, put an arm round my neck and gave me a big wet malty kiss on the lips. Then she stepped through her bedroom door and slammed it shut.

XVIII

She didn't appear for breakfast. I sat on my own reading the paper. The usual pile of junk mail flopped through the letter box. I shovelled it up for immediate transit to the recycle bin, scanning for bills, adding a couple of unopened Christmas cards to the neglected pile I was accumulating.

Somebody had written me a letter. How unusual to see the handwritten name and address on the sealed blue envelope. I opened it with curiosity.

5 Willow Grove
Kingseat
Dec 18th.

Dear Dr Cameron-Strange,
I hope you don't mind my writing to you personally. I believe you were seeking the whereabouts of a patient of Mr Trubshaw. His name is Alan Stobo and he lives at East Cottage, Claverton Estate, East Neuk. He is one of the lecturers at the college. His mother is a friend of mine. She has been worried about him and she thanks you for your concern.

I don't think he's on the phone. Best to enter the estate by the west gate house and follow the drive, keeping left. Mind the potholes.

Yours sincerely,
Elspeth Mayhew (one of the cleaners at the hospital)

The letter had been written neatly in a female hand that had lost its youthful curves. The spelling and punctuation were meticulous. Nothing reminded me more sharply than that letter of the grotesque upsidedownness of a society whose leadership is characterised by puffed-up pomposity, crass ignorance, and bumbling incompetence; while down in the rank and file, Elspeth Mayhew kept the hospital floors scrupulously clean, had her finger on the pulse, and was a mine of information. And there was I, wasting my time going cap in hand to consultants, lawyers, senior police officers, academicians, and Members of Parliament whose soul preoccupation was in ticking the box that would satisfy their own superiors and progress their 'careers'. And all the while the information was available, if only I had known who to ask.

I wasn't rostered on the floor until the afternoon. I gathered up my things and got going.

Caitlin's bedroom door was still closed.

Alan Stobo lived in a tired cottage in the shadow of an ancestral pile squat in a hundred hectares of wood and parkland. The big house was unoccupied and belonged to some absentee landlord who lived in an apartment in Paris and who visited twice a year to collect his rents and open the local village fete. The gatehouse had almost been obliterated by ivy. I nudged my car between the rusted gates and crept along gingerly amid the potholes like a bare-foot man walking over gravel. The Seat itself, an exuberant and crumbling Scots baronial folly, loomed up and slid away behind me. There was a fork in the drive and I veered left towards the woods. Here was a slight elevation. *Chez* Stobo was little more than a log cabin. The tenant was at home. I could see him chopping lumber. He was wearing an unfashionable corduroy suit in dark brown. He had taken off the jacket, opened the waist-coat, and rolled up the sleeves of a collarless blue pin-striped shirt. He looked more than ever like Lawrence. Or perhaps like the gamekeeper in *Lady C*. What was his name again? Danvers? No, that was that bitchy housekeeper in *Rebecca*. Mellors. He caught sight of the car as he was swinging his axe and he let the rhythm and the arc of his motion quietly decay as he straightened up and watched my progress. He kept a hold of the axe. I parked the car and got out.

'Good morning.'

'Oh, hello.' The frown was replaced by a shy look of recognition.

'Mr Stobo? It's Dr Cameron-Strange. I hope you don't mind this follow-up visit?'

He dropped the axe. 'You'd better come in.'

The interior was so gloomy that I had to pause inside the threshold until my eyes began to adjust. The ceilings were low and all the walls and floors were at a slightly jaunty angle. I had thought the hallway was absurdly narrow until I realised it was almost full of stacks of papers. Stobo led me through to his study at the back. Here the walls were completely hidden by shelved books, floor to ceiling. There were more stacked papers on the floor. There was a littered desk and a decrepit swivel chair that had broken at an uncomfortable angle. There was a typewriter, not a laptop. It was a Lettera 22. The rest of the world was going paper-light, but Mr Stobo was definitely going in the opposite direction. I wondered if he had a hoarder's obsessional condition: Diogenes Syndrome. He removed a great stack of documents from a chair I hadn't noticed, and bade me sit. 'Tea?'

'That would be very nice.' He went through to the kitchen. I sat down and glanced at the nearest bookshelf. It was crammed with Churchilliana: the six volume history of the Second World War in the handsome yellow covers of the Reprint Society edition, *My Early Life*, *Great Contemporaries*, and the four volume *History of the English Speaking Peoples*. From the Second World War history I opened

Volume 1, *The Gathering Storm*. I leafed through the pages at random.

Stobo brought in the tea things. I looked up and put the volume aside. 'Do you admire Winston?'

He looked round for somewhere to lay the tray down. I made some space, lifting *The Herald* off the corner of his desk. I noticed he was halfway through the crossword. Then I was completely taken aback. The monosyllables had been replaced by great tracts of Macaulayan periphrasis.

'Churchill?' He screwed up his face. 'As a politician, no. As an Imperial aristocrat, no. As a writer, yes. Utter clarity. Short words and vulgar fractions. But I would not have cared to meet him. And I would have hated to work for him. An egotistical, bumptious bully. Wouldn't you say? Yet there's something else there. There's a vulnerability. An apprehension. Maybe because he was an outsider. When you see these pictures of him, posing with a cigar and a submachine gun, you realise he was really an American. One thirty-second Iroquois!'

He was lecturing me. I might have been one of his senior honours students, required to submit an essay once a fortnight, and privileged to attend for an hour's one-on-one tutorial, sitting at his feet.

'You know, when Winston was very young, he jumped an immense height off a building while playing a game of tag. He was laid up in bed for weeks with internal injuries. He had this propensity for insane suicidal abandon. He wanted to placate his father, who despised him. I think he was so wretched as a child that he decided to risk everything in a game of pitch and toss. It was all or nothing. So all through his army career he took steps repeatedly to put himself at risk. He really ought not to have survived. I suppose it was a kind of self-advertisement but I rather admire it. At the back of it lay an apprehension, a terror of his Black Dog. He didn't like to stand too close to the edge of station platforms with the express coming through, in case something mad gripped him and it would all be over. I empathise with that.'

'You contemplate self-harm?'

'Of course.'

'Or perhaps you wish to harm others?'

'Sometimes. Don't you?'

He poured the tea. I was reminded of the first chapter of Henry James' *Portrait of a Lady*. It was impossible to do other than see Stobo through the prism of the world of Letters. Ensconced here in his ramshackle cloister, Stobo was entirely at home, at one with himself. What a difference from our first meeting. Yet I could not say that the virtual plate glass window that had seemed to sit between us in the Gloom Room had completely disappeared. He wasn't good at eye contact; and his chat more resembled a Quintilian apostrophe, addressed to an invisible third party, than small talk. We sipped the tea. He seemed in no hurry to ask me my business. I strove to make light conversation.

'I see you're doing the crossword. I had a quick look over breakfast. I struggled with 13ac.'

'Well for God's sake don't tell me. Black ten on red knave and all that.'

'Talking of crosswords . . .' It was a clumsy enough segue. He cocked an eyebrow. 'Talking of crosswords, I solved *The Bottom Line*. Are you really going to shoot up Clerk Maxwell?'

'That depends.' He didn't pause for a moment.

'Depends on what?'

'Depends on how far the Vice-Chancellor drives me over the edge.'

'Horton?'

'I see you've done your homework.'

'What is it about Horton?'

He calmly lay down his cup and paused to gather his thoughts. 'Horton is a monster. Horton is Churchill, without the wit, without the tears, without the penetrating shaft of insight, without the grand cause, and above all, without the language.'

'So what does he have? What are his strengths?'

'Ah. You are conducting a SWOT analysis on Professor Sir Douglas Horton. Strengths, weaknesses, opportunities, and threats. First, his strengths. Opportunism. Guile. An eye for the main chance. An instinct for the way the wind's blowing. Combine that with an appetite for relentless work. He's the complete workaholic. He's one of these people who can survive on four hours sleep a night. Winston again, but without the siestas. Never takes a holiday, unless he fits it in with a conference, or some junket he can offset against tax. And he expects the same of his staff. He drives them. I see he's organised a *Conversazione* for Christmas Eve! School of Information Technology. They'll love him for that.'

'What about his academic credentials? Is he sound?'

'I couldn't possibly say. His background is in computing. I couldn't possibly judge. I don't own a computer. Of course I have to grapple with them at college. I don't even have a television set. I gather he is well known in his field. He's on the international conference circuit. He has found a niche. It's a gravy train. Something to do with the processing of information. Everything is data. There is nothing outside data. And everything must have utility. Everything must be value-added. Everything must be win-win. You may well appreciate that under that philosophy, the School of English cannot possibly survive. That is why Horton is a portent, and it is why he has to be stopped.'

'And his weaknesses?'

'That's easy. Horton is portentously ignorant. Oh, he may be able to give papers and read lectures and chair university senate committees and hold office in any variety of ways. I dare say undergraduates appeal to him for help and guidance. He has the ear of politicians. I am prepared to acknowledge he may have a certain mathematical facility. He is a good media man, always available for a quick sound bite. He's very prize-worthy. I dare say he will end up with a Nobel in – what would it be – economics? Peace, heaven help us. But you know, none of that can disguise the vast lacuna of emptiness that is his ignorance. Of literature, of history, of the history of ideas, of culture, of humanity, of all the things that combine to make us human, he knows, precisely, nothing. That is his weakness. The trouble is, in the topsy-turvy world in which we now live, his weakness becomes his strength. Ignorance is strength. Orwell saw it all coming. And that is why it is so alarming and distressing that the good professor now occupies a position where he senses he has an opportunity.'

'Opportunity to do what?'

'To destroy the School of English in this university. Do you know that Horton recently chaired a meeting with the Faculty at which he pretty well announced, unilaterally, that assessment in the School would henceforward be by Multiple Choice Examination? Can you imagine what that would mean? Let's see now . . .'

He stood up. He assumed a thespian pose and stared at the ceiling. I could imagine the tights and doublet.

'Hamlet is

A. a comedy

B. a history

C. a tragedy

D. a tragicomedy

E. a farce'

He sat down again and gave me a mischievous smile. 'You see. You can always get it down to the last two.'

I had to laugh. I suppose in my own undergraduate and postgraduate career I must have trawled my way through tens of thousands of five-stemmed posers. I always thought of MCQ exams as surreal experiences. For a couple of hours you inhabited a world of falsehood. Your mission was to discover the truth by discarding the lie. But the lies outnumbered the truth by four to one. Hence you were in a world of treachery and deceit. It was like being in the hall of mirrors at a fun fair. It was a vertiginous world of altered perspective. After a while your sense of judgment and balance became clouded. Occasionally a question would be thrown in that turned the game on its head. Four truths and one lie. Double negatives. A nightmare for the migraineur. You would forget the nature of your mission. Why am I here? What am I trying to find out?

After I left Med School and embarked on a career I kept thinking a five-stem poser would crop up in reality. But I never found one. Maybe I had an urge for over-simplification. I inhabited a two – or at most a three – dimensional world. Do this. Do that. Do nothing. My world was the world of the Monty Hall problem. Stick with your decision or change your mind. I put it to Stobo that in the real world there was no such thing as – what would you call it? – a 'quinlemma'.

'A quincunx.' It was a strange word. Quincunx. It was the number five as it is depicted on a playing card, with four symbols delineating a rectangle, and a fifth placed at the intersection of the diagonals. It was a beautiful word. It sounded to me like a taboo word, a luscious, fulsomely erotic Elizabethan word denoting the female sexual apparatus. I gathered he had attributed it with a special meaning. I put it to him that *The Bottom Line* was a kind of quincunx. A. Aramoana B. Hoddle St C. Columbine D. Dunblane E. . . . . . .? Did he know of any others?

'One other. Matthew 16:13.'

'Yes?'

He smiled the mischievous smile again. 'Look it up. But one thing you must understand. I didn't compile *The Bottom Line*. It was submitted to me as course work.'

'One of your students?'

'I can't even be sure of that. I have an Ordinary English class of one hundred and fifty. I think I got about 145 scripts. There are always a few defaulters. *The Bottom Line* was anonymous. It could have come from anybody.

'What was the assignment?'

Stobo fished around amid the papers on his desktop. 'Precisely what we've been discussing. Let's see . . . where is it? Ah! Here we are.' He extracted a sheet.

'The Vice-Chancellor wishes to introduce assessment by

170

MCQ to the School of English. Discuss the implications for this University.'

'And back came *The Bottom Line*?'

'Just so. By email. Most of the students now submit electronically. I gave it an alpha minus.'

'Did it alarm you?'

'Yes. No. Maybe. I can't really remember. There was a lot going on at the time. I was getting pressure from Horton. I was holding out against him. I was an obstacle. He doesn't like that. He was trying to wear me down. And he was succeeding. I'm a depressive. I'm very easily undermined. I remember the night I solved *The Bottom Line*. I realised I hadn't the energy to do anything about it. So I posted it on the Internet, the way a castaway on a desert island might throw a message-in-a-bottle out into the ocean in the hope it might turn up on a foreign shore. I walked through the campus with the solution in my head. There was a frightful din because a rock band was playing and the place was crammed with students. I was making my way to the railway line, but they all looked so innocent, and so vulnerable. So I came to see you instead.'

'I'm afraid I wasn't much help. I'm sorry.'

'What are you talking about? I'm all right, now.'

'I can't believe you worked yourself into a lather over a bunch of MCQs.'

'That is because you cannot see that Horton's MCQ initiative is an attack on culture itself.'

I pointed out that the man I'd heard on *Private Passions* could not be entirely antipathetic to culture.

'You heard that too? Rich man's toys. I'll tell you who Horton is like. Hermann Göring. Göring said that whenever he heard the word "culture" he wanted to pull out his revolver. But it's not just the MCQs. There was something else.'

It started one afternoon when he was conducting a tutorial on Chaucer's *Canterbury Tales*. There had been a discussion about the Latin tag *Amor vincit omnia*. Love conquers all things. I had always thought of such a sentiment as a benison.

Two young people starting out on life would together face and overcome all difficulties because of their mutual love. But, as one of Stobo's students pointed out, *Amor vincit omnia* had a dark connotation. Love was such an overwhelming force that it destroyed everything else in its path. Love undermined you, unseated you, unhinged you. If you were undone by love, you would be useless to the state. You would not be able to wage war.

And while this dark view was being propounded, there was a distraction. The Head of School had appeared in the corridor outside, looking perplexed, standing on his toes to reach the window, summoning Stobo with rapid come-hither jerks of the arm. Mystified, Stobo went out.

The Head of School looked distraught. He embarked on a long and convoluted tale about one of the overseas students. He had failed his English exam. It was a catastrophe. It appeared to be a catastrophe as much for Head of English as for the student. But there were special factors. They were sensitive. No need to go into them now. But necessary and sufficient in order for the student to be bumped up, to be pushed over the pass mark. University regulations needed first marker to rubber stamp this, if Stobo would be so kind.

Well that's all well and good but, as Stobo pointed out, the student had failed the exam, and second marker had concurred, and the external had not intervened, and if some Extraordinary Measure was being invoked, should not the Senate too be involved?

Stobo returned to his group, and Chaucer.

Stobo got the summons from Ms Muir Foye the following day. 'The Vice-Chancellor would like to meet with you in his office at 2pm today.'

'I'm afraid that's not going to be possible. I have classes all day. To-morrow would be good for me.'

'I've already contacted Head of School to change your timetable. That's all arranged.'

So. It was to be an audience by Royal Command.

Horton himself was late for their meeting and kept Stobo

waiting in the anteroom for twenty minutes. When he arrived it was clear he intended to use blunderbuss tactics, to breeze in, exert his will, and breeze out again. 'Ah – Stobo! Good of you to give up your time.' Stobo thought, did I have a choice? It was the first time Alan Stobo had met Professor Sir Douglas Horton one on one. He didn't take to him. When they entered the inner sanctum, he thought, this is the power-house of an empire. Horton *qua* Caligula.

'Now look here, I need your signature. Here's the chit. It's a special factors issue. Sorry I can't keep you in the loop, but the matter has gone to Senate. Can I ask you to take this on trust?' Horton had a fixed expression of disgust on his face. He looked as if he was chewing sand. It was intolerable to him that he should have to go cap in hand to a minion, with a chit, for a signature.

'I can't do this, Professor. You must understand that in the School of English we use anonymous exam scripts. This candidate is only identifiable by me as a number. I have no remit to evaluate special factors. All I have to go on is the candidate's script. And I can assure you, this candidate has failed the examination.'

Horton stared at Stobo icily. 'You're just chaff, aren't you?'

'What?'

'One moment.' Horton reached into a drawer and took out a slender buff A4 folder. He slid it across the red leather desk top.

'Open it.'

Stobo did so. It contained copies of his annual appraisal for the past three years. He felt as if he were in a headmaster's study, receiving a brief lecture prior to a caning.

'Not very satisfactory, is it?'

'Sorry?'

'Your results. Pass rates between 70 and 80%. You have been asked annually for three years now to devise an Action Plan to ensure pass rates exceed 85%. You have not pro-duced any plan.'

'There is nothing wrong with my pass rates. They indicate a maintenance of standards. Besides, I don't see the relevance of all this.'

'Don't you see I'm trying to help you? We can increase your pass rate at least by a percentage point. I know it's modest but it might indicate an upward trend which will take you to your next appraisal. Otherwise we might have to let you go.'

'That is outrageous. That is blackmail.'

'I would be very careful if I were you of the language you use. There's something else in that folder. Take a look.'

It was a copy of the contract Stobo had signed five years previously. Stobo stared at it in bewilderment. He only stayed in the room with the reds and golds, the Art, the ticking clock, the big window, for a few minutes longer. He knew this because at this point Horton had produced a small sandglass and inverted it on the desk top. It served as a reminder that the veiled ultimatum Horton was issuing had a limited shelf life and an expiry date. The secretary, Muir Foye, was sitting in shadow.

'You're not really a team player, are you, Stobo?'

'I suppose not.'

'Mm. And yet you must know that we at Clerk Maxwell operate very much as a team. Yes? After all, you signed up for it.' Horton then directed Stobo's attention to a single paragraph, a gagging clause, buried deep in the text. It had been added into everybody's contract after a maverick lecturer had taken early retirement and made a speech at his leaving do after a few glasses of wine. 'I just want to set the record straight on a few issues . . .'

Stobo reread the paragraph. 'I still don't see the relevance.'

'No? It's just that, if we have to let you go, you'll be left without recourse.'

'I don't think the union would see it that way.'

Horton had raised his eyes to the ceiling. Suddenly Stobo realised the truth. Horton had the union in his pocket.

He didn't sign the chit. The last few grains of pink sand disappeared into the sump of the sandglass. Horton had gazed at him for a few seconds longer and then passed a remark which Stobo later had some difficulty recalling. It was a terse rejoinder, an abstract, key words: tenure, censure, dismissal, pension rights. Its import did not strike Stobo immediately. Getting a piece of bad news is a bit like stubbing your toe. The sharpness of the initial impact is quite tolerable; then it is followed by that dull, sickening, protracted thalamic ache. The ensuing onset of symptoms had been rather insidious: the loss of sleep, the early morning wakening, the loss of energy, appetite, motivation, the inability to concentrate. By the time you realise you have fallen into an abyss, it is too late; you have sunk down so deep that you cannot find your way out. Stobo's GP signed him off with work-related stress. The convening date for the industrial tribunal had not yet been set.

'So there you are, doctor. As far as I'm concerned, *The Bottom Line*'s on the back burner.'

Maybe he's right. Maybe it's time to draw a line. Give it up. Let it go. 145 scripts! The job had become too vast. Was *The Bottom Line* a warning? Was it a call to arms? Maybe this was the way terrorist organisations worked. There were little isolated cells, barely aware of one another's existence, occasionally picking up a murmur. Vague, half-baked ideas floated around, all the more so in this age of the Internet. Pathogenic ideas hung in the air like spores waiting to be picked up, to find a conducive environment, to hatch, to multiply, to break loose. And the rest of us were really helpless to do anything about it. You can't legislate for the flick of a switch in somebody's head. I asked Stobo if he thought somebody was planning a Columbine on Clerk Maxwell.

'I don't know. But it doesn't really matter. You can't fight shadows. That's why I've decided to take on Horton. To resist him. At least he's tangible. I'm not going quietly. That's all I can cope with. Maybe that's why I came to see you that night in PMH. To pass the torch.'

You can't fight shadows. Maybe he was right. And, by

implication, Pearson, Walkerburn, Hoddle, and all the others had been right. It had been paranoia. Here, amid the banal surroundings of a tumbledown cottage stacked full of paper and amid the scattering of the tea things, time to let it go. I looked at Stobo. I still thought of him as Bletchley. Stobo-Bletchley. He seemed perfectly stable in his mood – 'euthymic', as the psychiatrists would say.

'So. Just to be clear: you're not going to shoot up Clerk Maxwell?'

'I don't think so. I might murder Horton, but that's another matter.'

I laughed. 'I might beat you to it. Well there you are. *The Bottom Line* solved.'

'Hmm.'

I had a very pleasant couple of hours with Mr Stobo. Our discussions were very frank and wide ranging, as the diplomatic attachés would say. We spoke of letters, of political affairs, of history, of culture. He was enormously well read. He was erudite. It occurred to me that the respective universes he and Horton occupied were utterly alien to one another. There was no point of interconnection. They could hardly mutually exist. I happened to mention that I, too, had recently been in Horton's office, and had caught sight of two very sophisticated African visitors.

'That would be "CLIMAX". Clerk Maxwell International.'

I couldn't see how the acronym worked but apparently there was some fancy logo.

'CLIMAX is Horton's baby. Clerk Maxwell started as a modest tec in a rickety building in Davidson's Mains. Then it outgrew its domain and attained university status and spilled over the bridge on to its present campus. Now we have an annex in London. There's big money in the foreign student market. People from developing nations will pay a lot for a British education. In fact some of them pay so much that they think they are purchasing a degree by right. That can be a problem. We have students from Africa, Eastern Europe, the subcontinent, the far east.'

'You're critical?'

'Of the students? Not at all. Many of them put our home grown lot to shame. But I am worried we are turning tertiary education into a sausage factory. There's too much pressure. Our students need time and leisure for contemplation and reflection. They need to be aware they are travelling in the Realms of Gold. Horton doesn't know anything about that. He doesn't know how desperately the students need to take their eyes off the computer screens and look up to the stars. But I fear it may already be too late. We're even issuing tablets to the children at kindergarten. Give a toddler a brick and he won't pick it up, he'll paw at it to try and scroll down the screen. No. We must destroy this target-driven tick-box IT-orientated gimmickry. Slough it off!'

He was back on his soapbox. He sensed it himself. 'I'm sorry doctor, I'm turning purple. I have a tendency to over-write. I must learn to murder my darlings.' He sighed. 'At any rate, it's either Horton or me. One of us has to go.'

And I had to go too. I was going to be late for work. I thanked him for the tea. I glanced at the typescript on the sheet of paper in the Lettera 22. I asked Stobo what he was working on. It was a piece on Orwell's time in Jura.

'I'm a great admirer of George. He saw it all coming – the death of language. What is Twitter if it is not Newspeak? The language of people who yell at their telescreens, shrunk to a series of incoherent tics limited to 140 characters. LOL! OMG!' He stuck a finger down his throat.

Stobo came outside to resume his wood chopping and to see me off. We shook hands. I suppose it was a form of closure. This man is okay, I thought to myself. Yet there was something nagging at me. Maybe I just don't like a sense of abandoning unfinished business. I said, 'I told the police about *The Bottom Line.*'

'They must have thought you were certifiable.'

'Do you mind if I tell them about the 145 scripts?' If I told Horton he'd have an apoplectic fit. And Chief Superintendent Hoddle? It didn't bear thinking about. But bite the bullet. Dot the *i*s and cross the *t*s.

He shrugged. 'As you please.'

I turned the car round and started off back down the pot-holed track towards the west gate. I could see the brown cor-duroy figure recede in my rearview mirror. So, what was my formulation? Student prank. Hadn't Forbes said as much? Wily old Forbes, with his years of experience. He had taken one glance at *The Bottom Line* and remarked, 'Student prank.' In the meantime I had flustered and blustered around and caused no end of confusion and mayhem. What a pity we hadn't been in old Middlemore the night Stobo-Bletchley fronted up. Sue, my old pal the liaison psychiatrist, would have shot through for a quick word and laid a hand on my arm and said, 'Relax Al, there's nothing to this.' Her assess-ment would have made mine look hopelessly pedestrian. And I recalled a remark Sue once made while giving a lecture on the assessment of the suicidal patient.

Whenever you interview a depressed patient, there is a question you should never omit. Ask, do you ever get high?

I reached the west gate house and turned back out on to the main highway, barely conscious of a vague sense of unease. I hadn't asked Stobo if he ever got high.

XIX

'MacTaggart wants you in the board room.'

'I don't think so. ELSCOMF is adjourned.'

'Prof Pearson's there.'

'I'll just change.'

'I think they want you now Alastair.' The staff nurse looked nervous, distractible.

'But I'll miss the handover.' I was so slow on the uptake.

'Now, Alastair. Here's Cecilia to take you along.'

Cecilia Bentley was the Patient Advocate. Oh lord, not another complaint. I didn't know her very well. She was a large, rumbustious woman who donned her mantle of hearty bravura like a suit of armour to protect her from the incessant torrent of abuse pouring in over the parapets day in day out. But even she was a bit low key. I asked her what I had done now, and I wasn't reassured when she replied briefly that Professor MacTaggart would explain.

At the board room, Cecilia knocked and went ahead. The Patient Safety Committee was sitting. There was a full complement. Even then I didn't think this was anything out of the ordinary. There must have been a critical incident. Something would have happened on the floor. This would be a fact-finding mission. I was a witness.

MacTaggart, seated at the head of the table, looked up briefly from his blotter. He didn't smile.

'Sit down.'

MacTaggart and I were at the top and bottom ends respectively of the mahogany expanse. If it had been a dinner party I would have proposed the health of the sovereign, and MacTaggart would have led the speeches. But this was not going to be a merry occasion. It slowly dawned on me; this was an interview without coffee. Cecilia sat to my left. Forbes was on my right. The members of the committee I did not know stared at me with vague curiosity. Those with whom I had a working relationship kept their eyes fixed on their agendas. As I sat, Forbes laid a hand on my sleeve and gave a gentle squeeze. MacTaggart began with his customary expedition.

'This extraordinary meeting of the Patient Safety Committee is now convened. Dr Cameron-Strange, it has come to light that some of your out-of-hours activities may be adversely affecting your professional performance and, as a consequence, posing a threat to patient wellbeing, not to mention the reputation of this institution, and the good name of the medical profession as a whole. I am referring to some work you undertook on a locum basis at PMH –'

'I wasn't moonlighting. I undertook that shift in a response to a request through official channels.'

MacTaggart raised his voice sharply. 'I'm not talking about the shift. I'm not talking about shoring up Trubshaw, though God knows why anybody would want . . . Well, I'm talking about the unhealthy obsession you have acquired over the pursuit, one might even say the stalking, of a particular patient, and your incessant badgering, in a wholly unofficial capacity, of various public servants. You can consider yourself very fortunate if you are not charged with a whole raft of misdemeanours: mischievous misuse of police time, conduct unbecoming the medical profession, harassment of public officials, unlawful entry into private premises, identity theft, and fraud.'

'He's got to you, hasn't he?'

'What?'

'Horton. He's reached you.'

'You were specifically instructed not to pursue your outrageous false hare. Professor Pearson specifically ordered you not to –'

Forbes spoke up. 'That's not quite true, Angus. I merely gave some advice. I had no idea this thing was going to run away.'

'Well with all due respect Forbes, I think you're being a little disingenuous. When a consultant gives his junior a piece of advice I think he may be justified in assuming the advice will be taken, unless the junior is intent on committing professional suicide, don't you?'

There was a sharp collective intake of breath round the table. It occurred to me that the last time this committee had met in plenary session as now, it was to confront an anaesthetist who had been so hooked on fentanyl that he was giving himself a fix every hour on the hour. Following the meeting, the anaesthetist had been suspended. Suspended – an unfortunate way of putting it. He promptly went home and hanged himself. There had been the hell of a stink.

'Sorry! Sorry!' The Patient Advocate broke the silence. 'This is not a court of law. We are not here to blame anybody. I'm sorry, but we're here to help somebody.'

She was referring to me. She was the Patient Advocate. I was her patient. I was the focus of attention, and yet I had an odd sense that my presence was quite immaterial to the proceedings. I was just an impartial witness to a box-ticking exercise.

'Quite. At any rate, doctor, you are suspended from working in this hospital until further notice.'

'Sorry! Sorry! Dr Cameron-Strange is not being suspended. He is to be signed off sick. Work-related stress.'

'If it's all the same to you, I'd rather be suspended. I'm not sick.'

MacTaggart opened his hands in a take-it-or-leave-it gesture. He couldn't have cared less. He just wanted me out.

'Sick or not, you are required to attend Dr Chaudhury before you leave. He's expecting you.'

Chaudhury was the head of psychiatry. They didn't want another hanging.

The unblinking eyes of the committee stared down at me impassively.

I took the remains of *The Bottom Line* out of my pocket and placed them on the table.

'Very well. If I am to be removed, you must be responsible for taking this forward. I tracked down Bletchley –'

'Oh for God's *sake*!' barked MacTaggart with real fury.

I unfolded the crumpled sheet of A4. 'We think there may be about one hundred and fifty leads . . .'

'*Desist!*'

The Bottom Line, abused, battered, and crumpled as it was, finally disintegrated. I suddenly saw myself as the committee saw me, a bereaved and broken man howling incoherently over some totemic fetish. Forbes laid a hand on my arm and said gently, 'Let me look after this for you. I'll take care of it.' He gathered the remnants of paper and quietly confiscated them. MagTaggart snapped, 'Dr Chaudhury. Now.'

'That's fine. I'll clear my desk.'

'No you won't. That has already been done for you. Leave your ID and swipe card on the table. Your personal effects will be returned.' I wasn't even going to be allowed back into the department. Personal effects. I was dead already. I stared stonily down the length of the room at MacTaggart. Forbes said in a low voice, 'I'll have your things dropped off at the flat. I'll call you.' He didn't look up.

24dn: Heavy metal executant,
or maybe executioner (6)

XX

I pushed the Yale key into the lock at Thirlestane but the door was already open. I stepped into the dull entrance hall. There was dead silence. I called. 'Caitlin?' The flat was mute.

I glanced at the fish tank. Tallulah was lying motionless, just below the surface, belly up. Some noxious effluvium seemed to seep out of the floor boards and through my feet to ascend into my body.

Search the flat. It didn't take long. I sat down in the front room and stared at the wall for ten minutes. Then I glanced at my watch. I was amazed to find it was not yet midday. The whole of the rest of the day yawned at me vacuously.

She should have left a note. Would she take the train down to Cheltenham? I should really phone Eric and Sally but what if she wasn't planning to go home? They would be beside themselves.

I sent her a text.

Katie where R U? Call me, Al.

I folded my phone away and wandered about the flat, sensitised, wired for a response, wanting to hear that chirpy double bleep as a lover longs to hear from a loved one. Nothing. I tried her again on the land line. My hands were trembling as I tapped out the number. I got voice mail. I left a brief message telling her to call.

She'd cleaned the place up. I suppose I should have been grateful but I was mortified. She had obliterated herself. She'd left the set of keys I'd given her in a little brass jug beside the late Tallulah. Maybe that was why Tallulah was belly up. She had died of a broken heart.

In the kitchen, she had taken all the dishes out of the dish washer and stacked them away. All the work surfaces had been wiped. In the bathroom all the porcelain and glass and chrome shone. There was bleach down the loo. All around the flat she had dusted and vacuumed. I wanted the place to be a mess and I wanted to find a note scrawled in her rounded girlish hand. 'Gone for a walk. See you for tea! XXX'

Abruptly the door bell rang. Thank God.

I threw the door open. It wasn't her.

They were standing together quietly at the door, two men in suits. My first thought was that they were Jehovah's Witnesses or maybe representatives of the Church of Jesus Christ of Latter-day Saints. Maybe they were just selling toilet brushes. But there was an air of officialdom.

'Dr Cameron-Strange? Major Forster. Special Branch.' He flashed a card momentarily. It disappeared as if by sleight of hand. 'This is my colleague Dr Parkinson. May we come in?' He sensed my hesitation. 'It concerns your recent enquiries. We may be able to help.' He lowered his voice. 'Clerk Maxwell.'

'Come in.'

I showed them into the front room. They stood politely, waiting. In the brighter light I could see they were an odd couple. The man named Forster was tall and fit, short fair hair, middle thirties. Well dressed, up-market gumshoe. He gazed at me with an air of detached amusement. The other man might have been Forster's father, an image of Forster two or three decades down a life fortified with booze to cope

186

with the constant exposure to degradation. He was heavy and shambolic and his off-white suit was sweat-stained and crumpled as if he had slept in it. The eyes were slow and watchful. He was surveying my flat as if it were in escrow and he in real estate. He gave an appreciative grunt and said, 'Nice unit.' Australian. Maybe I had been too quick to let them in.

'It's rented – could I see your card again Major Forster?' I hadn't invited them to sit down and they hadn't presumed to do so.

'Of course. Keep it for reference.'

He removed a card from his wallet. In a piece of dumb-crambo resembling a high wire act he took out a very expensive-looking gold fountain pen and scrawled an illegible endorsement, in racing-green ink, across the elaborately embossed card details. Then he carefully removed the top right corner of the card by ripping through a diagonal line of perforations. It was as if he were disabling a passport. Then he waved the card through the air to dry the ink and then handed it over. I read it line by line. 'The rank of Major – that's not a police rank.'

'No. I've been seconded. I work for the Ministry of Defence.' True enough. There on the card was the Whitehall address.

'Which department?'

'Antiterrorism falls within my jurisdiction. My bailiwick.'

'I see. Dr Parkinson, do you have identification?'

He fumbled around his suit and found his card, crumpled and dog-eared, in the lapel pocket. It read 'Dr Ralph Parkinson PhD FRCPsych FRANZCP, Negotiations Pty.' The address was the Maudsley Hospital in London. Under the contact details there was a jingle in italics:

'You don't get what you deserve, you get what you negotiate.'

I said, 'What's the Maudsley got to do with this?'

'I've also been seconded. I do some work for The Home Office.'

'In what capacity?'

'Conciliation and arbitration.'

'I don't follow.'

'I have a special interest in hostage situations.'

'Your doctorate?' I'd taken in the details of his card.

'The Stockholm Syndrome.'

He was a negotiator. The relevance still escaped me.

We sat down.

Major Forster said, 'We just want to clarify a few things.'

'. . . just a few things.' It was an echo from Down Under. Parkinson had a bass voice rich as matured Caboolture cheese and Hunter Valley merlot, dark and mellow, with hints of cinnamon and chocolate.

'You've caused a bit of a stir.'

'. . . quite a stir.' It was like a duet from a Gilbert and Sullivan operetta.

'Trouble is, we haven't been able to get past you. The trail runs cold with you. For example, we haven't been able to find *The Bottom Line* on the Internet. D'you follow? Everything just peters out. The upshot is, if we are going to keep an eye on anybody, it's you.'

'You.'

'Mind if I take a look around?' Forster smiled briefly and got up without waiting for a reply. 'Dr Parkinson needs to crosscheck a few references.' He disappeared into the foyer.

'Now look here –'

'No worries. The major's very tidy. He won't disturb a thing. You like crosswords yourself, doctor?'

'Yes, as a matter of fact I do.'

'You any good?'

'I'm not bad.'

'An aficionado.'

'Maybe.'

'Bit of a buff.'

'I wouldn't go that far.'

'Ever make them up?'

'Dr Parkinson, I did not compile *The Bottom Line*.'

'You sure? You sure you aren't Bletchley?'

'Positive.'

'If you say so. But you can see where I'm coming from. You're all we have to go on, mate.'

Forster slid silently back into the room. Parkinson looked up enquiringly and Forster shook his head. A platinum laptop, my Vaio, was under his arm. He handed a little cellophane bag of herbs over to Parkinson. Caitlin's stash. Parkinson glanced at it, turning down the corners of his mouth.

'This your shit?'

'No.'

'Whose then?'

I shrugged. 'The previous tenant?'

He grinned broadly at me. Forster tapped a finger on my laptop.

'Mind if I borrow this?'

'Yes as a matter of fact I do.'

'Sorry. It's just the way it is.'

'You can't do this. Do you have a search warrant?' It was a line I'd borrowed out of countless police dramas. I had no idea what a search warrant was.

'We always have a search warrant. Our warrant is open-ended.'

'That's rubbish. This is theft. You can't stroll in here and take my stuff. Without an order from a high court judge.'

'We can get that, if you wish. Retrospectively.'

'. . . retrospectively.'

'I didn't think we were living in a police state.'

Forster raised his eyes briefly to the ceiling as if to question what on earth bloody kind of state I thought I did inhabit.

'You're on a mission, aren't you?'

'What?'

'You've been working outside the box. Pushing the envelope.'

'I don't know what you mean.'

'You've pushed the boat out. You're flying a kite.' Major Forster was not shy of mixing his metaphors. I couldn't help but smile. He didn't like it. The amused expression on his face vanished as quickly as a bullet from a gun barrel. He suddenly looked like a professional killer. Oh God – he's in the SAS.

Parkinson said, 'Got any flat mates?'

'No.'

'Nobody staying with you?'

'No.' It was a measure of the completeness of Caitlin's departure that I could say this with a degree of conviction. She had been scrupulously and fastidiously tidy as if she had wanted to obliterate any echo of her stay. And she had succeeded. Apart from the hash.

'Sure?'

'Yes.'

Parkinson sniffed. 'It's just I thought I could detect the scent of a lady. *Amouage* if I'm not mistaken. You a poofter?'

'Why don't you mind your own bloody business?'

'I guess that's a no. I thought I could smell a Sheila. Not just the perfume. *The smell of the stench behind the perfume.* If you know what I mean. Must have been a visitor. It does tend to linger.'

'Just exactly what government department did you say you represent?'

'We're a small department. Kind of a think tank. Loosely affiliated. Quango if you like.'

'. . . quango.'

'What are you called?'

'We don't have a name. It's policy. Quite deliberate. We find we can work better that way. Anyway, thanks very much. You've been very co-operative. Should get this back to you pretty quickly. We'll let ourselves out.'

They moved out into the hall.

'What happened to the fish?'

'I don't know.'

'Can't see any bubbles. Looks like asphyxiation.'

Caitlin wouldn't have done that.

'Oh! One last thing. Meant to ask. Have you got a firearms licence?'

'No.'

'So I take it you don't have any firearms then?'

'No I don't.'

'Mm. Thought not. Well. All the best! And take it easy. We'll be keeping an eye on things.'

'. . . things.'

They stepped back out on to the landing. Major Forster paused momentarily on the threshold. I had the odd sense that he was about to go out of his way to do me a favour. Over the years he and Parkinson would have perfected their hard man soft man double act. He was stepping momentarily out of role. 'This pushing the boat out business . . . There is a tipping point. Cross it, and you have passed the point of no return.'

He closed the door with exaggerated politeness. The flat resumed its customary quietude. Tallulah's upended corpse ogled the ceiling.

XXI

It's very subtle, the Monty Hall problem. Remember, three doors, two goats, one BMW. You choose your door. The compere opens another door to reveal a goat and offers you the chance to change your mind.

There was a correspondence about it in *The Herald* not so long ago. A distinguished professor of mathematics wrote in rather snootily to pour scorn on people who felt it was worthwhile to change their minds. But he was wrong. Why? Why is it not just a fifty-fifty chance?

Think of it this way. Say there aren't three doors. Say there are a hundred. You make your choice and then the compere opens up ninety eight doors to reveal ninety eight goats. Then he asks you if you want to change your mind. Not only that: you get the chance to play the game a hundred times. Let's say you play the game in that format a hundred times and each time you stick with your original decision. Then you play it another hundred times and each time you change your mind. Which strategy is going to win you the most BMWs?

People don't like to change their minds. It's such an

upheaval. It requires a relinquishment of all you hold dear. You don't think the earth's flat? You must be certifiable. There's me, the enemy, and the authorities. I'm in the middle of a Monty Hall problem. We actually need a *dramatis personae* of five to re-enact this – a guest, a compere, and three people concealed behind doors. There's me, Stobo-Bletchley, Forster-Parkinson, Caitlin, and the white-faced man in the black cape. I don't even know whether I'm a guest, a host, or one of the prizes. I'd thought I was hunting Stobo-Bletchley but now I'm forced to change my mind. Stobo-Bletchley turns out to be *simpatico* but I have a distinctly queasy feeling about Forster-Parkinson. And all the while, like a fevered patient tossing and turning through a night of delirium, I try to force this conundrum into the template of the Monty Hall problem.

Two things. The open door. And the dead fish. Caitlin wouldn't have done that. She might have drowned Francesca but she would never have drowned Tallulah.

I know what you're thinking. You're thinking I'm blowing the demise of a carp way out of proportion.

Please send me a text Caitlin.

Text! In a distracted way I hunted round the flat for my ancient Holy Bible. And all the while I felt this terrible mounting sense of fury pitching in my guts. I had tried to warn them. I had acted in good faith. I had uncovered a potential health hazard much as a Community Medicine Specialist in the Department of Public Health might have detected a pathogen at large and advised everybody on simple hygiene measures. Forbes had dismissed it, Walkerburn had vacillated, the police had been positively antagonistic, Horton had clearly taken steps to harass me. And now, somehow or other, Caitlin and I were being harmed. I wasn't going to stand idly by. I couldn't get my thinking to join up. What had Stobo said? Matthew 16:13. I fumbled with the wafer-thin pages.

When Jesus came into the coasts of Caesarea Philippi, he asked his disciples, saying, Whom do men say that I the Son of man am?

And they said, Some say that thou art John the Baptist: some, Elias; and others, Jeremias, or one of the prophets.

He saith unto them, But whom say ye that I am?

He had been right. Jesus had posed a quincunx before his disciples.

And then it dawned on me. Horton had engineered all this, just as he had said he would. 'Not only will I break you . . . I will *destroy* you!' And he was doing so, with extraordinary expedition. In the course of an hour I had been suspended, removed from my work place, and now I was more or less under house arrest. Had he not done something similar to Stobo? Stobo had been removed from his classes, was also under house arrest, pending his tribunal, his show trial. Stobo had realised that Horton was the real enemy. He had dropped *The Bottom Line* and turned his attention to Horton. No! He had actually taken on the challenge of *The Bottom Line*. I must do the same. Stobo and me, we're not going to take this lying down. Together, we can get back at Horton. A two-pronged attack. We could wreak havoc across his demesne. We could attack Clerk Maxwell.

Because the fish is dead, Caitlin has to be in great danger.

The phone gave a single yelp and I snatched it up.

'Ally?'

My heart sang.

'Something's come up. Where are you? No, don't say. Can you meet me at Golf Echo Charlie Kilo Oscar – same place as last time don't say where.'

She sang some spoof melodramatic film music in a minor key ending on a triad.

'Da da ra da . . . DAH . . . .' Whatever spat we had had last night appeared to have been forgotten.

'I'll explain. Can you make it under an hour?'

'Yup.'

'Don't talk to anyone. Have you got money for a taxi?'

'How can I tell the taxi man where to go without talking to him?'

'Caitlin I haven't got time. Be as quick as you can.'

I hung up, suddenly consumed with a new anxiety. What if there were no aircraft available? I called the aero club. I got lucky. Aaron Jackson answered the phone. He was from Auckland, on the big OE. Maybe we could cut through some red tape.

'Aaron! Alastair.' I tried to sound as if I hadn't a care in the world. We would have one of these kitsch-Kiwi conversations that seem to lack any sense of irony.

'G'day mate!'

'Can I borrow a 172?'

'Oooh . . .' I could see him pursing his lips, looking at the booking sheets. 'They're all out mate. Not an aircraft to be had.'

My heart sank.

'Except the Slingsby.'

'She'll do.'

'All yours. When d'you want her?'

'Now?'

'Sweet.' God bless New Zealand. 'Where you off to?'

'Tiree.' It was the first destination that came into my head.

'Mint.'

'I'm taking my sister-in-law. Only she doesn't know. Mystery tour.' You fabricate a lie and immediately it starts to crumble and you need to shore it up.

'Good as.'

'Spotcha.'

I left my car parked outside Thirlestane and got a taxi too. Why would I want to leave an audit trail? And as the taxi carried me west through Corstorphine towards the Maybury Roundabout and Ingliston I fidgeted in the back and thought, is this a step too far? Is this Major Forster's tipping point?

Caitlin had got there before me. I had a surge of relief when I caught sight of her profile. She was sitting quietly in the aero club coffee bar scanning a copy of *Pilot* magazine. There was a Christmas tree beside her, and some model aeroplanes hanging from the ceiling were festooned in Christmas decorations. I had forgotten all about Advent. It had completely passed me by. Caitlin looked up and gave me one of these waves a girl does as if her hand is inside a glove puppet. So we were still friends. Jackson had gone flying. I would have to negotiate with the CFI. He didn't know me, and he was an older, careful man.

'You current?'

'Yes.' What a stroke of luck we had gone aerobating just a few days ago.

'Got your licence and log book?'

I handed them over. I tried to look nonchalant while all the time consumed with anxiety about the narrowing window of opportunity, the failing light. I might have been an escaped POW, handing my forged documents to the Gestapo. The CFI scrutinised them with his careful eyes, checking the medical certificate, checking the expiry dates. He checked my hours. 'You've done a bit of flying.' He flicked through the log book and looked at my type ratings on the back page. He read through the whole list. 'Have you filed a flight plan? Got your weather and Notams?'

'Yes.' Blatant lies, now.

'Ah! A Nanchang. Chinese military training aircraft?'

I nodded. 'Same as a Yak.' I had an image of one landing at dusk in Ardmore, with its high nose attitude, elegant as a pelican.

He snapped the book shut and handed it back.

'Have a good flight.'

I had some difficulty prising Caitlin away from the guys. In the end I grabbed her by the wrist.

'Ouch! You're hurting me!' I remember as we disappeared through the door the CFI gave me a sharp look.

Airside, I got through the preliminaries as quickly as I could, Caitlin singing, 'The magical mystery tour is coming to take you away!' I parried her banter with monosyllables. We got in.

'Buckle up.'

'Fasten your seat belt, we're in for a bumpy ride!'

The engine sprang to life and I secured the cockpit and ran automatically through the ground checks, all the time thinking, how can I slip out of here without anybody noticing? How can I ensure we're not missed until Christmas morning? How can I disappear off the radar screens without anybody alerting Search and Rescue?

The joystick thumped against my thigh. The CFI had come out to the aircraft and was attracting my attention by waggling the aileron. My heart missed a beat. I was going to be grounded. I pulled the throttle back to idle and opened the canopy. He leapt up on to the wing root, his grey hair tousled in the slipstream. He was shouting to be heard, gesticulating at a map, flapping like a sheet on a blustery line.

'The Princess Royal's chopper's at Faslane. There's purple airspace all the way up to Oban.'

'No worries. I'll stay north of the Glasgow zone.' This was panning out. I could become invisible. The CFI nodded, smiled briefly, and pulled the canopy over our heads, dropping it carefully it into place. I locked it, and he jumped clear.

And now the careful, unobtrusive taxi out to the holding point. I told the tower we were off to Tiree, and we would vacate to the north-west. They weren't particularly interested. They were preoccupied with the jet traffic and just wanted us out of the way. The delay waiting for some incoming traffic and then letting the London City shuttle go before us seemed interminable. Even after the jet was airborne we had to wait two minutes for the invisible jet turbulence to decay. Finally we were cleared and I flew out west and made a climbing turn to the right at 500 feet, kept climbing and, somewhere to the north-west of the Forth road and rail bridges, announcing my intention of switching frequency to Scottish Information on one two niner decimal eight seven, said goodbye to Edinburgh.

They acknowledged. 'Squawk 7000 g'day.'

7000 on the transponder. The conspicuity code. We were not uniquely identified. We might yet become invisible. I listened out on the Scottish frequency, but I didn't give them a call. Here were the familiar landmarks Caitlin and I had previously encountered – the Kincardine and Clackmannan bridges, the Grangemouth Refinery. We crossed over Bannockburn and Stirling Bridge and I thought of all the battles waged below us seven hundred years ago. Stirling Castle and the Wallace Monument fell away behind us. There were fewer recognisable features ahead. I felt we were slipping out of a zone of comfort into an undiscovered terrain. Over the mysterious Flanders Moss I descended to 500 feet and, as we neared the Highland fault line I picked up the main trunk road that would let us snake through the mountain passes and the glens. I switched the transponder off. We had vanished.

Caitlin seemed to have recovered her *joie de vivre*. She said in a conversational tone, 'Ladies and gentlemen, the captain has switched off the seat belt sign. You are free to move about the cabin. However . . .'

I was concentrating on the flying. I wanted to keep off the radar screens. How low could I drop?

'There will be a complimentary bar service, and then we will be serving dinner.'

If I flew much lower the CAA might start getting calls from irate owner-occupiers whose roofs I'd buzzed.

'Our flight time this afternoon is . . .'

And then there was always the possibility of meeting an RAF Tornado screaming up the glens at 500 miles an hour and at 250 feet.

'Our flight time this afternoon is . . .'

'Two hours.'

'Two hours! Where we going? America?'

'Caitlin, shut up. I'm trying to think.'

'Why are we so low?'

'For God's sake!' I was too busy to reassure her. I was 'maxed out', looking for unexpected elevations, power lines, and RAF jets.

'Are we going to crash?'

'Only if you keep wittering on.' I could feel her chirpiness suddenly plummeting away.

'I wanna go home.'

'Not now.'

She started to cry. Fine. Just so long as she doesn't have a tantrum. Not at 250 feet. I might have to give her a slap. We lapsed into our respective morose, brooding, moody silences. She pretended to sleep. Then she slept.

And everything was deteriorating. There was a heavy dark grey ceiling barely above us, enveloping us, oppressively, like a shroud. I was getting some spots of rain on the canopy. Normally I would have turned well before now, sought clearer skies, diverted, gone back to base. But there could be no question of going back. Every sortie has its point of no return. I remembered Forster's expression. A tipping point. I was well beyond it. I would keep heading north-west and be driven lower and lower by the weather, until the failing light compelled me to land.

An hour later she opened her eyes. It was the turbulence that woke her. We had run into a major depression. She stared out at the gloom.

'God.' She peered down at the coastal fishing town beneath us.

'Where's that?'

'Mallaig.'

'Looks like Murmansk.'

'Not long to go now.' The land fell away behind the trailing edge of the wings. Ahead, dusk had filched all the colour out of the landscape of the island that I now realised I had wanted to reach. The water was oil black. And we were low on fuel. Armadale, Tarskavaig Point, Strathaird, Soay, and then Rubh' an Dùnain. A series of short hops and at last we were on the island's west coast.

'Ladies and gentlemen, at this time the captain has commenced his descent.' Caitlin was always quick to rediscover her laconic poise. 'Please return to your seats, fasten your seat belts, ensure your tray table is fastened and your hand luggage stowed away in the lockers or beneath the seat in front of you . . .'

Loch Eynort. Suddenly it was dark. There was a single cough from under the cowling, and then the little Lycoming engine resumed its steady beat. I held the nose of the aircraft on a westerly heading and let the coast recede behind us. That remark Major Forster had made, about a point of no return, preoccupied me. How far out to the west did it lie? And I thought of my lord Hamlet's soliloquy, and started to recite it to myself, in snatches, piecemeal.

'Be . . . not . . . question . . .'

'Are we really going to New York?'

We were back in the cockpit of the Slingsby, spinning between its twelfth and thirteenth rotation. Another opportunity to let go. Relinquishment. It was possible to forgo everything. Desirable even. How wonderful to make a tidy exit, to be found in one's hermit's cell, dressed in rags, surrounded by bare walls, one's sole personal effect a battered cup. Slings . . . sea of troubles . . . heartache.

'What's the fuel situation?'

I've always found the idea of dumping baggage deeply seductive. I've never been a collector. It had all started as a mere affectation, a refusal to hoard. It was something I had learned from my father. He had been an efficient man, a great user of the waste paper basket. 'The three Ds!' he would say. 'Deal with it, delegate it, ditch it!'

'Alastair?'

Consummation, rub, shuffled . . . So clear out the loft, get rid of old diaries, old love letters. It's past. Let it go. Give your old suits to Oxfam, take all these useless mantelpiece trinkets to the charity shops. Clear your shelves. The second-hand book shops will be delighted. What a liberation it will be.

'Ally, please . . .'

Whips, scorns, contumely . . .

But it's not merely a question of material possessions. Work, wealth, ambition, music, love, desire, (disprized, fardels . . .), even hope itself . . .

'Alastair you're frightening me.'

The undiscovered country from whose bourn . . .

Abruptly Caitlin seized the joystick and yanked it over to the right. The aircraft's nose responded obediently and tracked steadily round the horizon. I snapped out of my reverie. We had come so far off shore that all I could discern was wind and rain and blackness. There was a violent lurch as we hit an air pocket and dropped 50 feet. My head actually struck the canopy. I suddenly woke up to the fact that we were in the middle of a storm. A flash of brilliant light briefly illuminated the cockpit and was immediately followed by a tremendous *crump*! The Slingsby lurched violently again, my headphones spluttered, and the needles on the instrument panel spun senselessly as the gyros toppled. Now we were flying east, blind, as an act of faith. The Lycoming gave another single, quiet cough. Then came the dark contour of the shore line, obliquely, 500 feet below and on the right. Caitlin said, 'You have control!' There was a tremor in her voice. I took the stick and banked to port. Tracking north-north-west now, looking ahead, questing. We're here. Abruptly my night vision switched on. We had arrived abeam the cliff face at the south-east rim of the bay. There is the carious tooth rock formation down at the water's edge. Now we are out over the bay on the downwind leg of a right hand circuit. Cliff face up ahead to the north. And there is the waterfall flowing backwards, casting spray over the cliff top. Mixture rich, carburettor air intake to warm, throttle back to 1500 rpm. I flew as near to the rock face as I dared and then banked right on to base leg. The paddock just off the beach looked tiny from here.

'Caitlin. Get your harness as tight as you can.'

Abruptly the engine died.

Endlessly you practise for this. Sometimes you undershoot, sometimes you overshoot, sometimes you get it right. I had to get it right. I pulled the nose up to gain some precious height and then pulled it round obliquely on to my round-out point. There was silence but for the spatter of rain on the canopy and the windmilling of the prop. Best glide rate? Maybe about 70 knots. I was muttering to myself. Brake off, undercart down, mixture lean, fuel pump off . . . I leaned forward and flicked off the master switches, the mags, and I closed the fuel cock. No going round now. So difficult to get perspective in the gathering darkness. Surely we're too high! Resist the temptation to pull on full flap. Only when you know you're going to get in. Bleed off some height. I pushed left rudder and applied right aileron and bled off 50 feet in the sideslip. Enough! Oh God, you've overdone it. There's a fence, and a stream, just at your round-out point. You're not going to make it. Maybe just . . . Full flap now. Coming in low over the black sand, the bracken remnants, and the diamond-hard boiler plates. A brief glimpse of the stream and the fence. I dumped the Slingsby down unceremoniously on the grass. She bounced and yawed into the air and then sank down again and stayed on the deck. I put as much pressure on the toe brakes as I dared and the aircraft juddered to a halt with her undercarriage intact.

The intensity of the silence. Then the incessant drumming of the rain on the canopy. Release the hood lock and pull the perspex bubble back over your head. Headphones off, and look up to the sky and let yourself be drenched by the wind and the rain. Yes. It's good to be alive. Somewhere in the distance there is the boom of the surf, echoing off the imposing cliff buttresses at each end of the field. An instant of broad daylight followed immediately by the one o'clock gun directly above us. We need to get out of this.

Now I am like an automaton. Release the buckle of the five point harness, pull yourself out of the cockpit and jump down. Grab the prop and pull. Already the Slingsby is settling into the saturated earth. The warmth of Caitlin's body beside me, pulling. Find a meagre recess of shelter, grab a torch, secure the cockpit, make the plane safe. There's a track, leading to a big house, and beyond it, further inland, a tiny hamlet. I saw it all from the air. There are no lights on in the big house. It looks unoccupied. Another series of flashes and

rumbles as we head inland up the path. Run! Another flash
– a five-barred gate and a million heavy rain drops bouncing
off the track and turning it into a river. Leap the gate. Here is
the great shadow of the house. Slither down an embankment
and off a short wall into the trench of the basement level,
coming up hard against the dank mossy stonework. Choose
a window, find a brick. But now Caitlin is prising the heavy
stone from my fingers, taking my hand in both of hers. And
then I watch her insinuate her fingernails under a sash and
pull it up ten inches.

It was enough. Caitlin slithered through. Clumsily I followed. As I slipped down towards the parquet floor she half
broke my fall and grasped me very tight in a prolonged hug. I
noticed the way her soaked T-shirt was clinging to her body.
She was trembling. There were no alarms.

Another flash from outside, as if a photographer were
recording our forced entry. It briefly illuminated a full-size
snooker table. We had broken into the low-ceilinged house
billiard room. There were storage heaters on at either end of
the room. We were back in darkness. Not quite. The heaters
afforded an eerie light by which I could make out the contour
of the table, the pockets, the flat expanse of the baize underneath the overhead gantry. It occurred to me dully that they
had been left on to prevent the table from warping.

I felt an exquisite flutter of excitement. I was losing control. I left Caitlin and carried out a quick exploration by torch
light of the rest of the basement. I found a kitchen, a pantry, and a linen cupboard. I grabbed some blankets. We had
everything we might need. I had a notion that if I ventured
upstairs I might trip an alarm. Back to the warmth of the billiard room. She was standing by the window through which
we had entered, looking out and up at a line of rhododendron
bushes and evergreen firs swaying extravagantly in the gale.

'Take off your wet things.'

She turned slowly and stared at me. For a minute we held
one another's gaze. Physical threat, mortal danger, these are
the great aphrodisiacs. Abruptly Caitlin peeled off her T-shirt.

She had nothing on underneath. Then, without removing her gaze from my face, she kicked off her shoes and snaked out of her jeans. Then she slipped her panties to the floor and kicked them away. A flash of sheet lightning briefly illuminated the firmly contoured body. The keloid scar seemed to glimmer like an ember and then to die away. She was back in the shadow. She turned her head slightly in the direction of the billiard table as if to draw my attention to its green baize surface. Then she turned back to hold my gaze again, quizzically, with a half-smile. There was a low rumble of thunder.

Sororate?

I moved towards her. I held out the blankets. 'Get some rest.'

I closed the door behind me. I made a tour of the basement, once, and settled on a cramped couch in the basement corridor, covered in a dust sheet. I stripped off my own wet things, covered myself in three blankets, and closed my eyes.

XXII

In my dream I couldn't get the blue to stay on its central spot. It kept meandering off to the side cushion, as if the floor sloped, or the table wasn't true. Yet all the other balls remained still. It tormented me, the blue's contrariness. The blue was a very important ball. It occupied a very pivotal role, midfield. A kind of quincunx role. It was the door of opportunity between the baulk colours and the high premium scoring balls. I spotted it again and reattempted the shot. This time it stayed still. That's how I knew I was awake again. I crouched over the baize and adopted my stance; relaxed posture, firm bridge, now align cue ball with object ball, a little left hand side. Pause . . . Not too much backward motion of the cue. Firm, confident strike, keep your head steady like a golfer and hold the posture. I watched the blue traverse the baize and flop into the top right pocket.

They were standing at the doorway, just beyond the corner of the table where the blue had disappeared. I hadn't heard them come in. They looked just as they had looked when I had opened the door to them at Thirlestane.

'Where's the Sheila?'

I laid the cue down on the baize.

'Eh? Where've you put her?'

'She's perfectly safe.' My voice was soft and remote. I hadn't spoken for a long time. I had been alone for many hours. 'She is beyond harm.'

I had forgotten about the lit Stuyvesant I had balanced on the edge of the snooker table. It had burned away like a slow fuse and was starting to damage the wood. I picked it up and took a last drag and stubbed the butt out in an ash tray that was already full.

The two men interchanged glances. Major Forster left the room. I had no doubt he would search the house. I wondered if he would find her. For a moment I couldn't remember where she was. Had I left her in the big drawing room upstairs? No, that might have been last night. So much had happened since. But it was jumbled in my mind. Had we been off the island? Surely we had. But I had come back on my own. First I hadn't been able to join up my tactics and strategies. Now my memories were all out of order. Retrograde amnesia.

I had woken in a terrible downer. The storm had blown itself out. I had fossicked in the pantry and boiled a jug and opened some tinned fruit. I let myself noiselessly into the billiard room. Caitlin had built a little wigwam for herself by one of the storage heaters. Her breathing was soft and even. I slipped back out of the window and walked back down to the bay to make sure the Slingsby hadn't blown away. The beach was littered with discarded fishing tackle. MacKenzie had got that right. I turned the aircraft into wind, a north-westerly. I made an attempt to cover the wings with old foliage. At least she might not be immediately recognisable from the air. Then I went back up the track to the house to explore the yard and the outhouses. There was a rusty old banger in the garage, a Hillman Hunter, about forty years old. The garage was full of junk. I remember a dry, friendly oil rag smell. An old dresser at the back was crammed with tools. I remember siphoning the Hunter's petrol tank to make sure there was some fuel. If I got under the dashboard I could hot-wire a start. I didn't spend a childhood on a Northland farm for nothing. There wouldn't be any computerised jamming systems in a 1970s car.

I got out of the vehicle and there was Caitlin's silhouette in the dawn light at the garage door.

'What now Captain?'

'Caitlin, I'm going to drop you off at Uncle Hector's.'

'Who the hell is Uncle Hector?'

I've never been interested in genealogy. I never could chart the convolutions of my late mother's extended family.

'You've been crying.'

She brushed her hair out of her eyes with the back of her hand. 'It's just the wind.'

'There's food in the pantry if you want to grab some. Best get going.'

For once, she didn't argue. I had the nagging sense that she had at last identified me as bad news. Like a lover, she had gatecrashed my life for a while. She had come along for the ride. When she finally realised the ride was going nowhere, she would get off without demur. Go and pick up the pieces of her life. Don't look back. Above all, don't stick around when things are about to go pear-shaped. We would have a parting by mutual consent. I was a loser. I carried the stench of death around with me. A dead man walking. And she was an encumbrance. I didn't need her. For what I had in mind, I needed 50 litres of aviation gas and a gun. And I had an idea where I might get them.

Major Forster slipped back into the billiard room and shook his head at Ralph Parkinson. He had done exactly the same in my flat, a hundred years ago. Dr Parkinson said, 'Aeroplane?' Forster nodded and went back out. I guess he would take a walk to the beach.

'You stay here last night?'

Did I? I can't remember. Was this my second night? I'd gone to get some fuel. There were two possibilities. First, the strip at Lower Breakish, but it had looked as deserted as a disused wartime airfield obliterated by grass. I hadn't wanted to cross the bridge to the mainland but I had to get to the strip by Duirinish, above Am Ploc. At Badicaul I spoke to two men outside a black croft, and came back to the car with a package.

'What's that?'

'Nothing.'

'Who are these people?'

'Benders.'

'Benders?'

'Travelling people.'

'Why are they called benders?'

'Because they bend saplings to make a skeleton for their tents.'

'You're kidding.'

'Caitlin, I need to take you out of the equation.'

'There's no such person as Uncle Hector, is there?'

I didn't say anything. She started to whimper. In that beautiful and unlikely triangle of wooded landscape between Badicaul and Duirinish and Am Ploc, with its palm trees and its promiscuous *crotal* splashes of broom, I accomplished my tasks.

I returned by another route. Never retrace your steps. Never go back. Balmacara, Eilean Donan, Inverinate. I thought I could hear music. *Divo Aloysio Sacrum*. St Aloysius. The patron saint of youth. *St Aloysius pray for us*. In my memory it is the setting of MacMillan that I hear, yet how could I play my CD in a 1970s car? All I can say is that the Gàidhealtachd seemed to resonate with it. It seemed to come out of earth and rock. I heard it echo back at me from the Five Sisters of Kintail, Mam Ratagan, and the ancient brochs of Glenelg. The ferryman who took me across the Stygian waters never gave the two big containers on my back seat a second glance. A nervous run back through Broadford, Luib, Sconser. At Sligachan I turned left and started to head west with the great mountain ridge frowning over my left shoulder, and then falling away behind me. Left again. Roads getting quieter but, ahead, a polished black BMW. I stayed well back. It headed for the distillery. I hung another left and commenced the long descent back down to the bay. I remember getting the Hunter back out of sight into its garage and then making two journeys to lug the containers down to the Slingsby. Three hours after I'd started, everything was as it had been.

Except I was alone.

Major Forster slipped back into the billiard room and shook his head again. He had drawn another blank. I asked him how he had found me.

'I knew you'd be under one waterfall or another,' he said vaguely, 'practising *taghairm*.'

'And you? What are you doing here?'

'Holed up in the Skeabost, old boy. I've taken a salmon beat on the Snizort.' It always seemed to me that Major Forster had twigged the great cosmic joke. He had moved beyond cynicism, into some quaint fey realm of surrealism I could only guess at.

'You've got to tell us where you put her.'

'You'll never find her.'

'I once told you, Cameron-Strange, that there is a tipping point. Stay this side of it, and the failsafe mechanisms still apply. Cross it, and the past is irrevocable.'

But I had long since crossed my point of no return.

XXIII

Dr Parkinson's slow eyes rested on the billiard table. 'Do you play?'

'Mm?'

'Snooker. Do you play?'

It was such an effort to remember. I practise medicine, I fly aeroplanes, go for a run, solve crosswords . . . anything else? There are gaps. Yesterday was a gap. This is what it is like when, piecemeal, you begin to lose your memory.

Then I thought of all these dusty afternoons in the hospital residency. 'Yes I play. A little.'

'Tell you what. One frame. If you lose, you tell me the whereabouts of Ms Roy. If I lose, I won't section you under the Mental Health Act. Deal?'

'Deal.'

We both knew we were each going to dishonour our respective sides of the bargain. I couldn't have cared less. I'd forgotten what I was trying to achieve. Something about the solution to a crossword puzzle. I had brought it to mind so often that surely, after all, I must have made it up. I was

Bletchley. Parkinson had suspected it from the start. It had been a weird night, the night Mr Uprichard and I had repaired a damaged heart. I had consumed a strange cocktail and concocted a conundrum. I am an addict. I am a cruciverbalist.

We got on with the charade. Forster assumed the role of referee. In my memory he has put on a pair of white gloves, but that is preposterous. Forster walked round the table and salvaged the balls from the pockets, sending the reds up to Parkinson who corralled them within the stout wooden triangle while I placed the colours. I fired the pink up the table and Parkinson balanced it on the apex of the pyramid of reds. Then Forster zeroed the counters on the oak scoreboard on the wall beside the rack of cues. We chose our weapons. There was a drinks cabinet beside the cue rack, empty but for one bottle. Parkinson took it out and frowned at the label.

I was thinking about St Giles, that early morning family service, the lovely Whangie and the way she charmed the children.

'Talisker. Local brew. Snifter?' Parkinson poured a couple of generous measures. I noticed he didn't offer any to the Major. I returned the compliment. 'Cigarette? I'm down to my last two.' I proffered the Stuyvesant packet.

'Thanks. I'm trying to give up.' Parkinson had long ceased to invest this cliché with any sincerity. He rolled his cue on the table to ensure it was true; I stared down the length of mine as if it were a sniper's rifle.

She had used *The Bottom Line* as a prop for her children's address. Surely that can't be right. Parkinson juggled the blue chalk like a conjurer and presented me with two closed fists. I chose the left. He opened his hand to reveal the chalk. I had the break. No, it was a piece of origami. The Möbius strip. You take the end, you join it to the beginning like that and hey presto, you have a false bottom. I played with the abandon of the disinterested, smacking the cue ball into the reds with a resounding *thwack*. The noise of the impact was so loud that it made me jump. Like the one o'clock gun. And it was at that precise moment of contact that – at last, and for the first time – I really did solve *The Bottom Line*. I felt the colour drain from my face.

'It's to-day.'

'Excuse me?'

'It's going to happen to-day.' I wondered if Stobo had also spotted it, that vital piece of information, sitting there, deeply concealed within the solution, smugly taunting us. 'We need to tell the police.'

'Sure we do, doc.'

If only I'd seen it earlier, before they'd all dismissed me to the lunatic asylum. Yet why choose today? Term's finished. The campus will be deserted.

No it won't. The *Conversazione*! What was it to be about? What had Stobo said? Information Technology of all things. What university faculty wouldn't show an interest in this day and age? The place could be teeming with people!

'They need to get over to Clerk Maxwell now.'

'Yeah yeah yeah.' He absently chalked his cue.

'No really –'

'Stop changing the subject. It's the whereabouts of Ms Roy that concerns me.'

It was no use. I was like a man caught in quicksand; the more he struggles the quicker he sinks. Time might be running out but I was going to have to slow down and play their game. Parkinson was busy studying the white that had wandered back down into baulk. He pulled a face as if I'd committed some unpardonable breach of etiquette teeing off at the Royal and Ancient. It was a terrible break. I was going to live to regret it. Suddenly it had become incredibly important to buy a little time and space. It was absolutely vital that I win this game of snooker.

Parkinson potted a red in the left middle bag and positioned himself on the black. I could see I was going to be taken apart. One. Eight. Major Forster intoned the litany.

'I've been doing a bit of research, doctor.' It was another Melbourne accent. It isn't true that Australian accents are classless and regionless. I could see Parkinson, hatless, in his crumpled suit, walking down Punt Road. I could narrow it down. St Kilda, maybe Toorak. He was posh, but deeply under cover.

'I looked you up. Hope you don't mind. You didn't make it particularly easy. You're kind of low key. No Facebook account, that's for sure. Not your thing. Maybe I can tell you what I came up with and you can fill in the blanks.'

Nine, sixteen, seventeen.

'Roger Strange, your father, met Susan Cameron, your mother, just along the road at Broadford Hospital where she nursed. He was a Kiwi on the big OE. Back home, an 'ag' pilot – a top dresser. Over here, the green keeper at Sconser. They stayed around long enough to have you and your sister. But Kiwis always seem to need to go back. So you lived on Ninety Mile Beach and he flew out of Kaitaia. Only two white kids in the class, you and – is it MacKenzie?'

Twenty four, twenty five, thirty two, thirty three, forty. He's a hustler. I watched him lean over the table to readdress the cue ball.

'Your folks retired now?'

'They're dead.'

It was impossible to tell whether Parkinson was pausing to absorb this information, or merely taking care over his next shot. Forty one.

'What happened?'

'Plane crash.' I really didn't want to talk about it.

'How old were you?'

'Eleven.'

Forty eight.

We got adopted by a Maori family. I stopped speaking Gaelic and I started speaking Maori. The whanau would laugh when I got my languages mixed up. *Tha mi às an Eilean Sgitheanach. He iwi kotahi tatou.* Then I went down to King's College in Auckland. Then I went up to Auckland Medical School. How quickly you could romp through the scant details of a life. It was just a montage of a few pictures. The lake at Ngatu, the pseudo-English playing fields at

Kings beside the swanky golf course in the improbable surroundings of Otahuhu and Papatoetoe. The big hospital up on the Domain.

Forty nine.

Parkinson finally miscued and the pink rattled on the lips of the top right pocket and slunk off down the table as if trying to take shelter on the cushion, blushing like a child who has just wet his trousers in class.

'Wiped its feet.'

Ralph Parkinson, forty nine.

I got up and surveyed the devastation of the balls scattered across the battlefield. I got down to it and began laboriously to construct a break.

One. Three. Four. Seven. Eight. I was pleased to make Major Forster scurry about. But I was stuck down at low echelon baulk.

'Is that why you got a transfer to Edinburgh halfway through your medical course? Keeping in touch with the ancestors?'

Twelve, thirteen, eighteen, nineteen, twenty five. Better. Much better. Twenty six. I'd got on the black at last.

'Then you met Ms Roy.'

Thirty three. Thirty four. But I'd overcued. Not the end of the world. I had a nice angle on the blue and could still get back on the black. Thirty nine.

'What was she like?'

He's taking a psychiatric history. And why not? I probably am mad. But not completely; I still have a flicker of insight. I had become the monosyllabic patient behind the plate glass window in the Gloom Room.

'Well. Give me a clue. Short, tall? Fat, thin? Blonde, redhead?'

'Tall. Long red hair.'

'With the temperament to match? I mean what was she *like*?'

'I told you.' Why's he doing this?

'Good doctor?'

'Very.'

'General Practice, or a specialty?'

'Paeds.'

'It suited her?'

'Uh-huh.' It was perfectly true. Mary had an uncanny ability to soothe frightened children.

'What was it about her that attracted you?'

What is this? Why is Parkinson twisting the knife? And besides, there's no answer to that question. It might be the look, the smile, the zest for life, the common interests, the sense of humour, it might be any or all of these things, but in truth it is none of them. Love is not the sum of its parts. Love is not an epiphenomenon. Love is a phenomenon. Inexplicable.

For about six weeks after Mary died she used to speak to me. I don't mean that in any paranormal or quasi-religious sense. I recognised her utterances as the hypnagogic and hypnopompic hallucinations that can occur on the cusp of sleep or wakefulness. Yet her young voice was extraordinarily real to me. She wouldn't say much. Maybe she would just say my name. It wasn't my imagination – at least, not in the usual sense of that term. I really did hear her voice. It wasn't a spooky experience. In fact it was *balsam*. Her voice filled me, if only briefly, with a sense of calm.

Then she stopped visiting.

Of course I took it very badly. I said to her, 'All right, Roy, if you're going to slope off with your fancy man with the white face in the black cape, don't expect *me* to come running after you.' And I forced myself to stop thinking about her. It's survival.

'Did she like sex?'

For pity's sake.

'Yes.'

'Were you good together?'

'Yes.'

'Did you fight?'

'Once.'

'What was it about?'

'Something trivial. Can't remember.'

'I don't believe you. Not if you only fought once.'

But it was true. The apparent cause of the spat was lost to me and besides it had only been a kind of code for an underlying tension. I think we both panicked because events at the time seemed to assume a momentum of their own. Caitlin told Mary she approved, and MacKenzie told me she approved, and then Caitlin and MacKenzie together told us both they approved . . . It was all too sudden. We took a break. At least we didn't have one of these ghastly 'it's not you, it's me' conversations. Mary was not short of admirers and I had the sense to leave her to get on with it.

One night in the Potterrow Bar opposite McEwan Hall some slightly inebriated guy was making a nuisance of himself and I could see she was being harassed. I went over and got him to stop. I don't mean I exercised any kind of machismo. I think I tried to crack a few jokes. At any rate it seemed to work. Later that night I got the shortest of texts from her.

'Look after me, Ally?'

The rest is history.

'What happened?'

'Car crash. Drunk driver.'

I swiped at the cue ball. There was a puff of blue chalk and the white wobbled uncertainly into the last red which ambled off into the cushion. A kick.

Alastair Cameron-Strange, thirty nine. I had it all, and I let it slip away. I was playing catch-up snooker. One red left on the table.

'Where was the crash?'

'Haddington.'

'What took her over there?'

'Her sister was playing her oboe at a Watch Night Service.'

'This is a poignant date for you.'

'I've never been one for anniversaries.'

He sank the last red and got on the black again. Fifty. Fifty seven.

Only the colours now. Eighteen points behind, twenty seven points on the table.

Fifty nine. Twenty points behind, twenty five points on the table. The game was running away from me. We both stared at the table and we both did the same piece of mental arithmetic. He only needed the green. Slam dunk. Sixty two. Thwack. I didn't want to look, but I heard the brown drop into the left middle bag. Sixty six.

'What was the last thing she said to you?'

That was an inspired question. I don't know what it was – probably a 'catch you later!' accompanied by a swift hug as she and Caitlin got into the car. But I do know the last time I heard her voice, one morning in the half world between sleep and wakefulness, and I know what she said.

'Look after me, Ally?'

The remaining colours were shimmering in a heat haze on the baize. I sat down and took a gulp of Talisker and put my head in my hands.

'There's something you're not telling me.' He was an excellent interviewer. I could see why he had been seconded as a negotiator. Always probing. Always looking for the deeper level, questing. What's the diagnosis? What is it you seek? What makes you tick? He played the blue with some finesse. The blue sauntered to the edge of the pocket with the insouciance of a French aristocrat on a tumbril, paused, and flopped in like a guillotined head into a basket. Seventy one. I had all the trouble in the world.

'Did they get the guy? Was he banged up?'

'No. There was a problem with the processing of the blood sample. A lab error. He had a very clever lawyer.'

'You mean he walked?'

'Yes.'

He got the angle wrong on an easy shot on the pink and missed by a mile. He didn't seem the sort of man to be easily distracted. Ralph Parkinson, seventy one.

Bit of a formality now. I would steal a quick glance at the position, concede, and put on the straitjacket. There were only three balls left on the table. They had all meandered down to baulk like three companionable drunks who had lost their way coming home from the pub. It was an unlikely scenario, but there was the possibility of a snooker. I was thirty two points behind with thirteen on the table, a lost cause. Yet somehow I had to win this game. Just had to. A million years ago, when I lived a life, I had been sentimentally fond of telling patients who had reached the end of the line, that no matter the mess they had got themselves into, there was always a way out. But was it true?

I stubbed out my cigarette. I sent the pink up towards the top cushion and the cue ball gently kissed the black and nestled behind it on the lip of the bottom left pocket. Parkinson gently tapped the shaft of his cue on the edge of the table.

'Do you know who he is?'

'Yes.'

'Do you know where he is?'

'Yes.'

'Have you had contact?'

'No.'

'Do you forgive him?'

What a question. Forgiveness. It was a word we bandied around. And we thought we knew what we meant by it. I never wanted to see the man who had killed my wife after I had left the court room. I never wanted to know of his whereabouts and of his progress through life and if I had been able to obliterate his name from my memory I would have done so. I had no plan to harm him just as I had no particular wish that he prosper. If he had tried to make contact with me to express his remorse I am not sure that I would have welcomed it. Insofar as I had not appealed the court decision, and I had not attempted to track him down and murder him, it might be said that I had forgiven him. But my sense of charity was not really being put to the test. If a Sharia court had sentenced him to be beheaded, and I had had the power to pardon him, there would have been a test of my forgiveness. What would I have done? I would never know. So how could I possibly answer Parkinson's question?

'Forgiveness?' I shrugged. 'It is not in my gift.'

I didn't want Parkinson to ask me any more. I will lose myself to the baize in this absurd endgame, I will deaden my senses. Snooker and crosswords and Talisker and Stuyvesant – narcosis.

Parkinson attempted a three cushion rescue, played with power and force. The white zig-zagged and ricocheted back and forth across the baize, gave the pink a glancing blow and went in off. The pink wandered back down to baulk. I might be able to do it again.

Foul. Alastair Cameron-Strange, forty five. Another gentle tap, another gentle kiss. I'd almost reproduced the same scenario. This time Parkinson attempted a one cushion rescue hoping to nudge the pink on to the top cushion and bring the white back down to baulk. He missed the pink by a hairsbreadth leaving the cue ball with sufficient momentum to come off the top cushion back down to pot the black.

Foul. Fifty two. Forster respotted the black. Wonder of wonders. I was snookered on the pink, sitting up on the top cushion. I could nominate a free ball. Black ball. I played it, dead weight. Too soft! My heart was in my mouth. The cue ball just made it. The kiss was almost inaudible. Forster shaded his eyes beneath the glare of the overhead gantry.

'Touching ball.'

Nineteen points behind, thirteen on the table. Just one more miracle. Now Parkinson tried to come off the side cushion to catch the pink with a thin enough angle as to keep it on the mid top cushion and bring the cue ball back down the table.

'Foul, and a miss.' The rules of snooker, the finer points, are rather subtle. I often wonder why Forster exerted his prerogative to call a miss. Maybe he was curious to know what I would do if I won. Fifty eight points! Thirteen behind, thirteen on the table. We hadn't made any provision for a draw. I gave a curt nod, and Forster re-sited the balls as they had been before Parkinson's last shot, like the recon-struction of a crime scene. This time the cue ball struck the pink but the contact was too full and the pink strolled up the baize like a flapper on a village green under a parasol eating an ice cream. Not only that, he had nudged the black a millimetre.

'Foul. Alastair Cameron-Strange, sixty five.' And the pink was on, to the left middle. Parkinson seemed to have snatched defeat from the jaws of victory.

'Do you forgive yourself?'

That was the crunch question. After the match, I could hardly recall the way in which I had peremptorily and per-functorily pocketed the last two balls and stolen it, in an atti-tude of suppressed rage. I told Parkinson that there was no possibility of personal forgiveness or atonement, when I had failed to resuscitate Mary. I had failed to resuscitate her, the night the paramedics had brought her into Little France. And when the futility of resuscitating the victim of blunt trauma arrest became apparent, I had taken a scalpel and gone ahead, perhaps inadvisedly, to deliver my child but not, as with his mother, to resuscitate him. And as I would persist in prolong-ing the pathetic two finger CPR on the tiny blue sternum, Forbes had gently put an arm round my shoulder and led me out of Resus, past the awed blanched stares of the nurses and the doctors and the paramedics. No. There could be no forgiveness for that.

Parkinson laid his cue down on the deserted baize. 'I see.'

'I win. You promised you'd leave me alone.'

'I promised I wouldn't section you under the Mental Health Act. But I still expect you to come voluntarily.'

I looked at my watch. It was six thirty in the morning.

'Can I have half an hour? To collect my thoughts. Please. You can see I'm trapped.'

I watched Parkinson and Forster weigh it up. It was a won-derful choice of hiding place, down here in the bay, always provided you weren't discovered. Once cornered, there was no way out. A hiding place became a prison. You could fly an aeroplane into a short paddock at night but only a lunatic would attempt to fly it out again.

'Just half an hour? You needn't worry. Caitlin's perfectly safe.'

'I know, mate. We'll wait in the car.'

The odd couple moved to the door. Parkinson turned. 'You know, you should forgive yourself.'

We stared at one another. For a moment I had the absurd notion that these two men were going to become colleagues of mine, even friends. What could I be thinking? I could only shrug at the man from Toorak, and repeat my words.

'Forgiveness? It is not in my gift.'

XXIV

Back out of the basement window and move away silently into the darkness. Don't hurry. Count steps and wait for your eyes to adjust. Rods and cones. It's a clear night and there's a new moon caressing the afterimage of the old. There's the dull gleam of the iron gate. Don't open it! Sounds like a soprano sax. Climb. Just under a kilometre to the beach. Count steps again.

Last bend on the track, strewn with sand. The surging swell of the bay, periodic, like a slumbering animal snoring in its lair. Off-shore breeze, maybe five to ten knots. Here's the little gully hiding the blessed Slingsby camouflaged under foliage. Cast it all aside. Port wingtip, leading edge, fuselage, dome of the canopy, prop, starboard wing leading edge, wingtip, trailing edge, fuselage, tail fin, fuselage, port wing trailing edge. So much for a pre-flight.

Now jump up on to the port wing root and turn the clasp of the canopy through ninety degrees and pull the canopy back. Release the port joystick where you'd secured it to the rudder pedals with elastic rope – an age ago – to stop the control surfaces from flapping in the wind. Parking brake off. Back down to the nose of the aircraft and grasp the prop in both hands and heave. Not too far. You'll need every inch.

There are old aviators and there are bold aviators. What would an old aviator do now? Retrieve the aircraft documentation from its pocket behind the pilot's seat and work out a 'P' chart. Take off performance, slope and distance of the strip, nature of the surface, all up weight, wind speed and direction, ambient temperatures and pressures . . . Forget it. One way or another, I'm leaving.

Now all of a sudden there's a light drizzle. At least access the oil dipstick under the aperture in the engine cowling. Five litres.

Get into the cockpit and don't think about it. Just do it. Left seat, hood closed and locked, rudder pedals out to length, five point harness secured low on the midriff. Put the key in the ignition! Start-up checks, hard-wired. Fuel on, brake on, throttle closed, switches off, instruments left to right . . . flicking on the masters, setting the mags on both, carb air cold, fuel pump on . . . Prime the engine with fuel using the throttle lever. Give it six strokes and set the throttle open half an inch.

Now to wake people up.

I pressed the starter.

There was a fractional pause, then the prop gave two great scything coughs, and then sprang obediently to life. Automatically I glanced at the oil pressure; it rose immediately. I set 1000 rpm and suppressed the compulsion to get on with it. I needed the engine to warm up to maximum efficiency. Never mind the fact that people would be opening their blinds, coming out to investigate. Get all the temperatures and pressures up. Therefore you have time to check the magnetos, for the pre-take-off checks, the vital actions. Keep the nav lights off. I set 1800 rpm and pulled the carb air intake to warm. The revs dutifully fell off by 100 and returned again to 1800 when I reset cold. Mag 1 – drop off 50. Mag 2 – dropped 200 and the engine started to run rough. I set mags on both and ran the engine up to full power. That would wake up the whole bloody island! I wished now I'd put my headset on. I was deafened. I gave it thirty seconds and then dropped back to 1800 and checked each mag in turn. This time there was a drop of 50 on each mag and the engine note was sweet.

Vital actions . . . I ran through the mantra automatically. Trim neutral, throttle friction nut finger tight, mixture rich, carb air cold, fuel pump on, instruments set, half a stage of flap . . . It may have been my imagination but I caught a glimmer of torch light out of the corner of my eye, and how could I have heard a shout above the engine note? But I abandoned the rest of the checks and thrust the throttle on to full power with my feet on the toe brakes. The engine roared to 2200 rpm. I glanced ahead. There was very little to see. A rock face ahead, alarmingly close, and a glimmer of light off the ocean on my left. I whispered under my breath, 'Dear Christ Almighty.' I do believe it was more of a prayer than a profanity. Then I released the toe brakes.

The aircraft surged forward. I used rudder to stay parallel with the line of the bay. The crosswind whipped at me. More right rudder, more right aileron – keep the wing down. Ignore the great slab of blackness ahead. Just get the nose wheel off the ground. There she goes. That's all you can do. Just wait for the machine to get airborne. How far ahead was that stream that cut across my runway on its way to the sea? Come on baby lift off . . . We're off! Keep the nose down. Get some speed. The pale silver of the stream flashed under me. Now the line of the seashore had vanished from view and the rock face occupied the whole of my existence. It was about to smash into the cockpit. Right aileron, right rudder, as much as you dare . . . keep the nose down! The stall warning light flashed and the stall warning horn screeched at me. Hold it there . . . hold it! I was hissing at myself through gritted teeth. Then the blackness of the cliff wall fell away and I could see a horizon ahead at the top of the valley and, above it, a blue black sky. Get the wings level. I had 50 feet and 60 knots. Bring the nose up, very, very gently. The screeching stopped and the stall warning light went out. The big house fell away to my right. There were a few lights burning in the cottages of the tiny hamlet inland. 70 knots. I put the Slingsby Firefly back into a climbing turn to the right, back over the house. Pick up the beach again. I could just make out two figures, one bulky and untidy with hands on hips, staring upwards, the other slim and fit, trying to make a call on his mobile. Would he get a signal down there? He's probably scrambling a jet to shoot me down. Surely they'd alert the police now! 500 feet. Release the flap. Climbing on full power. Fuel pump off. There's the beach, the surf. Turn south. You've done it. You've made it.

All the danger and tension fell away as the bay with its waterfalls and scarred rock basilisks disappeared behind. Prosaically, I retrieved my headphones from the tiny luggage space behind me, put them on, plugged them in, and turned on the radio. Not that I had any intention of talking to anybody. I thought I'd catch the seven o'clock news headlines.

XXV

Barry Trubshaw has tried to take his own life.

There is a terrible simplicity about the pattern of one's life that only becomes apparent to most people during middle age. Prior to this, even amid the heartbreaking anxieties of one's youth, there is, if only intermittently, a life-giving sense of omnipotence that, despite everything, one will wake up in the morning full of beans, one will move on to a higher plane, one will live abundantly. With courage and industry, there is no limit to what one might achieve. It is only later that one becomes guarded by a sense of one's own limitations and the realisation that, after all, all things were not possible.

Such a realisation is not entirely bitter. While it may seem to prescribe the path of one's future, and proscribe other, heretofore potential futures, at least it absolves you of some of the sense of guilt over the past. You have been blaming yourself for the way in which you played your hand. But how could you play for a Grand Slam when you were dealt a chicane?

Well, perhaps not quite a chicane. It was, after all, a biddable hand, if in a modest way.

Life is a game of contract bridge. Bridge is not like patience. Patience is a procession – like one of these Formula One Grand Prix events in which nobody is overtaken. The outcome is already ordained within the pack. But there remains some room for manoeuvre during a game of bridge. You can influence the future. Yet, most of that influence has to be exerted during the bidding. After that, there is very little opportunity for finesse.

In an interesting hand of bridge, you might bid two or three times. Is this also true of life? Imagine if the sum total of the pattern of your life were determined by two or three critical decisions you made during your youth.

Career. Spouse. Environment. I will be a surgeon. I will marry Veronica. I will live in Edinburgh. Such was the bid of Mr Barry Trubshaw.

Or, to put it another way, I will be a professional fake. I will make a fake match, and sire a fake dynasty. I will move in a fake world.

So it can clearly be seen that Mr Trubshaw's opening bid, his enrolment at Edinburgh Medical School, had been only a manifestation of an underlying theme. He always made the same bid. Did chance play any part in it? Of course he might not have met Veronica during rehearsals for the medical ball cabaret. But he would have found another Veronica.

Could he have been ploughed, could he conceivably have failed his medical course? Unlikely. He was academically bright and had a fine, retentive memory. Not that it mattered, but he even had an apt degree of motor skill for a surgeon. But his hands were at their best turning wood. Furniture making was his hobby; one could not say it was his passion. But there was exquisite tactile pleasure in the texture and grain of polished wood, just as there was something repellent for him in the handling of diseased or damaged tissue. The look of distaste as the layers of yellow fat spilled out over the incision site could not be seen behind the surgeon's mask. The examiners of the Royal College of Surgeons are not adept at discriminating between a surgeon and a wood-carver masquerading as a surgeon.

And Edinburgh? Well, it's such an incestuous place. And once the career and the dynasty were in place . . . Veronica takes tea in Jenners. Max and Carolyn are down for the Academy and St George's. Edinburgh was inevitable.

Freud teaches us that, beneath the superimposition of the rationality of intellect, all human motivation is ultimately child-like. Love, hate, greed, pride, humility. Why did Mr Trubshaw choose to lead the life of a dissembler? To attain wealth? Prestige, the respect of colleagues, power, a position in the community, security for his family? No.

To placate his father.

So it is that you make your life decisions, dimly aware of the way in which their resonances will reverberate down the years. You made your own bed – now lie in it! And you grow seasoned to the rigours of the life you have constructed for yourself. And after a time you become resigned to the impossibility of re-inventing yourself.

Yet, you realise, change is still possible – change for the worse. When you professed a predilection for hepatobiliary surgery you could have had no idea of the revolution in laparoscopic techniques which would radically alter your chosen sub-specialty. Then, after two decades, the need to reascend 'the steep part of the learning curve' had returned, and how much more difficult, this time, seemed the ascent, and how much less accessible the plateau of competence.

Perhaps if he had taken advice then, sought counselling for what he admitted to himself was his 'predicament', things might have turned out differently. But the self-reporting of inadequacy has never featured prominently in the medical curriculum; actually it did not feature at all in Mr Trubshaw's formative years as an undergraduate. The ethos of 'soldiering on', on the other hand, still has credentials. Thus it was that Barry Trubshaw found himself on that fateful afternoon, in the Grange, 'soldiering on', wielding the ungainly laparoscopic tongs and incinerating not the cystic duct, as his anaesthetist was so sharply subsequently to remind him, but the common bile duct, thereby bringing to an end with one swift stroke the burgeoning career of one of Edinburgh's more dynamic young entrepreneurs.

He had been philosophically aware that this simple and devastating act would usher in the twilight of his career in Edinburgh, but he had not been prepared for the brutality of his peers, and the collegiate ferocity which was turned upon him.

He was closed down. Anaesthetists with unpronounceable names from dubious schools in outlandish provinces might gas for him, but the stream of referrals from local general practitioners dwindled to a trickle and then dried up altogether. His operating privileges within the NHS were gradually withdrawn. After a time he was credentialed to perform only a handful of simple elective procedures such as the repair of an inguinal hernia – but not by laparoscope. His need for beds on the wards diminished and management apologetically but firmly farmed them out to the hard-pressed physicians and geriatricians. His university commitments were curtailed and, in any case, as word got round, the medical students had stopped attending his rounds.

It never rains but it pours. Just as the work was drying up, his investment portfolio began to perform less well. But the shopping bills and the school fees kept going up and up! That was the final nail in the coffin. But for ever pressing financial commitments he might have been able to sweat it out. As it was, his erstwhile colleagues took pity on him.

There was, they said, a 'Cas' across in the dark kingdom. A big shambling run down Victorian hospital. Very busy. Disadvantaged community. Low socio-economic status. High infant mortality. High unemployment. Drugs. Crime. Trauma. 90,000 patients per annum, 35% of them children. High service commitment. No medical students. Young nursing staff with a high turnover. Medical staff? Either foreign graduates or post graduate year 2. Six of them. Well, five really. There's a rotation for a month through neurosurgery. The present chairman, a retired orthopod with a predilection for the bottle, has just resigned, burnt out. Care to take it on?

Knowing full well that this was the final humiliation, that it solved little for him, nothing for the 'Cas', and that far from being an act of kindness this was a supremely cynical act on the part of the surgeons, whereby they could wash their hands of him, he accepted. His parlous financial state drove him to it. He accepted, knowing full well that he knew nothing of, say, asthma, croup, the anticholinergic toxidrome, acute dystonic reactions, occult bacteraemia, febrile convulsions, parasuicide, and the million and one other slings and arrows he would be bound to come across. He knew nothing of them and, worse still, the hospital management, who also knew he knew nothing of them, took him on.

Thus it was that, about a decade ago, Barry Trubshaw chose to re-invent himself essentially under the same dissembling guise as before, perhaps cognisant, even then, that resonances would once again reverberate down the years and that, once again and with absolute certainty, he would find himself in an impossible situation.

And here it was. He was like an actor on stage who has not properly learned his lines. Should he mumble and stamp and filibuster and look desperately to the prompt for help? No. This time he would step calmly over the footlights, apologise to the audience and prostrate himself before its mercy. This time, he would corpse.

I steered the Slingsby in from the north, very low, and landed uphill on the Claich, the field on the periphery of Clerk Maxwell that Farmer Bain hired out for gigs. I cut the engine as soon as I'd landed. I don't think anybody saw me. The haar was gone. The campus was radiant in winter sunshine.

Barry Trubshaw had taken home with him a Venflon, a bag of saline and a drip-giving set, a vial of thiopentone and another of suxamethonium. Nobody could say this was meant to be 'a cry for help'. Veronica found him. The drip had tissued. He couldn't even do that right. Poor bastard. Over in ICU at Little France they were squirting ice water in his ear, looking at one another and shaking their heads. It wasn't looking good. They would do it all again tomorrow, on the day of a nativity.

Trubshaw. I remembered the man in the tightly buttoned white coat, the quivering jowl and the forced bonhomie. He was my doppelgänger. Twenty five years down the track, I wouldn't be Pearson, I'd be Trubshaw. Pearson was too urbane, too accommodating, bending with the breeze, going with the flow. I struggled away at life like a man pushing his way through a crowd with his elbows, always about to miss my footing, slip, and be trampled. We are all of us impaired.

If I were a loner, disgruntled, disaffected, malcontent, camouflaged in my army surplus fatigues, interested in guns and the internet, and with a massive chip on my shoulder, I would choose to carry out my mass shooting on a university campus.

These places are so vulnerable – not like an airport, where policemen stand on corners with index fingers curled round the triggers of semi-automatic weapons, where the bored customs officers x-ray you with their icy stares; or a bank, or a mall, or a hospital emergency department. Even a garage forecourt has CCTV.

But look at this. I strolled past a Checkpoint-Charlie-style security barrier for vehicles where the attendant didn't give me a second glance. Now I have the run of the place.

Near the entrance to the Joseph Black Building I ran smack into Dumyat and Whangie Horton. I could see them both make a double-take. I hadn't washed or shaved for three days. They both stared at me open-mouthed. When Whangie found her voice she spoke so slowly that each disconnected word had its own independent existence.

'*Oh*

'*My*

'*God . . .*'

'Dumyat. Get out of here, man. Whangie, I like you. Go

home. No. Not that way. Get off the campus. Quick. Do as I say.'

They began to retreat in the direction I'd indicated. If they stuck to my advice they'd be down on the public road within two minutes.

I slipped into the Joseph Black Building. The place was deserted. I took the stairs, not the lift. All the way up, I never passed a soul. My footfalls echoed in the stairwell; I thought I could hear other steps, then a series of thuds. It seemed to come from outside. Somebody's car was back-firing. On the eighth floor I moved with complete silence along the carpeted lobby, placing my feet with the fastidiousness of a big hunting cat. I noticed the carpet wasn't an Axminster at all. It was a Wilton. The door to Professor Horton's office suite was slightly ajar. I pushed it wide open. The anteroom was empty. I walked across. I could see three blurred silhouettes through the frosted glass. One, with the slim profile and the Belisha beacon scalp, was unmistakable. I had no plan. So I just walked right in.

The room was as I remembered it, spacious, well appointed, with the smart luxury of a five star hotel penthouse. The reds and golds, the art, the oak furniture, the huge triptych picture window, the grandfather clock, just as they had been on my last visit. Tick . . . tick . . . tick . . . Professor Sir Douglas Horton, Muir Foye, and Alan Stobo sat in frozen immobility. It was a tableau. A Vermeer. Sunlight was slanting in from the east in broad beams, spilling across Horton's desk. Horton and Stobo posed in stultified silence opposite one another; Ms Foye had adopted her secretarial pose in the grey twilight zone of the Horton penumbra. Her gaze was directed toward the few objects that occupied the great expanse of the red leather desk top. They sat, strategically placed, like chess pieces in an endgame in which all extraneous complications have been spirited away to leave a distilled situation. White to play and mate in two. A paperweight; a Toby jug; a telephone; a Webley service revolver. Ms Foye fixed on the point on the desk where the light seemed to focus most sharply, glinting off the blue-grey gunmetal of the handgun Stobo had placed before him. She stared fixedly at the long barrel. Her face was a skull wrapped in papyrus. Nobody spoke.

Professor Horton had adopted a negligent pose. He sat back from the desk, slightly slouched in his chair, both hands gripping his right ankle which rested on his left knee. He was staring at the ceiling as if he was monumentally bored, absently whisper-whistling a vaguely familiar tune. He was very smartly turned out. Checked shirt, green tie, sports jacket, fawn cavalry twills, brown brogues. Immaculate. The sooner we work through this pantomime, said the demeanour, the sooner we can get on with life. He'd be late for *Conversazione!* Absurdly, both he and Ms Foye were wearing paper hats of the sort you pull out of Christmas crackers. It occurred to me there must have been an end of term breakfast meeting. Horton wore a blue crown and Ms Foye a pink tiara. Maybe they would offer a modicum of protection. Surely you couldn't shoot somebody wearing a funny hat. Horton carried on whistling his nervous tune through his teeth. *All the nice girls love a sailor.* He was trying to impose his own agenda at a meeting where he was definitely not occupying the chair. I shifted my gaze away from Horton and over towards Stobo and my heart sank. I'd seen the piercing eyes before but not quite with this mad gleam. Stobo on steroids; out to lunch.

Nobody registered any surprise at my entrance. I wasn't even sure that I had been noticed. Something compelled me to walk over to the picture window. It was like walking round the edges of a hologram. I gazed through the double-glazed panes towards the unbearable chatoyance of the diamond blazing low in the south-east sky. Reluctantly I turned my attention and looked down at the silent world one hundred feet below. A group of people were lying in various attitudes of abandonment, strewn around the quad, as if they were taking part in some kind of protest demonstration, against global warming, or the rape and pillage of the third world. When I spoke, my voice sounded unnaturally loud.

'Alan. What have you done?' But it was as if I wasn't there.

Then Horton seized the initiative. The clasped hands released the grip on his ankle and he sat up from his casual slouch. I noticed he was deliberately unhurried, eliding each movement. He kept both hands clearly visible above the desk top. He reached across it for the Toby jug. It was a representation of a stout, jolly frock-coated trencherman enjoying a frothing stein of beer. He flicked open the lid with a thumb.

'Sweet?'

Stobo didn't move.

Horton extracted one, unwrapped it, and jammed it into his cheek. He returned the jug to its original position on the desk. He spoke with his mouth full.

'"Curiously strong" mints. Werther's Original. Or is it Callard and Bowser? Can't tempt you?'

'*What, the fair Ophelia!*

'*Sweets to the sweet, farewell!*'

The compulsion to laugh was almost irresistible. I jammed a palm over my nose and mouth in case twitchy Alan decided to silence me with the Webley. I realised I had made a gross misdiagnosis. Pressure of speech! Flight of ideas! The textbook description issued me with a sharp reprimand.

There followed an eerie silence. Horton's aghast stare had frozen on his face. He was racking his brains, recalling the countless interviews that had taken place across this desk, trying to remember the last candidate or supplicant craving an audience who had behaved remotely like this, and how he had dealt with it. He looked like a man with a toothache, a Callard and Bowser dental abscess. The applicant had wandered off script. Now Stobo was joining in the desk-top dumb show. He had extracted a small article from his inside jacket pocket and was laying it down beside the paperweight. It was as if he had queened a pawn. A small sandglass.

Now he was grasping the handgrip of the Webley and rising to cross behind Horton to move to the triptych window.

I was aware that the revolver had dragged Ms Foye's stare along with it. Horton's eyes were fixed on the egg timer. I could see Stobo taking care where he placed his feet, taking his time, keeping his balance with quick darting movements of the head, keeping the barrel of the gun trained on his cornered quarry. He stole a quick glance down to the quad. Simultaneously, I watched a figure in camouflaged army fatigues suddenly emerge from the Cultural Arts Centre and commence a quick darting run, swerving to avoid the bodies, in the direction of the Joseph Black Building. The carrot red hair above the dark face evoked a vague memory. There was something pathetic about the camouflage gear. In the wide open space of the campus and in the brilliant winter sunshine the figure might have been visible from ten miles. As if in confirmation of this, it suddenly stopped in its tracks, threw up its arms in an absurd salaam gesture, and fell stock still. It was such a poor enactment of a death scene that if the figure had been a film extra on set the director would certainly have cut and ordered the scene to be retaken. Yet the body remained quite still. Stobo whispered something almost inaudible. It sounded like '*Peace on earth*'.

He moved back to the desk and resumed his seat.

'Why didn't you take steps to prevent this?'

Horton was still staring at the sandglass.

'Why didn't you – how did you put it? – keep me in the loop? Why did you expect me to – what was it you said? – "take it on trust"? Can't you see? It wasn't a fake degree this man needed. It was help! We could have found a way.' He placed the revolver back on the desk top and reached forward for the stout glass paperweight.

'Something could have been *done*!' The crash of the paperweight on the desk top, splintering its wooden edge, was simultaneous with the harsh bray of the telephone. I saw Horton start and Ms Foye uttered a short, involuntary, stifled scream. Horton's toffee bounced off the desk top with the expedition of a tennis service ace and landed somewhere on the carpet.

We all stared at the phone. The din did not relent. It was a retro-tone, reminiscent of an emergency vehicle of the fifties, a Black Maria. Nobody moved. Perhaps it was a cold caller. They would hang up in a moment. But the caller was very persistent. I prayed, Oh God, make that noise cease.

Stobo was irritated. 'You had better answer that, Ms Foye.'

The relief when the ringing stopped was immense. Ms Foye spoke in a breathy whisper.

'Yes? . . . Yes. . . . Yes? . . . Yes . . .'

She held the receiver towards me. 'It's for you.' She couldn't control the coarse tremor in her arm. The receiver danced around as if she were discharging a canister of air freshener. I raised my eyebrows at Stobo.

'Put us on speaker phone, Ms Foye.'

She fumbled to press a button and replaced the receiver. It clattered as she tried to control it with both hands. The acoustic of the room seemed to change.

'Dr Cameron-Strange? Is that you? It's Ralph Parkinson.'

'I hear you, Dr Parkinson.' I hadn't moved from the picture window.

There was a fractional pause. Parkinson had noted the change in timbre. I could see him mouthing silently to the officers around him. 'Speaker phone.'

'Do you have Professor Horton with you?'

'Yes. He's here.'

'Is he unharmed?'

'He's perfectly all right. We're all unharmed here.'

'Cameron-Strange, it's over.'

'What?'

'Your accomplice is –. Your accomplice has been incapacitated.'

I said nothing.

'Who've you got there?'

I made the introductions. 'Ms Foye, Dr Stobo, Professor Horton . . . Dr Parkinson . . .' I thought I was going to have a fit of the giggles. It sounded like a teleconference for academics.

I could just see Parkinson scratching his head, revising his appreciation of the situation. I remembered the legend on his business card.

You don't get what you deserve, you get what you negotiate.

I could sense Parkinson constructing scenarios, gesturing wordlessly to those around him. The assault team would be taking up their positions around the building, waiting for the word.

'This thing has gone far enough. You can stop it now. Alastair, you still have a future. We want you to come out of the building. Leave your weapon. We can sort this all out.'

But I didn't have a weapon. I had left the package that I had picked up in Badicaul down in the back of the Slingsby. I just couldn't envisage any scenario where I would choose to point it at somebody and pull the trigger.

I said, 'Give me ten minutes.'

'I'd like to trust you, Alastair. But do you remember the half hour we gave you this morning? We're here to help you, Alastair. But you must promise us, no funny stuff.'

He was getting very palsy-walsy. I decided to reassure him. 'That's all right, Ralph. No more shenanigans.'

'Okay. I'll give you a call in ten minutes if you're not out.' The line was disconnected.

'Alan, I think we should go out now.'

I don't believe anybody in the room heard me. Perhaps I wasn't there. I was like a time-traveller in a science fiction story, afforded the privilege of witnessing a famous historical scene, so long as I made no attempt to change the course of events.

'Now look here, Stobo. This has gone quite far enough.'

I thought, Horton, you idiot, shut up.

'I can't say it's not a serious matter, coming in here and threatening us with a deadly weapon. But we can still sort this out. I know you've been under a lot of strain. God knows we all have. I dare say you've had rather a rough ride. We can look at that. We can start again. What has happened, has

237

happened. The important thing is that we draw a line under it, and learn by our mistakes.'

He was blabbing.

'I fully admit I'm not immune to the odd cock-up. I'm fallible. Oh yes, by Jove. I've made some real howlers in my time. Like underestimating you, for a start. I own up – I treated you with a certain flippancy. Now I see I must regard you with a certain – caution, not to say respect. You've got backbone, Stobo. I admire that in a man. I like people who stand up to me. Your talents are clearly languishing in your present position. You certainly ought to have a senior lectureship. That can be arranged. Perhaps even a readership. That can free you up. It would afford you time and freedom, to pursue your own interests. Research and so forth. Perhaps with an eye to a Chair.'

Then he made a tactical blunder.

'What is it you want? Money? Compensation? Muir, write out a cheque for Dr Stobo. He can name his price. I'm sure it will be reasonable.'

Ms Foye made no move. I believe she was still taking the minutes. It was all she knew. It was her way of maintaining self-control. It was she who had first taken note of the last visitor to slip unobtrusively into the room; the man with the white face and the black cape. Stobo stared incuriously at Horton the way he might have watched unmoved as a drama student failed an audition.

'You'll find the cheque book in the filing cabinet Ms Foye. Top drawer. What would you consider an adequate out of court settlement, Alan? For stress and harassment in the work place I mean. One hundred thousand?' Horton had lost perspective. He was beginning to sound ridiculous.

Stobo remained perfectly still.

'All right, two hundred, dammit.'

The Lawrencian stare was unblinking.

'A quarter of a million. That's my final offer.'

'Professor Horton, you can't afford me. Ms Foye, you are free to go.'

She shook her head dumbly. Abruptly, Horton pushed his chair back and made to get up.

'Wait here, Ms Foye. I'll get this all sorted out. Shouldn't be more than a few minutes.'

'Not you, Professor. You aren't going anywhere.'

Stobo reached forward and flicked the little figure-of-eight sandglass over. The pink sands of time began to trickle. Horton froze, white knuckles on the arms of his chair, half seated, half standing. Now Stobo picked up the Webley in his bloodied right hand – he must have cut himself when he smashed the paperweight – and with his arm fully extended over the desk top directed it at point blank range at Horton's chest. I was reminded of another tableau, a picture I'd seen in some art gallery – was it a Manet? – of a firing squad taking aim on a condemned prisoner. It wasn't seemly. Surely the perspectives were all wrong. How could you possibly stand that close to someone you intended to annihilate? Blood was trickling from Stobo's palm down the handgrip to form large crimson droplets at its butt. They fell to the leather desk top with regular periodicity and bounced up in transient rose petal blooms. I was still standing by the picture window somewhere behind Horton because in my memory I seem to share his view of that tumescent gun barrel. I will not dwell on the way in which Horton finally lost his poise. In fact he lost control of his bladder. It is a hard thing to disguise in a pair of cavalry twills. Suddenly all my antagonism towards him fell away. In his shoes, I don't suppose I would have done any better. When he spoke his strangled voice – the harsh falsetto I had heard once before – was no longer human. The poor wretch had become Winston – the other Winston – in Room 101.

'Don't point it at me! Point it at Foye! Foye! Not me!'

It released Muir Foye from her mesmeric trance. She was able to withdraw her stare from the barrel of the Webley and turn it in the direction of Horton with an expression of utter disgust. Was it his appalling lapse in behaviour, or the pungent odour of ammonia? She had been undone by the sudden realisation that her last twenty five years had been wasted.

I heard myself speak. 'Look at him. He's finished. It's enough.' This was going right down to the wire. I had the notion that I might still diffuse this situation if only I could stumble on the right utterance, but that I would only get one shot at it.

The clock, the blood . . . tick . . . tick . . . drip . . . drip . . . I even thought I could hear the trickle of the sand in the glass. In the dazzling light the trigger of the Webley started to move.

'Remember! Göring and the revolver!'

Stobo's index finger stayed.

'You're not one of *them*!'

Ten excruciating seconds elapsed.

'No.' He relaxed his grip. He let his arm fall slowly downwards. He placed the Webley back down on the desk and turned it round, politely, so that the barrel faced away from Ms Foye, the way you might extend the handle of a knife when passing cutlery.

'Enough.'

Stobo acknowledged my presence for the first time since I had entered the room. He nodded briefly.

I edged back round the hologram towards him and we moved together and in parallel towards the door. I still think we might have made it if we'd been afforded a few more seconds.

The judder of the telephone was submerged in a deep subterranean percussive thump from somewhere under the Joseph Black Building and the entire picture window hurtled in tiny fragments across the length of the room. Kosh playing Clerk Maxwell? The one o'clock gun? I couldn't figure out why Miss Foye's face had suddenly erupted in a bloody rash. Horton was on his feet, making a lunge for the revolver. Another inhuman sound was coming from the back of his throat.

'Nhaarg'

Stobo pushed me forcibly to one side. I fell awkwardly between an ottoman and a davenport. It had been a firm push, but a curiously gentle one. For a moment I thought he was casting me to one side so that he could defend himself. God knows he had time enough. Horton made heavy weather of picking up the firearm, pointing it, finding the safety catch on, switching it to live, and pointing again.

Stobo smiled his serene, mischievous half-smile.

Then there was a series of deafening crashes, so rapid they almost elided into one another. They batted to and fro and died away to give way to Muir Foye's strident and sustained scream.

And Horton kept firing. He had emptied the chambers but he kept firing.

Then the echoes and the crashes and the screaming died away to silence. But the man in the sports jacket and the stained cavalry twills, in the improbable double-handed commando posture, kept firing away.

Click . . . click . . . click . . . click . . . click . . .

XXVI

James Clerk Maxwell University College Massacre

Ck/geohack.php?pagename=ClerkMaxwellshooting&params=
39_37_12_N_105_04_29_W_region:UK-Fyfe_type:landmark)
Extract from Wikipedia, the free encyclopedia

Location: James Clerk Maxwell University College, Fife,
              Scotland, UK
Date: December 24, 20__
Target: Students and faculty
Attack: Shooting spree
Weapon(s):   Carbine, Savage 67H pump-action.
              223 Norinco AK-47
              Webley Mk IV .38/200 revolver
              9kg propane improvised explosive device
Death(s) 13 (including two perpetrators)
Injured 4
Belligerent(s): Purchase Gentleman, aka Noxolo Pacharo and
              Alan Stobo

The **James Clerk Maxwell University College massacre**, or Christmas Eve massacre, occurred on the campus of a Scottish university located on the north side of the Firth of Forth. Purchase Gentleman, also known as Noxolo Pacharo*, a 19 year old liberal arts student from East Africa, was attending university on a scholarship under the auspices of Clerk Maxwell International (or 'Climax'), an ambitious program of international student recruitment spearheaded by the University Vice-Chancellor, Professor Sir Douglas Horton. Gentleman's background and provenance was of high social standing and wealth. Much was expected of him. He had previously however been admitted to hospital with a psychotic episode, and more recently had developed a behaviour pattern of frequent attendance at drop-in clinics and hospital emergency departments in central Scotland with presentations relating to substance abuse and self-harm. His academic credentials were undistinguished. When his academic performance began to suffer, he developed an inappropriate relationship with a faculty member. This was Alan Stobo, lecturer in English Literature, who initially befriended Gentleman but later attempted to disengage himself and may even have hampered his student's academic progress in order to remove him from the University. Stobo, who had a history of bi-polar disorder, fell foul of the University authorities when he failed to submit an Action Plan in response to poor academic performance by his classes. He harboured a deep grudge against the University Vice-Chancellor and this may have resulted in a reconciliation between himself and his student, culminating in a joint act of revenge. Gentleman's own position became precarious as his scholarship, and thus his UK visitor's visa, depended upon his continued attendance at College. A failed academic module, with a subsequent appeal rejected, was thought to be the trigger propelling Gentleman on his brief but deadly rampage at the close of the Michaelmas term. The University campus might have been deserted on Christmas Eve, but a Research *Conversazione* had been scheduled for that morning in the University's Colin Maclaurin Conference Centre.

Deaths and injuries

Gentleman arrived on site shortly after 8 am. He drove through a checkpoint on the campus south entrance where he was not challenged. He parked on a driveway on the northwest side of campus. He remained motionless at the wheel for an hour. At 9 am he left the car, wearing military combat gear. He carried a sports bag which contained a pump-action shot gun with a sawn barrel, a semi-automatic weapon, and ammunition.

Gentleman's shooting spree is estimated to have lasted 57 minutes. It has been reconstructed as follows:

09.07 . . . Gentleman enters the student halls of residence on the northwest perimeter of campus, where a handful of foreign students remain in residence. Four fatalities**.

09.16 . . . crosses a bridge spanning an artificial lake to the science laboratories and lecture theatres where he pauses to reload. Enters the science atrium. Three persons wounded, one fatally.

09.27 . . . passes the University sports complex but does not enter. Approaches the Colin Maclaurin Conference Centre where the School of Information Technology are setting up stands to showcase research project work as part of the annual *Conversazione*. Gentleman is about to enter, when he encounters a student who had previously lent him a translation of Chaucer's *Canterbury Tales*. She, thinking he is taking part in a paint-ball game, wishes him a merry Christmas. He in turn wishes her a happy New Year. She is unharmed. Gentleman elects to bypass the Conference Centre.

09.31 . . . turns towards the arts centre and students' union. Encounters a group of students between the student union and the Joseph Black building, heading towards the Conference Centre. Four wounded, three fatally.

09.36 . . . enters the main cafeteria of the student's union, firing indiscriminately. Two deaths and one major injury.

09.53 . . . First 999 call to the emergency services logged.

09.36 – 10.00 . . . Gentleman's movements uncertain. It is believed he made a single, brief call on a mobile phone to an unlisted London number. (Citation needed here.)

10.03 . . . emerges from the students' union and proceeds in the direction of Joseph Black building.

10.04 . . . Gentleman fatally wounded by a single bullet to the head from a high powered sniper's rifle. At the subsequent inquiry, a member of the emergency response team was granted anonymity.

Activities of Alan Stobo

Shortly after 9 am, Alan Stobo had entered the Joseph Black Building housing the offices of administration of the University. Stobo gained access to the Vice-Chancellor's office on the eighth floor, where he held Professor Horton and his Personal Assistant, Muir Foye, at gunpoint. Horton distracted Stobo and slowed his progress using techniques of negotiation. At 10.12 am, Horton succeeded in overpowering his assailant and fatally wounding him with his own weapon. Simultaneously, a suicide belt of high powered explosive worn by Gentleman and operated by a pre-set timing device, detonated, causing the death of an attending paramedic, widespread damage to neighbouring buildings, and the loss of valuable forensic evidence. Muir Foye sustained minor injuries from broken glass.

The University Vice-Chancellor, Professor Sir Douglas Horton, declined a bravery award. 'It was a team effort. We were all in this together. The emergency services were sublime.'

Shortly after the incident, Muir Foye took early retirement from her position in James Clerk Maxwell University College.

Conspiracy theories

Shortly after the incident a correspondence ran in the letters column of *The Herald* newspaper in which it was pointed out that the 11 minutes that elapsed between the first 999 alert call, and the fatal shooting of the main perpetrator, could not possibly have afforded the emergency services sufficient time to be in place. This conjecture was angrily rejected by the police officer in charge of the operation, Chief Superintendent Brian Hoddle, with the terse remark, 'Damned if you do, damned if you don't.'

The Herald correspondence, and other speculations within the media, were unexpectedly and abruptly silenced when the Prime Minister intervened to inform the nation that such speculation was 'not in the national interest'. Theories that the Clerk Maxwell massacre impinged on issues of high diplomacy (the so called Oil for Arms Theory) have effectively been silenced by the issuance of government Defence Advisory notices. Responding to a 'third man' theory, the police, the office of the Procurator Fiscal, and the government have been adamant that no such individual exists. The police are not looking for any other individuals in connection with the Clerk Maxwell shooting spree. The case is closed.

* 'Noxolo' means 'peace' in Xhosa. 'Pacharo' is a Malawi name meaning 'on earth'.
** I redacted the victims' names. Too painful. ACS.

Epilogue

Department of Emergency Medicine
Little France
January 6th

Mr David Walkerburn
Cardwell Walkerburn, Writers to the Signet
48 Heriot Row
Of this city

Dear David,

As discussed, please find enclosed Dr Cameron-Strange's memo. This is one of two copies; he asks that it be held in perpetuity. The second copy has been forwarded to the MSP for the Clerk Maxwell constituency. There is no electronic record.

Alastair took a flight to Auckland on New Year's Eve. Charges, incidentally, of violation of Civil Aviation Authority regulations, illegal possession of a firearm, found improperly secured in an abandoned aircraft, and, preposterously, child kidnapping, have been dropped. In fact he is quite air-brushed out of the official account. I suppose the security services wish to pursue enquiries undistracted by the glare of publicity. Purchase Gentleman could not possibly have composed *The Bottom Line*. He must have had sponsors. Perhaps he was even state-sponsored.

Ms Roy spent Christmas Day in Kyle of Lochalsh at the home of Hector Sutherland, Alastair's third cousin, twice removed. She's back at school in Gloucestershire now, rehearsing, I'm told, for auditions for the National Youth Orchestra of Great Britain.

Alastair is very exercised that Alan Stobo's reputation has been trashed. He says the official account is quite wrong; that he and Stobo both went to Clerk Maxwell on the same day in an attempt to avert a tragedy. How did they know? He says it's all in *The Bottom Line* but blowed if I can see it. And he says he's too tired to explain it. I'm afraid he has finally lost patience with us. Who can blame him?

I wonder if he'll ever come back? I let him down. I suppose we all did. Why didn't we listen? I am afraid we all seem to have lost our ability for thinking outside the box. All we seem to be able to do with boxes these days is tick them.

Oh well . . .

My best regards to Hester.

Cordially,

Forbes

The Rt Hon George Grierson MP
Ministry of Defence
Whitehall
Westminster
London SW1A 2HB
15th January

Angela MacVicar MSP
The Scottish Parliament
Horse Wynd
Holyrood
Edinburgh EH99 1SP

Dear Angela,

Thank you for your enclosure. The sensitive contents were fully discussed at a recent COBRA meeting in Downing Street. The documents will be protected under the terms of the Official Secrets Act.

My current advice to you holds.

George

Appendix

The Bottom Line, by Bletchley

1	2							3	4		5
6		7	8		9	10	11			12	
13			14	15							
	16				17				18		
	19						20			21
22		23					24			
	25							26	27	
28	29		30			31				
32		33				34				
	35	36	37			38				
39					40					
41										

*Twelve clues are "two in one" and code for twin solutions. One solution may be
converted to its twin by dropping a letter. The shorter twin should be entered into
the grid. The twelve redundant letters, when unjumbled, form* The Bottom Line
which is thematically related to and also predicted by four (unclued) lights.

ACROSS

1 Wrap up little Stanley in money. Some chance (12)
6 Gross gong to the Home Counties (5)
9 Succeed? I've collapsed in pain (7)
13 Back saint to confirm no-nos (5)
15 Expression of disapproval before golf start footwear ... (6)
16 ... or footballers' retro haircut (4)
17 Muddle sly Lily, and break up first love? Yes, maybe (4)
18 Princess' rubbish Frisbee record (4)
19 Mash an ugli, tongue of tongues, with Lagavulin distilled outwith the V & A (7)
20 Burst into tears over tulip, maybe (4)
22 Turn up poem (Nigerian) about the party makeover (4)
25 Hot spot: feel the pressure on TV (8)
26 First bake a French patisserie (3)
28 Three thousand make an arduous journey (4)
30 Stein from me because I deliver (6)
32 Maybe Abies and Picea, loud tax collectors, steady company (4)
33 Say oboe stop pianist, one fifty fifty indisposed (4)
34 Rubaiyat writer, in Cromarty, grants ... (4)
35 ... some wiseacre O level Spanish, French or Portuguese patois (6)
38 First person on a first holiday returning to city (5)
39 Paraphrase Hortens – the last shall be first (7)
40 Shrive Elena back (5)

DOWN

2 A ouija on deck (6)
3 Pause, audibly to assign greater importance to backing Spanish aunt an inch (4)
4 Grand Aberdeen ecstasy joint originally named straight from the horse's mouth! (4)
5 Ernie Els at the finish can be electric (4)
7 Bedeck with blooms river beyond the outskirts of Elgin (8)

8   Reinvent satire along these lines (6)
11 After old man place a wax plant (4)
12 Obscure curtain – archaic Roman standard 59th backed after victory in Europe (5)
14 Noise level among three Bridge players – O boy, back numbers (4)
15 Light music for pinball (9)
21 Ends up in drab mini, topless panto girl; toe curling! (8)
24 Heavy metal executant, or maybe executioner (6)
27 Peacekeepers' turn to disclose gradually (6)
29 Well off? Utterly ridiculous (4)
30 Cast lots for regular time on air (4)
31 Sound like a female deer, a bearer of brick back from Qatar (4)
32 Formula 1's about the purse (4)
36 Say Hamlet turn to the audience; caviar to 50% proles (4)
37 Run in – Emergency Room mistake (3)